D0356524

Dead Ringer

Dead Ringer

A MUSIC LOVER'S MYSTERY

SARAH FOX

WITNESS
IMPULSE
An Imprint of HarperCollinsPublishers

This is a work of fiction. Names, characters, places, and incidents are products of the author's imagination or are used fictitiously and are not to be construed as real. Any resemblance to actual events, locales, organizations, or persons, living or dead, is entirely coincidental.

DEAD RINGER. Copyright © 2015 by Sarah Fox. All rights reserved under International and Pan-American Copyright Conventions. By payment of the required fees, you have been granted the non-exclusive, nontransferable right to access and read the text of this e-book on screen. No part of this text may be reproduced, transmitted, decompiled, reverse-engineered, or stored in or introduced into any information storage and retrieval system, in any form or by any means, whether electronic or mechanical, now known or hereafter invented, without the express written permission of HarperCollins e-books.

EPub Edition JUNE 2015 ISBN: 9780062413024
Print Edition ISBN: 9780062413031
10 9 8 7 6 5 4 3 2 1

To my parents and my sisters.

Chapter 1

THE CACOPHONY THAT hit my ears was as familiar as a favorite song. I stood at the top of a set of stairs inside an old church, a faint musty smell tickling at my nose. The still air pressed in around me, a little too warm to be comfortable, but the discordant sounds drew me onward.

The wooden stairs creaked beneath my feet as I made my way down into the church's basement. It wasn't hard to figure out where to go next. All I had to do was follow the clamorous sound of multiple instruments playing out of sync.

With my violin case in one hand and a bag slung over my shoulder, I entered a small gymnasium. The sound of warring instruments came from the stage at one end of the room. Chairs and music stands had been set out in concentric semicircles, and several of the chairs were already occupied. Some of the people present chatted with one another, but most were busy tuning their instruments or warming up by playing snippets from various pieces.

Three violinists and a violist plucked and bowed while two clarinets and a French horn ran through different melodies. They were almost—but not quite—drowned out by the tuba player, who was by far making the biggest racket of all.

The clashing notes and melodies didn't bother me in the least. As a violinist in a professional orchestra, this was one of the soundtracks of my life.

My stand partner, Mikayla Deinhardt, waved to me from her seat. I waved back and headed for the open door on the far side of the stage. As I had suspected, it led the way up to the wings.

Carrying her violin and bow, Mikayla threaded her way through the chairs and music stands, the tight curls of her hair bouncing and bobbing around her face. She met me just off stage.

"Hey, Midori." She nodded down a dimly lit corridor. "We all stashed our stuff down the hall."

She led the way, the high heels of her black boots tapping the scuffed wooden floor, the sound audible even amidst the noise coming from the stage.

She opened a door and we passed into a large room with folding chairs and tables scattered around. More members of the orchestra milled about inside, chatting and unpacking instruments. I claimed an empty spot on one of the tables and set down my violin case.

"It's not much, but it'll do," Mikayla said, her gaze sweeping over the mismatched furniture and water-stained walls.

"As long as we've got a place to rehearse." I dumped my bag on the table next to my violin case.

"As long as we're not stuck here for long, is more like it." Jeremy Ralston, cellist and general annoyance, came over to join us.

Mikayla rolled her dark eyes while her face was still angled away from him. I shared her sentiment but managed to stifle a groan.

"How many professional orchestras do you know that rehearse in a dingy church basement? It's bad enough that the youth orchestra I help out with plays here on a regular basis." Jeremy stood between Mikayla and me, his lanky frame looming at least a head taller than either of us.

"What's the big deal?" I snapped open the clasps on my violin case and removed my bow.

"The acoustics are crap, for starters," Jeremy said, crossing his arms over his chest. "And I'm pretty sure this place is older than sin itself."

This time it was my eyes that rolled, and I didn't care if Jeremy noticed.

"It's only for a couple of weeks," Mikayla reminded him. "Once the renovations are finished, we'll be back at the Abrams Center, where you and your grandiose needs will be appeased."

"Thank God."

"Yes," I said with a sardonic smile as I tightened my bow and rubbed some rosin on it, "we *should* thank God, since the church provided us with rehearsal space."

Jeremy snorted and stalked off to the corner where he'd left his cello.

"What a prima donna," Mikayla said once he was out of earshot.

"No kidding." I tossed the rosin back into my instrument case. "And notice how it's the ringer who's complaining, instead of us regular members?"

"Oh, I noticed." Mikayla's words referred to Jeremy but her eyes lit on Dave Cyders, one of the bassoonists, as he entered the room. She checked her reflection in a dusty mirror on the wall, fluffing up her curls and using one finger to wipe at an imagined imperfection on her flawless brown skin. Her eyes going straight back to Dave, she said, "I'll see you on stage."

Even though I'd been all but forgotten in the space of a few seconds, I couldn't help but smile. If Mikayla had set her sights on Dave, he didn't stand much chance of resisting. Mikayla always got what she wanted. Not that he would want to resist. Mikayla was beautiful and vivacious, and never short on male attention.

I set down my bow long enough to twist my long black hair up on the back of my head and fasten it in place with a hair clip. That done, I gathered up my violin and bow in one hand and grabbed my folder of music with the other. Leaving Mikayla deep in conversation with Dave—a conversation that involved much eyelash fluttering and tinkling laughter on Mikayla's part—I headed out into the hallway.

My intention was to head out onto the stage, but the sound of angry voices made me pause. Two men were arguing somewhere not too far off. I walked quietly along the dim corridor, farther away from the stage, and stopped just before a corner. The voices were closer now, their words discernible.

"You don't want to take long to make it happen. Trust me."

Somehow I wasn't surprised when I identified Jeremy Ralston's voice. He wasn't exactly Mr. Congeniality. I was, however, surprised when I heard the second voice.

"Are you seriously trying to threaten me?"

The Danish accent was unmistakable. Jeremy was arguing with our maestro, Hans Clausen.

"What do you think?"

I stepped around the corner before the maestro could respond. An ancient floorboard creaked beneath my feet, and both men turned sharply at the sound.

"Everything okay?" I asked, trying to keep my voice light. It wasn't easy. The tension in the corridor was almost smothering.

Without acknowledging that I'd spoken, Jeremy stormed past me, not bothering to apologize when he bumped my shoulder on his way by. I was sorely tempted to say something biting, but the intensity of the glower on his face stopped me. He was a jerk, but I had no desire to provoke him into violence. And from his furious expression, I didn't think it would take much to do so.

I watched him disappear toward the stage before I turned back to Hans, both curious and concerned. "What was that all about?"

The maestro ran a hand through his blond hair, leaving it disheveled. "Nothing to worry about."

I moved a couple of steps closer to him. "Are you sure? He seemed awfully angry."

The maestro attempted a smile, but it didn't reach his eyes. "He has an unpleasant personality. He's not the first of his kind I've had to deal with."

"At least he's only with us temporarily," I said. "As soon as Janice recovers from her injury, Jeremy will be gone, and you won't have to hire him again if you don't want to."

"Yes, that's true. We won't have to deal with him much longer."

Despite his words, his expression remained troubled, his ice blue eyes clouded by some emotion I couldn't quite identify. But before I could question him further, he smiled—a real smile this time—and brushed his thumb along my cheekbone. My heart skipped a beat and I forgot all about Jeremy Ralston.

"You look beautiful." He moved closer until our faces were only inches apart.

"You say that every time you see me," I said, surprised that I could speak normally. My body had gone so floaty and tingly that I hadn't expected my tongue to work.

"That's because you look beautiful every time I see you."

He brushed his lips against mine, and my music folder slipped from my right hand. It dropped to the floor with a thump. I almost dropped my violin and bow as well but tightened my grip on them just in time to prevent disaster.

"Are you sure we should be doing this?" I whispered when his lips broke contact with mine.

"We're alone, aren't we?" His mouth never moved more than an inch from mine. "No one will see us."

Even if I had wanted to argue—which I didn't—I wouldn't have had the chance. His lips met mine again and all coherent thoughts went out of my brain like birds flying through an open window. I snaked my free hand up between us and around the back of his neck, my fingers curling around a handful of his hair. My mercury was seriously on the rise when he pulled back, leaving me wanting more.

He grinned at me. "As much as I prefer this type of rehearsing, we should probably get on stage." He brushed his thumb along my cheek once more and, still grinning, left me standing there in the corridor.

Somewhat breathless and struggling to get my mind back in working order, I patted my hair to make sure it was still held in place by its clip. Satisfied that it was, I retrieved my music folder and followed after the maestro.

IT WAS A tight fit to get the entire orchestra on the stage but I was determined not to grumble about it, mostly because I didn't want to be a complainer like Jeremy. I also knew full well that the alternative to the church basement was a long commute downtown through rush-hour traffic—a commute that would have wreaked havoc on both my schedule and my sanity.

The orchestra had voted on the options before temporarily having to give up our regular rehearsal space at the Abrams Center for the Performing Arts. While the Abrams Center was our home base, we'd had to vacate the building for a couple of weeks while it underwent renovations. About a third of the orchestra had voted to move our rehearsals to a swanky theater downtown, but the rest of us had preferred to stick to the same general part of the city so we didn't have to reschedule our other jobs.

Even though the basement auditorium wasn't exactly the ideal place for a professional orchestra to rehearse, it would do for the time being, whether or not a certain cellist agreed. So I got cozy in my seat next to Mikayla and tuned my violin.

As I made a final adjustment to my E-string, Mikayla leaned toward me and said over the noise of tuning instruments, "Dinner. Friday night."

Since her gaze was aimed across the stage at Dave the bassoonist, I knew she wasn't referring to a girls' night out with me.

"That's great," I said with a smile.

"I'm betting it will be."

Mikayla set out the sheet music for Brahms's Double Concerto in A Minor and started to play, adding to the clashing sounds of different snippets of music coming from the various instruments around the stage. Although I was happy for my friend, I had to bite my tongue to stop myself from asking her if she was sure it was a good idea to date a fellow orchestra member.

I'd heard enough horror stories over the years to know that mixing work and romance often ended in disaster, but Mikayla was two years my senior and plenty old enough to make her own decisions. Besides, who was I to talk? I'd just locked lips with the maestro, and not for the first time. When it came to workplace romantic liaisons, I was pretty much going for the jackpot.

Maybe it wasn't the best idea to strike up a relationship with the maestro, but I knew that wouldn't stop me. Our connection was too electric, too exciting to ignore.

Still, I knew we would need to be careful. If anyone found out about our relationship, even while it was in such an early stage, things could get uncomfortable for both of us.

I didn't think anyone connected to the orchestra was likely to find out, though, at least as long as we didn't make a habit of kissing backstage during rehearsals. So far, we'd managed to maintain the appearance of a strictly professional relationship whenever in anyone else's presence. All we had to do was keep that up. And not get caught kissing backstage.

The act of pretending that there was nothing between us continued as Hans took up his position at the front of the orchestra and tapped his baton on his music stand to get everyone's attention. He made no special eye contact with me, gave no indication that he noticed me at all, and I expected nothing else.

After making a few preliminary announcements, Hans started the rehearsal. We worked our way through the first movement of the Double Concerto, the cello and violin soloists providing the highlights. Next we moved onto the second movement, my favorite of the three. I loved the rich dignity of the andante movement. It had a way of filling me with a sense of peace, reminding me of quiet, happy evenings spent outdoors in pleasant weather.

Our concertmaster, Elena Vasilyeva, and cellist Johnson Lau wove the solo parts together with a seamless beauty that never got old for me. Even though we stopped and started as part of the usual rehearsal process, the movement didn't fail to exert its calming effect on me.

After about an hour of rehearsing, the maestro set

down his baton. "Take a ten minute break and then we'll move on to the Symphony No. 2."

As soon as the words were out of his mouth, the stage area filled with the sound of scraping chairs, shuffling feet, and chatter. I couldn't say I was surprised when Mikayla made a beeline for Dave Cyders. I didn't have the same luxury, and didn't even cast a glance in Hans's direction as I made my way offstage and toward the back room where I had stored my belongings.

Setting my violin and bow in my instrument case for safekeeping, I removed a bottle of water from my bag and took a long drink. I exchanged a few words with a couple of my fellow second violinists and then headed off in search of a washroom. I made my way back up to the main floor of the church, certain I'd seen a ladies' room on my way down to the auditorium when I'd first arrived.

I was right. At the top of the stairs and halfway down another creaking corridor, I found the women's washroom. Both of the two stalls were already occupied, so I checked my hair in the mirror while I waited. As I tucked a few flyaway strands behind my right ear, I heard a muffled thump from somewhere out in the corridor.

Curious, I left the washroom and peered up and down the hallway. There was no one in sight. There was, however, another thud, followed by the sound of hurried, retreating footsteps.

I might not have Spidey senses, but I definitely had an inkling that something was amiss.

Ignoring my less-than-urgent need to return to the washroom in favor of satisfying my curiosity, I tiptoed

along the hallway, away from the stairway that led down
to the basement.

I reached the end of the corridor where it joined the
narthex. I knew from entering the church earlier that
there was a staircase right around the corner, leading to
the upper level. Pausing for a second, I listened for any
further sounds, but all was quiet. Eerily so.

Goose bumps formed on my arms, and my heart thudded like a drum beaten on by an overzealous percussionist.
I drew in a deep breath and moved around the corner.

I was met by a pair of feet. The feet were, unsurprisingly, attached to legs, and the legs were attached
to a body. Jeremy Ralston's body, to be precise. He was
sprawled on his stomach on the worn red carpet of the
staircase, his feet near the bottom, his head higher up. He
wasn't moving.

"Jeremy?"

He didn't so much as twitch when I said his name.

Gripping the railing for support, I took two tentative
steps up the stairs. That was far enough to allow me to get
a good look at his face.

Never the most attractive man to begin with, Jeremy
now qualified as hideous. His face was splotchy, mottled
with red, and his eyes were open a fraction of an inch.

I barely took the time to register the angry red marks
on his throat before I hastily backed down the stairs.

Jeremy was dead.

Murdered.

Chapter 2

"HELP!"

I spun in a frantic circle, not sure which way to turn. I reached to the pocket of my pants for my cell phone, but I'd left it in my bag.

Find someone!

I was about to retreat to the washroom or, if that proved empty, to the basement, when a blond-haired woman appeared at the top of the stairs, a pink cashmere cardigan buttoned haphazardly over her white blouse.

"Oh, dear!" She paused on the landing, five steps above Jeremy's head. "Has there been an accident?"

I swallowed, finding it hard to breathe evenly. "I'm pretty sure he's dead."

The woman's blue eyes widened with shock and one hand went to her mouth. "Dear Father in heaven!"

"Do you have a phone?"

Before the woman had a chance to respond, which I wasn't entirely sure she was going to do, a man came down the stairs behind her, stopping when he saw Jeremy's body. He wore a black clergy shirt and clerical collar. Even in my panicked state, I was able to conclude that he was the reverend.

"What's happened here?" he asked with concern.

The woman grabbed his arm. "Darling, he's dead."

"Heavens! How did that happen?"

"Telephone!" I shouted, perhaps a little louder than strictly necessary. "Do either of you have a telephone?"

"Oh, ah, yes." The reverend seemed to get somewhat of a grasp on the situation. He addressed the blond woman. "Cindy, dear, go up to the office and call 911."

The woman clasped her hand to the collar of her cashmere cardigan. "Yes, yes, of course."

With one last glance at Jeremy's unmoving form, she turned on her low-heeled pumps and retreated up the stairway.

The reverend was about to continue downstairs and pick his way past Jeremy's body when I stopped him.

"Wait!"

He halted, his expression bewildered.

"You shouldn't walk through a crime scene. Is there another way down?"

"Oh. Yes, there is." The reverend retreated up the stairs and disappeared around the corner of the landing. Seconds later he reappeared, descending a parallel stairway that I hadn't noticed earlier. It was only twenty or thirty feet from the one where Jeremy lay dead.

The reverend came over to stand beside me, eyeing Jeremy's body. "Any idea what happened?"

"This is how I found him." I hugged myself, an unpleasant chill working its way through my body. "Look at his neck."

The reverend leaned closer to Jeremy but drew back quickly. "Oh dear. Murder? In a house of God?" His eyes darted about, as if expecting God to appear in person to express His displeasure.

Or maybe he was looking for the murderer. He or she could still be lurking inside the church. Why hadn't that occurred to me before?

Another chill ran up my spine and I hugged myself more tightly.

"Midori!"

My heart nearly leapt out of my chest when Mikayla appeared from around the corner.

"What are you doing?" she asked. "Rehearsal's starting again in about ten seconds."

All I could do was point at Jeremy's body. She stepped into view of the stairway and her jaw dropped. "Is he . . . ?"

"Dead? Yes," I said. "And it looks like murder."

"Oh my God." Her gaze flicked to the reverend. "Oops. Sorry, Reverend."

Eyes closed and head bowed, the reverend was too busy murmuring a prayer over Jeremy's body to notice what Mikayla had said. As he closed with "Amen," Cindy reappeared. She'd descended the parallel staircase, wisely avoiding the scene of death.

"The police will be here any moment." She glanced in Jeremy's direction, but then winced and averted her gaze.

Mikayla put a hand on my arm and gave it a quick squeeze. "I'll go tell the others."

"Make sure they don't all come swarming up here."

"I will."

As soon as Mikayla left, I wished she'd stayed. Standing there staring at Jeremy's body gave me the creeps. So did the thought that whoever had killed him could still be nearby. I tried to turn away, to focus on something other than Jeremy, but my eyes remained glued to him.

A police siren became audible, wailing in the distance, drawing closer every second. I shivered, wishing I could go home and soak in a hot bath. But then I felt guilty for wishing that. Jeremy had died. He'd been murdered. Thinking of myself was selfish.

Still, I was cold and could have used something to warm me up.

"Midori?"

I hadn't realized how tense I was until a wave of relief washed over me at the sight of Hans rushing toward me. I was tempted to hug him, to hold onto him tightly, but I managed to restrain myself. I didn't want anyone thinking our relationship was anything but professional, and I didn't want to play the role of a damsel in distress. But that didn't mean I couldn't appreciate the strong hand that came to rest on my back.

"Mikayla told me what happened." He stared hard at Jeremy's body for a second or two before turning his ice blue eyes to me. "Are you okay?"

"I think so."

The police siren grew louder and cut off abruptly. The reverend hurried off toward the front of the church, most likely to meet the officers. Whatever tension had left my body on Hans's arrival returned with a vengeance. My muscles were taut, like violin strings strung too tightly. I closed my eyes and focused on the feel of Hans's hand on my back. That helped to calm me.

When several sets of footsteps thumped on the floor, I opened my eyes. The reverend had returned, with two uniformed police officers accompanying him.

"Please stand back," the taller of the two officers cautioned the reverend, who was about to guide them over to the body.

The reverend stopped and Cindy moved quickly to his side. He put an arm around her, but his gaze followed the officers to the stairway.

The police officers made a cursory examination of Jeremy's body, confirming that he was indeed dead. While the shorter of the two officers spoke into his radio, the taller one addressed us onlookers.

"We'll need everyone to remain in the building until we've questioned you," he said. His eyes roamed over the four of us. "Which one of you found the body?"

I lifted a hand. "I did."

"Your name?"

"Midori Bishop."

The police officer nodded and jotted my name in his notebook. "Come with me, please."

"Can I come with her?" Hans asked, his hand still warming my back and keeping me anchored.

"Sorry," the officer said. "You'll all have to be questioned separately."

I glanced at Hans, and he gave me what I guessed was meant to be a reassuring smile. It struck me as more distracted than anything else, but maybe that wasn't surprising. There was a dead body sprawled out a few feet away from us, after all.

Leaving Hans behind, I followed the police officer through a set of double wooden doors and into the nave.

"If you'll wait in here, ma'am, a detective will come talk to you shortly."

"Thank you," I said, as the officer retreated back through the double doors. They closed with a dull thunk behind him.

I stood for a moment in the aisle between the two back pews, gazing up at the stained-glass windows. Even in the evening, with little natural light coming through them, the windows were beautiful. On a sunny day they were probably breathtaking.

I took a few steps along the aisle and slid into a pew on my right. I already felt more relaxed than I had out by Jeremy's body. I wasn't a religious person, but the nave had a calming effect on me. It was peaceful, serene. Sitting there in the polished wooden pew, it was hard to believe that someone had been murdered just down the hall. But it had happened. And now that I thought about it, I probably hadn't been far from the murderer.

The thumps I'd heard could have been Jeremy struggling with his attacker or his body falling to the stairs. The hurried, retreating footsteps had probably belonged to his assailant.

For the first time since I had discovered Jeremy's body, my thoughts cleared. Which way had the footsteps gone? Up the stairway, I thought, although I couldn't be sure. Certainly not toward the washroom, otherwise I would have encountered the killer.

I shuddered at the thought of that happening. It would have been helpful to the police if I'd caught a glimpse of the murderer, but the thought of getting in his or her way was not one I wanted to dwell on.

I sat back in my pew and let my eyes wander over the stained-glass windows again. Now that I was more relaxed, new questions popped into my head.

Why would anyone want to kill Jeremy?

Sure, he wasn't the nicest guy in the world. In fact, he could be downright annoying. But that wasn't reason enough to kill someone. There had to be more to it. Maybe he'd angered someone. Maybe he'd been mixed up in something criminal or, at least, unsavory.

No matter what the motive, why was he killed here in the church? Had the killer followed him and simply waited for an opportunity to strike? Or—and this thought chilled me more than any previous one—was the killer a member of the orchestra?

I shook my head, frustrated. All I had were questions. No answers.

Behind me, one of the wooden doors creaked open. I turned in my pew to see who was there, my heart rate speeding up a notch. Despite the nave's calming effect, the thought of the killer lurking about in the shadows still had me jumpy.

The man who came into the nave was dressed in a gray suit, his jacket unbuttoned and his white shirt strained across his wide girth. He had gray and white hair and a bristly gray moustache to match. Everything about him seemed gray, except for his skin, which was a little too ruddy to be healthy.

Behind him followed a woman in her mid-thirties, also dressed in business attire, but her honey blond hair and the bright blue of her shirt peeking out from beneath her navy suit jacket made for a far less depressing color palate than that of her older companion.

"Ms. Bishop?" the man said as he approached.

I stood up. "Yes."

The man extended his hand. "I'm Detective Bachman and this is Detective Salnikova."

I shook his hand and then Salnikova's.

"Please, take a seat." Detective Bachman nodded at the pew.

I sat back down, and he settled himself into the pew directly across the aisle from me. Salnikova took the pew in front of him, and they both angled their bodies to face me.

"I understand you're the one who found the victim," Detective Bachman said as Salnikova removed a notebook and pen from the pocket of her tailored jacket.

"That's right."

"That must have been quite a shock for you."

I swallowed, remembering the red marks that marred the flesh of Jeremy's throat. "That would be an understatement."

Bachman nodded. "Of course. Did you know the victim?"

"Yes, but not well."

"But you know his name?"

"Yes. Jeremy Ralston."

"He was a member of the same orchestra as you?" This time the question came from Salnikova as she wrote in her notebook.

"Temporarily," I replied. "He was a ringer."

Detective Bachman's bushy gray eyebrows drew together. "A bell ringer?"

I might have imagined it, but I thought Salnikova had to fight to suppress a smile. Had the circumstances been less serious, I might have been tempted to roll my eyes. Bachman's mistake was one I'd heard many times before.

"No, he was a cellist. A ringer is someone who is hired to add to an orchestra temporarily. One of our cellists is out with an injury so we needed someone to stand in for her for our next concert."

"And that person was Mr. Ralston."

"That's right."

"So he was in the church this evening for a rehearsal?" Salnikova asked.

I nodded. "We're using the basement as a temporary rehearsal space. We normally rehearse at the Abrams Center, but it's being renovated at the moment."

Salnikova wrote another note.

There was a brief pause and then Detective Bachman said, "Can you explain how you came to find Mr. Ralston's body?"

I took in a deep breath to prepare myself to relive the unpleasant experience. I told the detectives how I'd heard the odd thudding noises and had gone to investigate, finding Jeremy's body on the staircase.

"And there was no one else in sight when you found him?" Salnikova asked.

"No one."

"What about the footsteps you heard? Do you know which direction they were heading?"

I repeated the answer I'd come up with in my own mind prior to the detectives' arrival. "I think they were heading up the stairs, but I can't be sure."

As Salnikova jotted notes in her notebook, Detective Bachman picked up the line of questioning again. "Are you aware of any enemies Mr. Ralston might have had, or any problems he may have been experiencing lately?"

I shook my head. "Like I said, I didn't know him all that well. We were just acquaintances, really."

"I understand," Bachman said. "But even when you don't know someone well, there can sometimes be an indication of a problem. Something said, certain behavior. That sort of thing. Did you notice any of that with Mr. Ralston?"

I thought carefully about that. "Jeremy wasn't always the most pleasant person to be around," I said. "He liked to complain a lot and his personality was a bit . . . abrasive. I guess it wouldn't shock me to find out that he had conflicts with other people. In fact . . ." I trailed off, realizing what I was about to say.

"In fact?" Bachman prompted.

I gave myself a mental kick. I didn't want to bring Hans into this. Then again, it wouldn't really cause much harm. There was no way that Hans had killed Jeremy, so telling the police about the argument I'd interrupted wasn't likely to get him into any trouble. Besides, now that the detectives knew I'd been about to say something, they wouldn't let it drop. I could tell by the sharp way their eyes watched me.

I let out a breath and finished my sentence. "I overheard Jeremy arguing with someone earlier today."

"Do you know who that someone was?"

I still didn't want to say Hans's name, but there was no getting out of it. "Maestro Hans Clausen."

Bachman's eyes flickered with interest but his expression otherwise remained neutral. "And what was it they argued about?"

"I'm not sure. I didn't hear much of what was said. But Hans—" I checked myself and started again. "Maestro Clausen did ask Jeremy if he was threatening him."

Salnikova's pen moved swiftly across the page of her notebook. I wanted to say more, to defend Hans, but I bit my tongue. I doubted that my opinion would mean much to the detectives, and they would find out soon enough that there was no significance to the argument.

"How angry would you say Maestro Clausen was during this argument?"

"Not particularly angry. When I asked him about it, he brushed it off as no big deal."

"I see," Bachman said. "And he didn't tell you what the dispute was about?"

"No, he didn't."

Detective Bachman heaved himself to his feet. "Perhaps the maestro himself can enlighten us."

Chapter 3

WHEN DETECTIVE BACHMAN stood up, my hope was that I'd be allowed to go home. I wanted nothing more than a hot bath and my bed. I wasn't sure that I'd be able to sleep after the evening's events but I at least wanted a chance to rest.

"Detective Salnikova will take your official statement," Bachman said as he straightened his suit jacket.

I'd been about to get up from my pew but now sank back into it.

So much for going home.

With a departing nod in my direction, Bachman lumbered out of the nave.

Salnikova shifted back one pew, taking the spot vacated by her partner so she and I sat directly across the aisle from one another. Her body turned toward me and her pen poised, she invited me to once again recount my story.

I did so, in as much detail as possible.

Once we finished with that, I provided Salnikova with my contact information.

"Thank you," she said as she snapped her notebook shut. "That's all we need from you at the moment." She handed me a business card. "If you remember anything else, please give me a call."

I accepted the card, glancing at it before slipping it into my pocket.

"You can go home now if you'd like."

There was nothing I wanted more.

Relieved to be free, I stepped out into the narthex. The scene of the crime was now cordoned off with police tape, and technicians were searching for evidence. Detective Salnikova pointed me in the opposite direction, telling me to use a different route to get to the basement where I'd left my belongings.

With one last, uneasy glance at the scene of Jeremy's death, I parted company with the detective. As I went in search of the basement's other access point, I passed Hans. He sat on a wooden bench between the two parallel stairways leading to the second floor. His face took on an expectant expression when he saw me, as if he thought I would approach. I gave him a weak smile but kept moving without a word. I could hear the detectives coming in our direction and didn't think they would appreciate it if I stopped to chat with another witness before they had a chance to question him.

Moving on, I found a narrow hallway leading to a descending stairway. I was about to head down to the auditorium when I heard Detective Bachman address Hans.

"Hans Clausen?"

"That's correct," Hans replied.

As Bachman introduced himself and Salnikova, I walked softly back along the hallway, stopping when I was around the corner from Hans and the detectives. I knew I shouldn't eavesdrop on a police interview. Maybe I'd even get dragged off in shackles if I was discovered. But I couldn't help myself. As sure as I was of Hans's innocence, I wanted to know what he and Jeremy had argued about.

I breathed as quietly as possible as I listened in on the conversation around the corner. At first I thought I wouldn't learn anything of interest. The detectives started out by asking Hans how well he knew Jeremy and how he had happened upon the scene of the crime. I already knew the answers to those questions. Patience wasn't always one of my dominant traits, but I managed to remain still until the conversation turned toward more interesting matters.

"I understand you argued with the deceased earlier this evening," Bachman said.

My ears perked up.

"I . . . well . . ." Hans seemed taken aback by the detective's knowledge of the argument, maybe even a bit flustered. He recovered quickly enough, though. "Yes, as a matter of fact, I did. However, I didn't kill him."

"What was the argument about?" Salnikova asked, ignoring Hans's last statement.

Hans let out a sigh loud enough for me to hear all the way around the corner. "It was nothing of consequence, really. Mr. Ralston wanted a permanent place in the orchestra. I told him I couldn't oblige, as our current opening was only temporary. Ms. Ellison—the cellist he was replacing—has an injured wrist, but will return to the orchestra in due time."

"And Mr. Ralston wasn't pleased with your response?" The question came from Bachman.

"No, he wasn't. But, in all honesty, not many things pleased Mr. Ralston. He was an unpleasant sort of fellow."

"Did he threaten you?"

There was a pause, and I guessed that Hans was again taken aback by how much the detectives knew. I hoped he wouldn't be angry with me for sharing the information.

"In a sense," he said after a moment. "He told me he wanted a spot in the orchestra and that I had better make it happen. He was no more detailed than that, and that's where our argument ended."

There was another pause, and I pictured Salnikova scribbling in her notebook.

"As I said before," Hans went on, "I didn't kill Mr. Ralston. I've been working with temperamental musicians my entire career. I certainly don't go around killing them for being arrogant or annoying. If I did, half the musicians I've worked with would be dead."

I couldn't help but smile a little at that. It was true that there were more than a few temperamental types among professional musicians. Jeremy was one of many.

"Thank you for that, Maestro," Bachman said in a bland voice.

As much as I would have liked to hear more, I didn't

want anyone to discover me lurking, and I decided it would be best not to push my luck. I eased away from the corner and made my way to the stairs as quietly as possible.

At the bottom of the staircase, I passed through a door and found myself in the corridor where Hans and I had kissed earlier. Where he and Jeremy had argued. As I made my way into the backstage room where I'd left my belongings, several of my fellow musicians swarmed around me.

"How was he killed?"

"Do they know who did it?"

"Was he really murdered?"

The questions came at me from all sides like balls from several pitching machines gone on the fritz. I covered my ears with my hands, overwhelmed by the bombardment.

"People! Give me a break!"

The questions broke off, but I could tell the lull was only temporary. It was only natural that they wanted to know what had happened, but I wasn't in the mood to fill them in.

Relief and gratitude replaced some of my tension when Mikayla elbowed her way into the crowd surrounding me and took my arm.

"Leave her alone, guys," she admonished. "Hasn't she been through enough?"

I let Mikayla lead me away from the others, over to my violin and my bag. I grabbed my bottle of water and took a long drink, only then realizing how thirsty I was. My fellow musicians still cast curious looks in my direction but they gave me a wide berth. That probably had something to do with the intimidating glare Mikayla sent in the direction of anyone who so much as took a step toward me.

I knew that Mikayla was as curious as everyone else, and I appreciated the fact that she held back with her questions.

"Thanks for that," I said, nodding toward the cluster of other orchestra members now murmuring among themselves.

"Any time."

I checked to make sure I'd loosened my bow earlier, then shut my violin case, fastening the clasps. "It's not like I really know a whole lot anyway. I mean, it was pretty obvious he was murdered, and I don't think the police know who did it, but I don't know anything else. All I want to do is go home."

"Of course you do." Mikayla put an arm around my shoulders and gave me a quick squeeze. "I get the creeps every time I picture his body on the stairs like that."

"How come you're all still here?"

"The police wanted to talk to each one of us so we had to wait around. Those of us in here have already had our turn, but I think everyone's shocked and wants to know what happened. I didn't want to leave until I knew you were okay." She picked up my music folder from the table and handed it to me. "Here, I brought this back from the stage for you."

"Thanks. And I am okay. But I'd really like to get out of here." I slid the folder into my bag before slinging the bag over my shoulder.

Mikayla grabbed her own belongings as I picked up my violin case. "I'm with you."

With her intimidating glare clearing a path for us, we left the room and headed for the nearest exit.

I WAS SURPRISED the next morning when I woke up to sunshine streaming in through the crack in my blue and white curtains. It wasn't that I had expected bad weather, even though Vancouver was known for its rain. What surprised me was the fact that I'd slept soundly through the whole night.

I wasn't about to complain. The rest had refreshed me, and I was relieved that I hadn't spent the night replaying my discovery of Jeremy's body.

I took a quick shower, dried my hair, put on some makeup, and dressed for the day. After that I didn't know what to do with myself.

Aside from playing second violin in the Point Grey Philharmonic, I also taught private violin lessons for a living. I did most of my teaching in the afternoons, after school hours. Although I taught a couple of adults and a few home-schooled children, even those lessons were scheduled for the early afternoons.

I could have stayed home and cleaned my tiny apartment, or I could have gone to the grocery store and stocked up on food to fill my sadly depleted refrigerator, but I didn't feel like doing either of those things. What I really wanted was company, so I grabbed my cell phone, planning to get in touch with my best friend, JT Travers.

JT was a musician, composer, and sound engineer. He had his own recording studio in the basement of his house in Dunbar, and also rented out a room on the main floor to me where I taught my violin lessons. Even though we were friends, the business arrangement still worked out well. He charged me a reasonable rate, less than I would have to pay elsewhere, and I occasionally helped him out by playing my violin for tracks he was recording without charging a fee.

JT was an easygoing guy, and that was exactly the kind of company I needed right then. Even though my solid night's sleep had left me refreshed, I was still preoccupied by everything that had happened at the church. I wanted someone to talk to, someone who would have a calming effect on me.

I had a key to JT's front door so I could come and go from my music studio as needed, but I didn't make a practice of showing up unannounced at times when I didn't have lessons scheduled. Since I wasn't due to teach for several hours, I sent JT a text message, asking if he was busy or if I could come by. I received a response less than two minutes later.

Not busy, his message read. *Come on over.*

Smiling, I sent back a quick reply: *On my way.*

I shoved my phone in my shoulder bag and grabbed a granola bar in lieu of breakfast. Picking up my violin case, I headed out of my apartment, munching on the granola bar on my way to the bus stop.

Fifteen minutes later I disembarked from the bus onto Dunbar Street and walked two blocks into a quiet residential neighborhood. The leaves of the large trees lining the street waved in the gentle morning breeze, and bright flowers planted in front gardens scented the air with the sweet perfume of spring. Amid such beauty, it was hard to believe there could even be such a thing as murder. But as much as I appreciated my surroundings, Jeremy's death was never far from the forefront of my mind.

When I reached JT's white, two-story house, I jogged up the front stairway and used my key to let myself in through the front door.

"I'm here!" I called out as I shut the door behind me.

I didn't receive a response, either from JT or his collie-malamute cross, Finnegan. I passed through a set of French doors on my right, entering the front room I used as my music studio. After transferring my cell phone from my bag to the pocket of my jeans, I left the rest of my belongings in the studio and followed the main hallway toward the back of the house.

"JT?"

As I reached the kitchen, Finnegan bounded into the house through the back door, tail wagging enthusiastically as he bounced around me.

"Hey, buddy," I greeted him, crouching down to give him a big hug.

He rewarded me with a sloppy kiss on the cheek and more wagging of his fluffy tail.

JT appeared in the doorway leading to the back porch, grinning as he watched Finnegan welcome me. "You'd think it was weeks since you last saw each other instead of less than twenty-four hours."

Giving Finnegan one last hug, I stood up. "It's nice to be missed."

My smile faltered, suddenly struck by the thought of someone missing Jeremy now that he was gone. Even though he hadn't been the nicest guy, surely there had been someone in his life who cared about him. Parents, siblings, maybe a significant other. Now they would have to face not only the loss of Jeremy, but also the fact that he'd been taken away so violently.

JT must have noticed the change in my face. "What's wrong?" he asked as he shut the back door.

"A cellist was killed at rehearsal last night."

"What? How?"

I perched on a stool at the dark granite breakfast bar, Finnegan settling on the floor by my feet. "He was murdered. I found his body."

JT stared at me for a moment while he processed that information. Then he ran a hand through his brown hair, leaving it slightly mussed. "That must have been awful, Dori. Are you okay?"

"Yes. No." I sighed. "I guess I don't really know. It *was* awful. I'd never seen a dead body before, let alone someone who was murdered." I shuddered. "Plus, I knew him. That makes it even worse."

JT came over to stand across the breakfast bar from me. "Do you know who killed him?"

"No. I think I just missed seeing the murderer, though." I explained how I'd found Jeremy's body and heard retreating footsteps right before my grisly discovery.

"I'm glad you didn't get there any sooner. Otherwise, who knows what would have happened."

A shiver went through my body. "I don't even want to imagine what the killer would have done if I'd seen him. Or her." I paused, thinking. "But at the same time, if I could have identified the murderer, he or she would probably be behind bars by now and I wouldn't have to worry."

"Are you worried?"

"Of course," I said, realizing only then how true that was. "Maybe there's a psycho out there who will kill again. Maybe the murderer is in the orchestra."

I didn't want to think about that last possibility. It was too creepy, too scary.

"Or," JT said, "maybe someone had a beef specifically with the victim. Someone who has nothing to do with the orchestra, and who followed the cellist to the church."

"I hope that's the case." I slumped over the breakfast bar, overwhelmed by all the possibilities.

Perhaps sensing my darkening mood, Finnegan lifted his head and whined.

"It's okay, boy," I reassured him. "Don't worry about me."

"But we do." JT's eyes were full of concern.

I'd always admired his eyes. They were such a unique shade of brown. Like root beer with sunlight shining through it. At the moment, the worry in them warmed my heart.

"No need," I said, trying to smile even though I felt weighed down by an array of emotions. "I'll be fine once the killer is caught."

JT didn't look convinced. I was touched by the fact that he cared enough to worry, and my spirits lifted, if only slightly.

"Really, JT. I'll be okay."

He didn't press the issue, instead crossing the kitchen to his fancy coffee machine. Even though he preferred plain old black coffee himself, he'd bought a machine that could make who-knew-how-many different drinks. It wasn't really for him, though. He'd bought it for all the musicians who came and went on a regular basis as they recorded albums in his studio. And for me. He knew I loved cappuccinos and lattes.

"Something to drink?" he offered.

"A cappuccino, please."

When my drink was ready, he set it on the granite countertop and came around to sit on the stool beside me. My cell phone chimed and I fished it out of my pocket. Hans had sent me a text message.

How are you doing today?

The fact that he had checked in on me warmed me on the inside. I tapped out a quick reply as I sipped my cappuccino.

I'm okay. You?

"Hans . . ." JT said, looking at my phone. "Isn't that your conductor?"

"Yes." I tried my best to sound casual.

"Since when does your conductor send you text messages?"

"He stayed with me after I found the body yesterday.

Until the police arrived. He's just checking in to see how I'm doing."

My phone chimed again as another message popped up.

Good. But I'd be even better if you'd have dinner with me tonight.

"Right," JT said with a wry edge to his voice. "And checking in on you includes asking you out to dinner?"

Against my will, my cheeks flushed. Without sending a reply to Hans, I shoved my phone back in my pocket.

"What does it matter?" I focused on drinking my cappuccino, careful to keep my eyes away from JT.

"Isn't he twenty years older than you?" JT's voice held a mixture of disapproval and disbelief.

"Seventeen," I corrected, downing the rest of my cappuccino in one gulp. "And what does that matter? We're both adults."

"Okay, sure. But he's basically your boss, Dori."

"So?"

"What if things don't work out? What if things go south and he kicks you out of the orchestra?"

"He wouldn't do that!"

"How can you be sure?"

"Because!"

"Because?"

I wanted to growl at JT. I was so frustrated and angry that it was hard for me to form any words. As I tried to come up with something to say to defend myself, JT's expression softened.

"I just don't want you to get hurt, Dori. I know how

much you love being in the orchestra. I don't want you to lose that, and I don't want you to get your heart broken."

Tears threatened to spill out of my eyes, and that only annoyed me further. "Why do you assume he'll break my heart?"

JT was silent for a moment. When he finally did speak, he avoided my question. "It's not a good situation, Dori."

Gritting my teeth, I slid off my stool. Finnegan jumped up from his place at my feet, and I rested a hand on his head. "It's my life, JT. I can make my own decisions." I took a step toward the hallway. "I'm going out for a walk." My words came out cold and hard.

"All right."

Something in his voice made me clench my teeth together even harder. Was it disappointment? Regret? I didn't even want to know.

"I'll see you later."

Exuding icy vibes, I set off down the hallway. As soon as I'd grabbed my bag from my studio, I left the house without another word.

Chapter 4

AFTER A BRISK walk followed by some window shopping, I decided to treat myself to an early lunch of Japanese food. As I sat at a table in a small restaurant, I tried my best not to think of JT or our argument. I was unsuccessful. JT was my best friend and I hated not getting along with him, whatever the reason. I was still frustrated with him, though. I was twenty-nine years old and knew how to look after myself. I didn't need his interference or disapproval, or even his concern.

I chewed harder than necessary on a piece of sushi, trying to drown out the voice in my head that told me I was lucky to have someone like JT who cared about me and that maybe he was right. I especially didn't want to listen to that last part. The most annoying aspect of the whole thing was the fact that he had simply voiced my own concerns, which I was trying to pretend I didn't have.

I wasn't about to admit that to him, however. I didn't even want to admit it to myself.

I set my phone on the table and stared at Hans's last message. I still hadn't replied to it, wanting to calm down before I committed to anything. But I wanted to accept. Whether or not there was some risk involved, the fact was, I was attracted to Hans. He was good-looking, talented, and intelligent. I'd enjoyed what little time we'd spent alone together, and I couldn't deny the spark between us. Not that I wanted to.

Besides, I didn't really believe that my job would be in jeopardy if our relationship didn't work out. Maybe I didn't know Hans all that well yet, but I knew he wasn't petty.

Thinking things over as I finished off my agedashi tofu, I came to a decision and picked up my phone to send a reply.

Dinner sounds great. What time?

Drinking down the last of my green tea, I paid for my meal and set off back to my studio to teach my first student of the day.

I DIDN'T SEE JT again that day. By the time I arrived back at his house, he and Finnegan had both disappeared, presumably down to his own studio in the basement. In a way, I was relieved. Part of me wanted to patch things up with him, but another part of me was still annoyed and didn't want to talk to him about anything.

Even if I'd wanted to talk to him, I didn't have a

chance. My first student arrived only a minute or two after I let myself back into the house, and I was busy teaching for the next few hours. When my last student of the day left my studio, I quickly packed up my things and set off for the bus stop.

Hans had responded to my last text message shortly after I sent it, and we'd arranged to meet at my place at seven o'clock that evening. He'd offered to pick me up at my studio, but there was no way I would have agreed to that. I didn't want to risk him and JT meeting, not now that I knew JT disapproved of our relationship.

I also had another reason for wanting Hans to pick me up at my place rather than at the studio. I wanted a chance to change into something nicer than the jeans and sweater I'd put on that morning. I didn't have a whole lot of time to spare, since my last lesson ended at six, so I didn't waste any of it, getting myself home as quickly as possible.

Once inside my apartment, I went straight to the closet and opened its louvered doors. I stared at my wardrobe, biting my lip with indecision. What should I wear? I didn't know where we were going for dinner and I didn't want to be too dressy or too casual. But I had to make up my mind or I'd run out of time and would have to go as I was. I grabbed a blue wrap dress off its hanger and changed into it. It was one of my most comfortable, and blue was my favorite color, as well as one of the colors that looked best on me.

After changing into the wrap dress, I touched up my makeup and switched my stud earrings for dangly silver ones. I brushed out my long hair and was slipping into a pair of strappy silver heels when Hans buzzed my apartment. He had perfect timing. I told him I'd meet him down in the lobby and then transferred my phone and keys from my quilted shoulder bag to a silver clutch. Smoothing my hair one last time, I took the elevator down three stories to meet my date.

I smiled when I saw him standing there, feeling certain I'd made the right decision in accepting his dinner invitation. When he noticed me stepping off the elevator, he smiled too, and butterflies fluttered in my stomach.

"Midori." He came to meet me, taking my hands and giving me a quick kiss that stirred up the butterflies again. "You look stunning."

"You're looking quite handsome yourself," I said, giving the collar of his brown leather jacket a little tug. I wanted to run my hands through his blond hair but somehow managed not to.

He kept hold of one of my hands as he led me out of the apartment building.

"Where are we going?" I asked, curious. I figured that neither of us would want to run into anyone we knew, and wondered if we would end up going somewhere far across town to lessen the risk of that happening.

"Actually, I was hoping you would allow me to cook for you."

I paused on the sidewalk, suddenly hesitant. "At your place?"

"That's what I had in mind." Hans squeezed my hand. "But if you'd rather we go to a restaurant, we can do that instead. As long as I get to spend time with you, I'm happy."

I was still hesitant. Although we'd stolen a few moments alone together here and there, this was our first real date. And even though going to his place would prevent anyone we knew from seeing us, it felt like too much too soon. What exactly was he expecting by inviting me to his home?

My hesitation must have shown on my face, in my body language. He gave me a reassuring smile and brushed his thumb along my cheek, making my knees weak.

"It's just dinner," he said. "No pressure. Time alone together is all I want. But like I said, we can go to a restaurant if that's what you'd prefer."

Relaxing, I shook my head. "I'd love for you to cook for me."

Smile lines crinkled at the corners of his eyes and he leaned toward me to brush his lips against mine. "Nothing would make me happier."

He opened the passenger door to his silver sedan and I settled into the seat. As Hans drove us away from my apartment and toward his place, I left all of my doubts and concerns behind. This was going to be a great evening, and I was determined to enjoy every minute of it.

WHEN WE FIRST set off in the car, I had no idea where Hans lived. I guessed it was probably on the west side of the city, but I didn't even know that for sure. It turned out that he owned half of a duplex in Kitsilano, a trendy neighborhood near the popular Kits Beach. When we stepped inside the front door and Hans flicked on the lights, I could see right away that the interior of his home matched the neighborhood.

Although not new construction, the duplex had been upgraded, and probably not too long ago. The hardwood floors were beautiful, and the tiled fireplace in the living room created a modern but charming centerpiece. When Hans led me through to the kitchen at the back of the duplex, I could tell that whoever had done the renovations had gone all out in that room.

There were dark wood cupboards, granite countertops, and tile flooring. The appliances were stainless steel and top-of-the-line. I wasn't an expert, but I guessed that the six-burner gas stove was a home chef's dream.

"Do you do a lot of cooking?" I asked, eyeing the fancy stove.

Hans grinned. "Whenever I get the chance." He nodded at the small round table in an alcove with a bay window. "Make yourself comfortable."

I pulled out a chair and settled into it, gazing out at the small backyard for a few seconds before returning my attention to the kitchen. Hans opened a built-in wine cooler and pulled out a bottle.

"Wine?"

"Yes, please."

"Sauvignon blanc?"

"Sure."

He took two wineglasses down from a cupboard,

filled them both, and passed one to me. "Are you allergic to shellfish?" he asked.

"No, I love shellfish."

"So shrimp scampi is okay?"

"Sounds perfect," I said.

Hans picked up a small remote control and hit a button. Music began playing softly, and I recognized the piece right away as Edward Elgar's Salut d'Amour. There were built-in speakers in the kitchen. I wasn't surprised. Hans was as much of a classical music lover as I was—perhaps even more so—and he likely didn't spend a whole lot of time without music accompanying his life.

I sipped at my wine and watched him as he worked, removing ingredients from his refrigerator and setting a pot of water on the stove to boil.

"So," he said as he poured some olive oil into a pan, "tell me about yourself."

"There's not a whole lot to tell, really."

"I find that very hard to believe."

I set my wineglass on the table. "Well, you already know that I'm a violinist."

"How about outside of music?"

I shrugged. "I'm an only child, born and raised in Vancouver."

"Have you traveled much?"

"Not as much as I'd like. I've been to England once, Japan three times. That's where my mother's side of the family is from. I've been to a few places in the U.S., but that's about it. How about you? You must be well-traveled."

"What makes you say that?" he asked as he added pasta to the pot of water.

"Well, you're from Denmark, and I think I recall hearing that you worked in a couple of other countries before coming to Canada." I tried to remember what I'd heard about Hans when he first took on the job as maestro of the Point Grey Philharmonic. "Weren't you working in Sweden before you came here?"

Although I could only see his profile, I thought I caught a flash of hesitation or wariness on his face. But it was gone so quickly, I wasn't sure I hadn't imagined it.

"That's right," he said, sautéing some garlic. "Uppsala. And I guess I am fairly well-traveled. I worked in Australia for seven years. Melbourne, to be exact. I also spent five years in Germany and a couple in California. I've done a fair bit of traveling in Asia, although that's mostly been in my spare time rather than for work."

"You must speak a lot of languages," I said.

"I can get by in several, but I'm best at Danish, Swedish, German, and English."

I shook my head. "The more I learn about you, the more amazed I am."

He grinned as he checked the pasta. "And the more time I spend with you, the more entranced I become."

My cheeks warmed and I took a sip of my wine to cover my sudden embarrassment. Fortunately, Hans wasn't looking at me at that moment, and I was able to recover without him noticing. We chatted some more about his time in Australia as he finished preparing our

meal, and soon he was refilling our wineglasses and setting out plates of shrimp scampi on the table.

The meal smelled delicious, and Hans lit two candles
on the table before sitting down, adding some romance to
the evening as the sun set and the natural light from the
bay window dimmed.

As I took my first bite of the shrimp scampi, I almost
sighed with pleasure. "This tastes amazing," I told him.
"You're a man of many talents."

"I'd like to think so."

His words, together with the glint in his eyes, made
me blush again. This time he noticed. He smiled, the
laugh lines at the corners of his eyes crinkling in a way I
found charming and attractive.

"What are we going to do now without Jeremy?" I
asked. "Do you have another ringer lined up?"

Hans swallowed a bite of food and nodded. "I have
someone in mind. I'm just waiting to hear back from her.
If all goes well, she'll be at tomorrow's rehearsal."

"I still can't believe he's dead," I said, twirling some pasta
around my fork. "Murdered. Who would do such a thing?"

"I don't know. But it wouldn't surprise me if Jeremy
had made several enemies in his lifetime. You know what
he was like."

I nodded. I did know what he was like. But still, dislik-
ing someone wasn't enough reason to kill them. At least,
not in my book. But maybe someone out there was missing a few pages from their mental symphony. Or maybe
somebody, for whatever reason, had hated Jeremy with a

passion. Who knew? Not me. I hoped the police would figure it out, though.

"In fact," Hans went on, after taking a drink of his wine, "he didn't even seem to get along with Reverend McAllister."

"Reverend McAllister? What do you mean?"

"When I arrived for the rehearsal yesterday, Jeremy was already there. I caught a glimpse of him having a hushed but very heated discussion with the reverend."

I took a second to digest that information. "Did you tell this to the police?"

"Of course."

"You didn't hear what they were arguing about?"

Hans shook his head. "I couldn't make out any words. When they caught sight of me, they broke off their argument rather hastily and went their separate ways."

How curious. I thought things over as I ate more of my dinner, and soon realized that something was nagging at me. "How did Jeremy even know Reverend McAllister?" I asked. "That was our first rehearsal at the church."

"Ah, but Jeremy helped out with the youth orchestra that rehearses there on a regular basis. He probably ran into the reverend from time to time."

Right. Jeremy had mentioned his work with the youth orchestra. I'd simply forgotten about it until Hans mentioned it. I almost forgot about it again when Hans reached across the table and covered my hand with his.

"Let's not talk about Jeremy or murder anymore tonight. I'm sure there are far more pleasant things we could do."

My heart did something crazy in my chest and my head felt light and pleasantly woozy. I didn't think it had anything to do with the wine. We finished up our meal, talking mostly about music and my work as a violin teacher.

After Hans had rinsed the dishes and put them in the dishwasher, he held up what remained of the bottle of wine. "Another drink?"

"No, thanks. I'm fine." I'd already had two glasses and wanted to keep my mind clear.

"How about we go into the living room?" Hans suggested. "I'll turn on the fireplace."

He took my hand and I let him lead me down the hallway to the front of the house. He switched on the gas fireplace and turned back to me, taking both of my hands in his.

"Thank you for coming tonight."

"Thanks for inviting me," I said. "It's been nice."

"I think we should do this again sometime."

I smiled. "Me too."

He leaned in to kiss me. His arms went around me and my right hand slid up his neck to the back of his head, my fingers raking through his thick blond hair. I was so caught up in our kiss, so focused only on the two of us, that I nearly jumped higher than a kangaroo when someone pounded on the front door.

Hans and I broke apart.

"Hold that thought," he said, moving away from me with reluctance.

I followed him to the edge of the living room but hung

back out of sight as he opened the door, just in case it was someone who knew both of us.

It turned out that it was someone who knew both of us, but not in the way that had crossed my mind.

"Evening, Mr. Clausen," Detective Bachman greeted Hans tersely.

"Detectives," Hans returned. "What brings you here at this hour?"

I stepped into sight. Detective Salnikova was on the doorstep along with Bachman and they both looked past Hans to me when I appeared.

Bachman nodded in my direction. "Ms. Bishop."

If he was surprised to find me there, he didn't show it. Neither did Salnikova.

"We'd like to ask you some more questions about the circumstances surrounding Mr. Ralston's death," Bachman said, turning his attention back to Hans.

"I've already told you everything I know." Hans sounded puzzled and slightly annoyed.

"We'd still like to ask you some questions." Detective Bachman wasn't about to back down.

Hans sighed but stepped back, opening the door wider. "Come on in."

The detectives didn't budge. "We'd like you to come to the station with us."

I gripped the edge of the living room doorway. "Why?" I asked. "Why can't you talk to him here?" There was an edge of panic to my voice.

Detective Bachman ignored me. "Mr. Clausen?"

A second or two ticked by before Hans responded. "I'll get my coat."

As he opened the hall closet, I went to his side, putting a hand on his arm. "Hans, why are they doing this?"

"I don't know." He took his leather jacket off its hanger and paused, meeting my eyes. "Everything will be fine, Midori. I'm sorry this has spoiled our evening. Should I call you a cab?"

"That's okay. I'll do it." I removed my hand from his arm and grabbed my clutch from the hall table while he shrugged into his jacket.

After Hans switched off the gas fireplace, we stepped out onto the front porch. I waited while he locked the front door. The detectives stood on the sidewalk, the yellow light from a nearby streetlight giving their faces a pasty, sickly appearance. My stomach clenched at the thought of them spiriting Hans away for what didn't seem like a friendly visit.

Slipping his keys into his pocket, Hans kissed me on the cheek. "I'll talk to you tomorrow. Don't worry. I'll be fine."

He descended the stairs and joined the detectives on the sidewalk, leaving me there on the porch. As the detectives' car set off down the street, all I could do was watch and wonder if Hans really would be fine. The police had taken him in for questioning, and despite what he'd told me, I had a feeling that he knew why.

Chapter 5

I DIDN'T SLEEP much that night. I kept tossing and turning, unable to stop worrying about Hans and thinking about Jeremy's murder. What interest could the police possibly have in Hans? He'd explained about the argument I'd overheard, so what else could the police want to know? I regretted ever telling the police about the argument. Then again, I couldn't have held information like that back. I never really thought it would get Hans in trouble, because I was so convinced of his innocence. But were the police?

Maybe Hans wasn't a suspect. Maybe the police simply thought he had some valuable information that hadn't even occurred to him earlier. I didn't quite buy that explanation, though. The detectives' demeanor had suggested that Hans was indeed a suspect, which was ridiculous.

Or was it?

I pushed that flicker of doubt aside, but it continued to tickle at my mind, working its way back into my thoughts slowly but surely. How much did I really know about Hans? He'd only started conducting the Point Grey Philharmonic three months ago, and last night was the first time we'd spent any real time alone together. What if he did have a reason to kill Jeremy?

Turning over and tugging at my blankets, I told myself that I was crazy to doubt Hans even for a second. He wasn't a murderer. He couldn't be.

Maybe everything would make more sense in the morning. I'd get in touch with Hans and he'd tell me that everything was fine, that the police had no more interest in him. At least, I hoped that was the way it would play out.

Holding onto that hope, I finally managed to drift off into a fitful sleep in the early hours of the morning. But even what sleep I did manage to get was troubled by restless, disturbing dreams, filled with shadowy dangers and a sense of being hunted. When I woke just after six-thirty, I didn't bother trying to get back to sleep. Throwing aside my blankets, I headed straight for the shower, hoping that the soothing, hot water would help to clear and calm my mind.

It didn't.

After dressing and eating a banana, I sent a text message to Hans.

Are you ok? How did things go?

I stared at my phone, hoping for an immediate reply. None came.

On edge, I worked away at cleaning my kitchen, putting away the dishes I'd left in the drying rack and washing the countertops.

Hans still hadn't replied.

I moved on to the bathroom, scrubbing all the surfaces until they shined.

Still no reply.

I couldn't stand it any longer. I was anxious and wound up, my nerves taut and strained like the hairs of a violin bow tightened too far. When I took a second to really think, I realized that the whole thing with Hans wasn't all that bothered me. I didn't like how I'd left things with JT. I didn't want to hear any more of his opinions about my relationship with Hans, but I also didn't want anything putting a strain on our friendship. It was far too important to me.

I picked up my phone—still without any messages from Hans—and sent a quick text to JT.

Sorry about yesterday. Can I come over?

This time I didn't have to wait long for a response. JT texted me back less than a minute later.

I'm sorry too. Come on over.

I smiled with relief, some of the tension easing out of my body. I gathered up everything I would need for the day, including my violin, and set off for JT's place. A quarter of an hour later, I arrived at his house and entered through the front door. This time, JT and Finnegan met me in the front hall.

After my customary hug fest with Finnegan, I stood up, leaving my violin case on the floor by my feet. JT gave me a lopsided grin that warmed my heart and eased away even more of my tension.

"Why don't we forget about yesterday?" he said.

I smiled back at him, feeling the best I had since the police had shown up on Hans's doorstep. "Sounds good to me."

He nodded toward the back door. "It's nice and sunny out. Finn and I were thinking of hanging out in the backyard for a while."

I looked at Finnegan and he wagged his fluffy tail, giving me his biggest doggie grin. I patted him on the head and picked up my violin. "I'll join you guys in a second."

I went into my studio and dropped off my shoulder bag and instrument. I checked my phone before slipping it into the pocket of my jeans. I hadn't received any messages. I tried not to let my anxiety make a comeback, but worry gnawed at one corner of my mind.

After stopping in the kitchen to make myself a vanilla latte, I joined JT and Finnegan out in the grassy yard. While Finn chewed on a rubber squirrel, I sat down next to JT in a blue Adirondack chair that matched his own.

"What do you have lined up for today?" I asked, blowing on my latte to cool it.

"I've got a new indie duo coming over later to work on their first album. Twin sisters."

I grinned at him over my latte. "Cute?"

"Sure," he said with a wry grin. "But they're also nineteen. That's a little young for me."

His words immediately brought to mind his comments about the age difference between me and Hans. I frowned, and when JT caught my expression, he seemed to realize the connection I'd made.

"I'm sorry, Dor," he said quickly. "I didn't mean anything by that."

"I know you didn't." I turned my face up to the sun and sighed as the warmth seeped into my skin. "To be honest, I'd probably be a bit creeped out if you started dating a teenager. I do think that age differences become less significant the older we get, but . . . . I guess I can see where you were coming from yesterday."

"And I can see where you were coming from," JT said. "You can make your own decisions and don't need me interfering."

I smiled, but my heart wasn't in it. My thoughts were with Hans again. I took another sip of my latte and tugged on my left ear.

"What's wrong?" JT asked.

"Wrong?" I echoed, distracted.

"You've got something on your mind." He gave his own earlobe a tug. "I can tell."

"Oh." I dropped my hand. I'd always had a habit of pulling on my ear when troubled or deep in thought. My grandpa had often joked that my earlobe would end up down by my knees if I didn't stop. I'd never managed to break the habit, but despite my grandpa's warnings, my left earlobe was still the same size as my right one. "It's Hans," I said after a moment. "The police took him in for questioning last night and I haven't heard from him since."

"Questioning? You mean he's a suspect?"

"I don't know. I hope not, but . . . I'm worried."

"Dori, if he's the murderer—"

"He's not!" I exclaimed, cutting him off.

"How do you know?"

I opened my mouth to reply but realized I didn't have a good answer. "He can't be," I said weakly.

JT let out a frustrated breath, no longer his usual laid-back self. "Dori, please tell me you won't spend any time alone with this guy until the police get everything sorted out."

A thought struck me. "I bet there are witnesses who can vouch for his whereabouts at the time of the murder." I brightened. "As soon as the police find that out, Hans won't be a suspect anymore. If he even is at the moment."

"Dori!" JT's voice broke through my spoken thoughts.

I blinked at him, not used to seeing his face so serious.

"Promise me," he said, his brown eyes burning into me in a way they never had before.

"I . . ." I set my cup on the arm of my chair, buying myself a second or two. My mind was suddenly muddled and my tongue didn't want to work properly. "I'm sure it wasn't him, JT."

His eyes didn't leave mine. "No, you're not. I know you'd like to be, but you're not."

I wanted to protest, but the niggling doubt that had bothered me in the night resurfaced. JT was right. I really wanted to believe Hans was innocent, but I couldn't be completely sure that he was.

I sank back in my chair and watched Finnegan roll around in the grass. "All right," I said finally, my voice resigned. "I won't spend any more time alone with him." I thought of the nice dinner we'd shared the night before and added, "For now."

Some of the intensity had left JT's eyes when I met his gaze again, but he still seemed less relaxed than usual. The only one completely at ease was Finnegan. He trotted over to us and sat at my feet, looking up at me expectantly. I scratched his head, thinking.

If I could find proof that Hans was innocent, that he hadn't been anywhere near Jeremy when the murder occurred, then I could rest easy and the two of us could resume our developing relationship. Surely someone had seen Hans during the break in our rehearsal. He often spent our break times chatting with the players, answering questions or discussing issues about upcoming concerts or the pieces we were playing.

All I had to do was ask around and find someone who remembered seeing Hans at the critical time. I'd have to be discreet about it since I didn't want to be the one to spread rumors about the detectives' interest in our conductor. But still, I thought I could manage it, and there was a rehearsal that very evening, so I wouldn't have to wait long to start my inquiries.

Now that I had an idea in mind, I couldn't wait to get started. I'd feel so much better once I could prove to myself and everyone else that there was no reason to suspect Hans. I bit down on my lower lip, wondering who would be best to approach first.

"Now what are you thinking?" JT asked as he leaned

over to pick up the rubber squirrel. He tossed the toy across the yard.

Finnegan bounded after it and pounced, picking up the fake squirrel and giving it a good shake.

"I'm sure I can prove Hans's innocence," I said. "It'll only be a matter of asking the right people a few questions."

"Dori," JT said, and I could tell right away that he disapproved. "That's for the police to do. Leave it to them."

"Oh, I'm sure they're asking questions too. But they're not going to tell me what they find out. And I need to put my mind at ease. I need to know for one hundred percent certain that Hans isn't the killer."

"Dori."

I rolled my eyes. "JT, don't worry. All I'll do is ask my fellow orchestra members a few questions. It's no big deal."

"No? And what if one of the people you start questioning turns out to be the killer? They might not be too thrilled with the idea of you sticking your nose into things."

"I doubt that will happen. The killer probably has no association with the orchestra at all."

"You don't know that."

Okay, so I didn't. That was true. But I needed to do this. I needed to reassure myself that the man I was developing strong feelings for wasn't a murderer. "I'll be careful."

I could tell that JT wanted to say more, but his phone rang then, interrupting our conversation. He glanced at the device, which sat on the arm of his chair. "I'll have to take this."

I got to my feet and smiled, my spirits lifting now that I had a plan. "I'll see you later."

Leaving JT to his phone call, I headed to my studio to await my first student of the day, anxious to get the afternoon over with so I could start asking the questions that would clear Hans's name.

ALTHOUGH I MANAGED not to usher my last student out the door, I didn't waste any time following her. It was only once I was on the bus, traveling toward the church, that my rumbling stomach alerted me to the fact that I hadn't eaten since breakfast. I'd been so caught up in my thoughts that it hadn't even occurred to me to grab some lunch before I started teaching.

I didn't want to stop somewhere to pick up food because I wanted to make sure that I arrived at the rehearsal early enough to ask my questions. At the same time, I didn't want to pass out in the middle of Brahms's Double Concerto. I dug around in my quilted shoulder bag and came up with a somewhat crumbled granola bar. It would have to do.

I munched on my makeshift dinner as I walked from the bus stop to the church, planning my first move. Mikayla was probably the best person to talk to. She was the one who had alerted Hans to the fact that I'd found Jeremy's body. Maybe she could tell me who else she'd talked to upon her return to the basement, and who had been present upon her arrival. Of course, several minutes had passed between the time of Jeremy's murder and the moment when Mikayla found me with the body. So if the killer was a member of the orchestra, he or she would have had plenty of time to return to the basement by the far stairwell before Mikayla reported the incident.

Crumpling up the wrapper of my granola bar and shoving it into my shoulder bag, I considered something else. I was quite certain the killer had fled up the stairs after strangling Jeremy. Why had he or she fled in that direction? Had the killer heard me coming and simply taken the only route available, or was there more to it?

Arriving at the church, I paused at the foot of the stone steps leading to the entrance. I recalled that there was another stairway leading down from the second floor, but the foot of it was in view of the staircase where I'd found the body. If the killer had run up the stairs, he or she had either remained up there awhile and then slipped down the other stairs without me noticing, or else had come downstairs in plain view.

Two people had done that—Reverend McAllister and Cindy, who I assumed was the reverend's wife.

But why would either of them want to kill Jeremy?

It was all quite confusing. The only way I could stop all those muddled thoughts from clogging my brain was to find some answers to my questions.

With any luck, I'd start getting those answers within minutes.

Chapter 6

When I entered the church, I hesitated inside the doors. I didn't have any desire to pass by the scene of the crime again, but fortunately I didn't have to. Heading to my right, I followed the same narrow hallway that had led me to the last rehearsal. I passed by the washrooms and descended the creaky stairs to the basement auditorium. The chairs and music stands were set up on the stage, but there was no one in sight. That wasn't surprising, since I was at least half an hour earlier than usual.

I crossed in front of the stage and climbed the eight steps that led up to the wings. I heard the sound of voices, and when I reached the back room, I saw that I wasn't the first to arrive after all. Ray, an oboe player, and Clover, a bass player, were lounging in folding chairs, drinking pop from cans.

I said hello to them and set my instrument and bag down on a table, sniffing the air. I wasn't an expert by any means, but I thought I smelled a hint of marijuana. It wasn't the first time I'd smelled it at a rehearsal, and I never appreciated it. The distinctive skunklike aroma tended to give me a headache.

"Were you the one to find Jeremy's body?" The question came from Ray.

"Yes," I confirmed, wondering how many people would ask me about that over the course of the evening.

Clover shuddered. "That's so awful. I didn't even want to come back here after what happened."

"Freaky," Ray said, nodding.

I decided I might as well start my inquiries right then, since they had provided me with an opening. "Do either of you have any idea who might have killed him?"

"No way," Clover replied. "Not a clue. I mean, the guy could be a jerk, but he was nice sometimes too."

He was? She must have known a side of Jeremy I wasn't familiar with.

Ray stared hard at the top of his pop can and then took a long drink.

"Ray?" I prompted, when it became clear he didn't intend to answer my question.

"Nah. I barely knew the guy." The oboe player's eyes wandered the room, focusing on anything but me. "Did the cops search his place?"

His question threw me off for a second. "I don't know," I said after a short pause, "but they probably did. Why do you want to know?"

He shrugged. "No reason."

He was trying to act nonchalant, but his eyes were now

shiftier than ever, and I thought I detected a few beads of perspiration on his forehead. I didn't know much about the pale, balding oboe player other than the fact that he'd been in the orchestra since before I'd joined. I couldn't recall ever seeing him with Jeremy, but the way he was acting now made me wonder if there was more of a connection between the two of them than he'd admitted to.

"Did either of you see Jeremy during the break in our last rehearsal?" I asked, focusing most of my attention on Ray, watching for his reaction to my question.

The perspiration at his hairline was more noticeable now, and he still wouldn't meet my eyes. "Nope. I went outside for a smoke." He got to his feet, the can of pop in hand. "Which is where I'm going right now."

He left the room without another word.

"He's an odd one," Clover said when Ray was gone. "It's probably the drugs."

"Drugs?"

"That guy smokes pot more than I drink coffee. And that's saying something."

That explained the odor of marijuana I'd detected.

"And I don't remember seeing Jeremy during the break," Clover added, her eyes not meeting mine. "The police asked us these questions on the night of the murder. How come you're asking them all over again?"

"I'm just trying to make sense of things in my head," I said, in no way willing to reveal that I was actually trying to clear the name of our conductor. "I guess it's my way of dealing with what happened."

Clover tucked her short dark hair behind her ear and

dug through her messenger bag. A moment later she came up with a Snickers bar. "I hope the police catch the killer."

I did too, but anxiety about a murderer being on the loose—possibly even in our midst—gave me even more incentive to do some investigating of my own.

Another bass player arrived and struck up a conversation with Clover, so I collected my wallet and cell phone and headed out of the room. As I stepped out the door, I nearly collided with Elena Vasilyeva, the PGP's concertmaster.

"Oops. Sorry," I said as I stepped aside.

Elena looked down her nose at me. "You're the one who found the ringer's body." Her accented words held a hint of distaste, as if I were somehow tainted by the unpleasant experience of finding Jeremy.

"Yes."

She tossed her thick blond hair over her shoulder and placed her hands on her hips. "This is all so inconvenient."

"Um . . . Jeremy dying was inconvenient?" I wasn't sure if that was what she meant.

She threw her hands up in the air. "All of it! The other evening was a complete circus, with the police running around. We lost an entire hour of rehearsal time."

Was she seriously more concerned with the loss of rehearsal time than the loss of life? I'd always found Elena to be snooty, but that was downright cold.

"Somebody did die," I reminded her. "I think that's a bit more important than an hour of rehearsal time."

She glared at me. "Maybe for you. But I don't want

to be embarrassed at the next concert when somebody messes up because they don't know their part."

I knew she wasn't suggesting that she'd be the one to mess up.

"Besides," she went on, "he was just a ringer."

My jaw nearly dropped to the floor.

Elena didn't notice my reaction, however. With another toss of her perfect blond hair, she brushed past me into the backstage room.

It took me several seconds to recover from the shock of my encounter with her. Sure, she was the leader of the first violins and a brilliantly gifted musician, but her personality left something to be desired. I didn't know how she could be so insensitive.

I shook my head, deciding not to waste any more time thinking about her. There were more important things I could be doing. Leaving Elena and the bass players behind, I followed the hallway past the spot where Hans and I had shared our backstage kiss and went upstairs to the main floor. From there, I walked along another hallway to the narthex.

Across from double doors leading to the nave were the two staircases. They were separated by an alcove that housed a long wooden bench with a potted plant at each end. The far staircase was the one where I'd found Jeremy's body. The closer one was the route Cindy had taken to get back downstairs after calling the police.

I headed for the latter set of stairs, still wanting to avoid the scene of Jeremy's death. As I climbed upward, I realized that both stairways led to a shared landing. A single set of stairs then led from the middle of the landing up the rest of the way to the second story.

I paused at the midway point between the two floors. The common landing meant that the killer could easily have fled up one staircase and down the other in a matter of seconds. Even though I found Jeremy's body less than a minute after hearing the retreating footsteps, his murderer could have escaped more readily than I had previously realized.

I could have given up on my explorations right then and stuck to asking questions to gather information, but I was curious about what I would find upstairs. After all, I didn't know for sure that the killer had escaped down the opposite stairway. There was still a possibility that he or she had fled to the second story.

If there was another way to get down from the church's upper floor, I wanted to know. If someone had seen anyone leave through a window or down yet another staircase, maybe that would lead to the identification of a suspect. A suspect who wasn't Hans.

I crept quietly up the second flight of stairs, my footsteps muffled by the worn red carpet. At the top of the stairway a hallway stretched off to my left and right. A total of four doors opened off of it, two on each side. I turned first to my left, peeking through the doors, both of which stood open. The rooms appeared to be small classrooms or meeting rooms, filled with mismatched chairs and scuffed wooden tables. Aside from the furniture, both rooms were empty. There were windows, but none that provided a realistic means of escape, with no rooftop or handy tree in close proximity.

Retracing my steps, I slipped my cell phone out of my pocket and glanced at the display. I still had plenty of time before I had to be back downstairs for the rehearsal. I figured I might as well do some more poking around.

I was about to investigate the remaining two rooms when a phone rang somewhere nearby. I froze. The ringing cut off and I heard a man's voice say, "Hello?"

Clearly, I wasn't alone on the second floor. The ringing and the voice had come from the right-hand side of the hallway. Not wanting to get caught sticking my nose where it didn't belong, I decided to give up on my snooping and go back down to the auditorium. Until I heard the man's voice again.

"I'm sure there's nothing to worry about. How would anyone find out?"

During the pause that followed his question, I tiptoed a few steps closer to the open doorway. That turned out to be a good thing, as the next time he spoke he lowered his voice significantly.

"By check."

I thought I recognized the voice as Reverend McAllister's. It wasn't surprising that he was present since we were in his church, but I was more than a little curious about his telephone conversation. I stood still and breathed as quietly as possible, listening for more.

"I didn't have any cash on me at the time and I didn't think . . . yes, yes, I know. But I'm sure no one will find out . . . I don't think she'll be a problem . . . yes, but . . ."

I shifted my weight and a floorboard creaked. I held my breath.

"I have to go," the reverend said. "We'll talk later."

I knew he was aware of my presence now, so I stepped forward into the open doorway, doing my best to keep my face neutral.

"Oh, hi, Reverend," I said. "I was hoping to find you here."

McAllister's face was flushed, and he cleared his throat as he stood up behind his cherrywood desk. "You're the young lady who discovered the, ah, unfortunate scene the other day."

"Yes. That's why I'm here, actually." I waited for a lightning bolt to strike me down for telling a lie in a church, but nothing happened.

"Please, come in." The reverend gestured to one of two chairs placed in front of his desk.

I left the doorway and settled into the offered chair. It was lumpy and I detected what I thought was a broken spring digging into my backside, but I wasn't about to complain. I had more important things on my mind. "It's just . . . I've never seen anything like . . . well, like what I saw on the stairs and . . ." I sniffled and blinked my eyes, hoping the reverend wouldn't notice that they were completely dry.

"Of course, of course," McAllister said in a soothing voice as he sat back down. "It was a terrible shock."

"It was," I agreed. "And it was all the worse because I knew him."

"Ah, yes. You're in the orchestra."

I nodded and added in some more rapid blinking. When I first stepped into Reverend McAllister's view,

I'd simply tried to come up with a way to explain my presence. Now, however, I recognized an opportunity to find out more about the discussion Hans had observed between Jeremy and the reverend. McAllister's phone conversation had also made me curious about the man. What was it that he didn't want anyone to find out about? Maybe it had nothing whatsoever to do with Jeremy, but then again, what if it did?

McAllister sat back in his chair and steepled his fingers beneath his chin. "Naturally, it's unsettling to see the results of such a violent act, to lose someone you knew in such a sudden and shocking manner. Have you prayed about it?"

"Er," I said eloquently. I didn't think it would be right to tell him that praying wasn't really my thing.

"Give it a try," the reverend suggested. "I think you'll find it a comfort to share your burden with the Lord."

"Um. Okay." I shifted in my seat in an attempt to escape the stabbing of the broken spring. It didn't work. "You knew Jeremy too, didn't you?" I asked, hoping to steer the conversation in a more illuminating direction.

McAllister was taken aback by my question. "No, no. I didn't know him," he said, his cheeks flushing again.

"Oh." I didn't have to feign my confusion, but I tried to make my next words sound innocent rather than accusatory. "But I thought you talked to him the day he died. At least, that's what I heard."

The reverend cleared his throat. "Oh. Yes. That." He fiddled with a stapler on his desk. "I wouldn't say that I knew him. He came to me for spiritual guidance, but we never had much of a chance to truly discuss things before he . . . well, before he passed."

That explanation didn't sit right with me, but I didn't let on. "Spiritual guidance? Oh dear. Was he troubled?" I pretended to find the idea distressing.

"Ah . . ." McAllister hesitated. "I'm afraid I can't divulge the nature of our discussion in any more detail."

"Of course not. I'm sorry. I didn't mean to pry into confidential matters."

Reverend McAllister waved off my apology, his eyes going to the door behind me. "Estelle."

I twisted in my seat—a mistake, I realized, as the broken spring dug deeper into my derriere—to get a look at the new arrival. The woman who stood in the doorway was probably close to fifty, her light brown hair cut in a sleek, chin-length bob.

"My sister, Estelle," Reverend McAllister said to me. "Estelle, this is . . ."

"Midori Bishop," I supplied. I stood up, grateful to escape the bite of the rogue spring. "I'd better be on my way. Thank you, Reverend."

McAllister got to his feet too. "Any time."

I smiled at Estelle on my way out the door and checked the time on my cell phone again as I made my way down the hall. Mikayla would probably have arrived by now, so I could ask her about Hans. My eavesdropping and my conversation with the reverend had been interesting but only left me with more questions.

There was something fishy about McAllister, but that didn't necessarily make him a murderer. Still, I couldn't help but wonder what kind of "spiritual guidance" would have led to the heated exchange that Hans had witnessed.

"Ms. Bishop!"

I glanced over my shoulder. Estelle hurried down the hall toward me, so I waited for her at the top of the stairway. When she reached me, she smoothed down her white blouse and navy skirt.

"I'm sorry to waylay you," she said.

"That's all right." I was curious why she wanted to talk to me.

"Peter told me that you're the one who found the body the other night."

I figured Peter must be the reverend. "That's right."

Estelle gave me a sympathetic smile. "I wanted to say how sorry I am that you had to go through that."

"Oh. Thank you." I was puzzled, sensing there was more she wanted to say.

She gestured at the stairway. "Shall I walk with you?"

"Sure."

Estelle shook her head as we started down the stairs. "Such a tragedy. That poor young man. First the troubles with his relationship, and then he ends up getting murdered. What a shame."

"Relationship?" I was still puzzled about the woman's interest in talking to me, but I picked up on that one word right away.

"With his girlfriend," she explained as we reached the landing. "He was concerned that she was cheating on him, and he didn't know what to do about it."

"You knew Jeremy?" I was surprised. I couldn't imagine Jeremy giving the time of day to the reverend's sister.

"Oh. Oh dear." Estelle seemed flustered. "I've said far too much, I'm afraid. You see, I overheard the young man speaking to Peter the other day. Accidentally, of course."

"Of course," I said, although I suspected it had been as accidental as my eavesdropping on the reverend's phone call.

"But no, I didn't know him. I didn't even meet him, officially. But I did think it was such a terrible tragedy."

"Yes," I said, descending the last few stairs. "It was certainly terrible." I shivered, the memory of what I had discovered only a short distance away resurfacing with disturbing clarity.

"I'm so sorry," Estelle said. "I didn't mean to upset you."

"It's all right," I assured her. Although the woman watched me expectantly, I didn't know what it was she wanted. I glanced at my cell phone. Time was getting on. "I'm sorry, but I have to go."

"Yes, of course. Don't let me keep you. I just wanted to express my condolences."

I forced a smile. "Thank you."

Leaving Estelle in the lobby, I made my way down to the basement, relieved to be away from the older woman. My exchange with her had left me confused, but at least I had more information to work with now. Could Jeremy's troubles with his girlfriend have somehow led to his murder? Maybe she wanted to be with another man and Jeremy didn't want to let her go. If that were the case, could the other man have killed Jeremy to get him out of the way?

That was pure speculation, of course, but it was something to look into, particularly because it was a scenario that didn't involve Hans. Hurrying into the backstage room, now crowded with other musicians, I retrieved my violin and bow from my instrument case. I recognized Mikayla's red bag sitting next to mine and guessed that she was already out on stage. Grabbing my music folder, I went to join her.

Even though my mind was spinning with thoughts about Reverend McAllister, Jeremy, and Jeremy's girlfriend, I hadn't forgotten the original questions I wanted answered. With any luck, I'd have those answers within a matter of minutes and could put any niggling doubts about Hans to rest.

Chapter 7

I TOOK MY seat on the stage next to Mikayla as she set out the sheet music for Brahms's Double Concerto. After greeting her, I looked around, hoping to spot Hans. I caught sight of Leanne, our assistant conductor, and experienced a wave of panic.

What if the police had never let Hans go? What if they'd arrested him?

But then Hans appeared, making his way to the front of the orchestra, and relief rushed through me, erasing my fears. I closed my eyes as my heart rate returned to normal.

An elbow jabbed me in the ribs and my eyes flew open.

"What's up with you?" Mikayla watched me with curious eyes.

"I . . ." My breath caught in my throat as Hans's gaze roamed over the orchestra, locking with mine for a split second. When he turned his attention elsewhere, I swallowed and tried again to answer Mikayla's question. "Nothing. I'm fine."

I don't think she believed me, but she let the matter drop, and for that I was grateful. I tuned my violin and then leaned toward her, lowering my voice so she would be the only one to hear me over the noise of the other players practicing and tuning their instruments. "Last rehearsal, when you came to tell Maestro about Jeremy, did you find him here on stage?"

"Yes. Why?"

I ignored her question and asked another of my own. "What about before you came to find me? Did you see him then?"

Mikayla narrowed her eyes at me. "Why are you asking me this?"

"Please, it's important." I didn't want to explain, especially not with so many other people around, even if our conversation was practically drowned out by the noise around us.

Mikayla's eyes remained narrowed, but she considered my question. "I saw him right before I went to find you. He came back on stage and I knew the rehearsal would start up again at any moment, and it wasn't like you to be late coming back, so I decided to see if I could track you down."

I thought that over. "So he did leave the stage during the break." That wasn't good. Unless somebody saw him backstage or wherever else he went.

Mikayla poked me in the arm with her bow. "Your turn. Tell me what this is about. You don't think Maestro had something to do with Jeremy's death, do you?"

I looked around, hoping no one had overheard her say that. Luckily, everyone still seemed oblivious to our conversation. "I don't," I said.

Mikayla's brown eyes widened. "But, what, the police do? Seriously?"

"Shh!" I admonished. "Don't tell anyone, okay?"

Mikayla mimed zipping her mouth shut. She raised her violin to her chin, but then lowered it to her lap again. "Hey, how do you know about this?"

Heat rushed to my cheeks. I glanced around again to make sure no one was listening and then leaned over to whisper in her ear. "I was at his house when the police picked him up for questioning."

"At his house?" Comprehension dawned on her face. "Midori! No way! You and—"

I shushed her again, frantically this time.

Maestro? she mouthed, finishing her sentence.

I didn't reply, but my flushed cheeks provided enough of an answer.

She stared at me. "I had no idea!"

"You weren't supposed to," I said.

Her eyes narrowed again. "I can't believe you didn't tell me."

"I would have eventually. I mean, if things . . . progressed."

Mikayla shook her head, still surprised. Hans tapped his baton on his music stand and the orchestra fell quiet, one instrument at a time.

"You owe me details," she said before focusing on the maestro.

I sighed, but not because she now knew my secret. I was disappointed that I was no closer to clearing Hans's name. I didn't want to interrogate every member of the orchestra, because someone else would be bound to catch on to the fact that Hans was a suspect, just as Mikayla had. Plus, questioning everyone would take ages.

Even though I'd promised JT that I'd avoid spending time alone with Hans for now, I knew I had to talk to him. Who better to tell me where he'd been during the break and whether anyone had seen him?

As Hans told us that we would start the rehearsal with Symphony No. 2, I made up my mind. Before I left the church that evening, I would speak to him and ask the questions that burned away in the back of my mind.

As MUCH AS I enjoyed the rehearsal process and playing in the orchestra, it wasn't easy for me to sit through the next hour. I had to force myself to concentrate as we worked our way through the movements of the symphony. At one point Hans cut us off mid-piece to ream out the bass players for not knowing their part. I watched him as he lectured Clover and her companions, not hearing his words. I was too focused on his strong profile and his thick blond hair. I remembered the way his lips felt against mine, the butterflies he stirred up in my stomach.

There was no way he could have harmed Jeremy. Was there?

I hated that I doubted him. Even if I proved to myself

that he was innocent, would my doubts eventually come between us in some way?

I considered throwing caution to the wind and going to his place after rehearsal, to spend some time alone with him. But then I thought of JT and dismissed the idea. I could never break a promise to JT. Besides, I knew that my best friend was right: I should be careful, no matter how much I wanted to believe in Hans's innocence. Once I was completely convinced that he was not the murderer, and once the police no longer suspected him, I could go back to enjoying his electric touch.

By the time Hans told us to take a ten minute break, I was already up out of my seat. Mikayla shot me a curious look, but I didn't wait around to talk to her, instead navigating my way through the chairs, music stands, and musicians.

"I need to talk to you," I said to Hans once I reached his side.

He glanced around. A cellist and a clarinet player were heading our way, intent on speaking with the conductor too. Hans saw them coming and nodded at me. "Give me five minutes."

I stifled my frustration, knowing that the delay couldn't be helped if I didn't want others listening to our every word. As I stepped back, I noticed Mikayla eyeing me from across the stage.

Details, she mouthed.

I rolled my eyes and mouthed back, *Later.*

It was her turn to roll her eyes, but she directed her attention elsewhere, making her way across the stage toward Dave Cyders. I chatted for a minute or two with Katie and Tabitha, two of my fellow second violin players, but excused myself when Hans left the stage, now free of the cellist and clarinet player.

I followed him into the wings. He kept going, and I knew he planned to continue on to where we had our last secret conversation. I put a hand on his arm to stop him, remembering my promise to JT that I'd stay within sight of the other musicians.

We were in plain view of the people coming and going from the stage to the back room, so I knew we were in a safe place. It wasn't exactly the best spot for a private conversation, but it would have to do.

Hans smiled at me and put his hands in his pockets. I wondered if that was because he was fighting the temptation to touch me. I hoped so, but maybe it meant nothing. I wanted to reach out to him but knew that I couldn't.

"How are you?" I asked quietly, holding my violin and bow in my left hand.

"I've been better." He sounded tired, and looked it too, unfamiliar dark rings beneath his eyes.

"How long did the police keep you?"

He waited for two first violinists to pass us by before responding. "Almost four hours."

I winced. No wonder he was tired. "But why? Why would they even suspect you in the first place?"

Hans shook his head. "They're barking up the wrong tree."

"But you have an alibi, right? Surely someone from the orchestra saw you at the critical time."

His eyes didn't meet mine, instead going over my head. "I stepped outside for some fresh air for a few minutes. I was alone."

That was bad news. I realized that he hadn't answered my question about why the police suspected him. "But—"

"We shouldn't talk about this here."

He moved to walk away from me, and I couldn't stop the small stab of rejection that hit me in the chest. But as he passed me, he brushed against my right arm, giving my hand a brief, subtle squeeze.

The stab of rejection eased away, replaced with gentle warmth. He was right. It was too risky to talk about such things here. Neither of us would want it to become common knowledge that he was a suspect. I ached to have some time alone with him, and regretted making my promise to JT. But then I remembered how Hans had avoided my question, how he'd avoided eye contact with me.

Was it simply a matter of not wanting to be overheard, or did he have something to hide?

I didn't know the answer to that question. I had hoped that speaking to him would put my doubts to rest, but that hadn't happened. Instead, they had only grown stronger, and that both troubled and frustrated me.

By the time the rehearsal wrapped up for the night, all I wanted to do was go home, fall asleep, and forget about Jeremy, Hans, and everything else. My curiosity had other ideas, though. As I packed up my instrument backstage, I caught sight of Andy Erikson. Andy was a cellist, and he was also one of the few people who actually seemed to be friends with Jeremy.

Remembering what Estelle had said about Jeremy's troubles with his girlfriend, I followed Andy out of the church and called to him as he unlocked his ancient and rusting station wagon.

"What's up?" he asked as he lifted his cello into the back of the car.

I bit down on my lower lip, unsure of the best way to get the information I wanted. "You knew Jeremy, right?"

The dark shadow of sadness that passed over his gray eyes was evident even in the dim light of the streetlamps. "We were in music together at university," he said. "I knew him for more than a decade."

"I'm sorry." My sympathy was sincere. Even though Jeremy hadn't been my favorite person, I knew how awful it was to lose a friend.

Andy shut the rear door of the station wagon. "You were the one to find him, right?"

"Yes." I'd lost count of how many times I'd answered that question over the past forty-eight hours. I didn't want to give him a chance to ask me anything more about my gruesome find, so I rushed on to say, "I've been thinking about his girlfriend."

"Shelley?" Andy headed for the front of the car, pausing by the driver's door and talking to me over the roof. "What about her?"

"I was hoping to give her my condolences," I said, having come up with that excuse moments earlier. "Do you know where I can find her?"

Andy paused for a moment, and I wondered if he'd refuse to give me the information. But as he opened the car door, he replied, "Her family owns the Green Willow Café. You can probably find her there." He nodded at me and climbed into his car.

"Thank you!" I called out as he shut the door.

I stood on the curb and watched him drive away, wondering if I should give up on the thought of approaching Jeremy's girlfriend. I didn't want to upset her, and I didn't know if she would even have any valuable information. It only took a few seconds for me to decide that I'd still try to talk to her. I needed more than ever to prove to myself that Hans wasn't guilty, and if nothing else, maybe Shelley could tell me if Jeremy had any enemies.

Holding my violin in my right hand and hoisting my bag over my left shoulder, I turned in the direction of the bus stop so I could head home. No matter how curious I was and no matter how many questions I wanted answered, it was too late to do anything except sleep that night.

ONCE I HAD showered and dressed in the morning, I opened the refrigerator, thinking I should probably eat a proper breakfast for a change. The only problem was, there wasn't much in the fridge. Aside from a bottle of ketchup, some wilted lettuce, and a can of root beer, the shelves were empty. The freezer held double chocolate ice cream, some frozen peas, and a tray of ice cubes. Something told me I needed to visit the grocery store.

First, however, I needed something to eat, and I wasn't

in the mood for one of the granola bars I so often relied on for meals. The obvious solution was to go out for breakfast. And the obvious place to go out for a meal was to the Green Willow Café. After all, I'd planned to go there anyway, and needing a meal gave me an extra reason to check the place out.

Grabbing my purse, I slipped my cell phone inside and scooped up my keys from the wicker basket on the entryway table. When I left my apartment for the outdoors, birds sang in the leafy trees and the sun shone brightly. There was a scent of freshly cut grass in the air, and the gentle breeze lifted tendrils of my long hair.

I smiled, the beauty of the spring day momentarily chasing away my troubles. When I arrived at a nearby bus stop, I used my phone to look up the exact address of the café. I had a general idea of where it was but had never actually visited the establishment myself. Once I knew its exact location, I boarded a newly arrived bus and rode it to my destination.

The Green Willow Café was on a busy street, but if it was a popular spot for weekday breakfast, I'd missed the rush. There were only a few other patrons present when I arrived, three workmen in paint-splattered clothing sitting at one table, and two young mothers with a toddler each sitting at another. The eating area was decorated in earthy tones, with wooden furniture and dark green willow trees stenciled onto the light green walls.

A petite young woman wearing a dark green apron called to me from near the kitchen. "Sit anywhere you like. I'll be with you in a moment."

I claimed a small table by the window and picked up the laminated menu that was propped up between the salt and pepper shakers. I perused the options, and the young woman in the green apron appeared at my table a minute later. Her name tag told me her name was Gina, not Shelley.

"What can I get you this morning?" she asked with a smile.

"A Denver omelette and an orange juice, please."

"Coming right up."

She disappeared back toward the kitchen, and I took time to observe my surroundings as I waited for my breakfast. The workmen got up from their table and ambled toward the counter near the back of the café. A moment later, Gina reappeared and worked the cash register, accepting money from each of the men. There was no sign of anyone who was likely to be Shelley.

A few minutes later, Gina brought me my breakfast, and I dug into my omelette, my stomach rumbling in anticipation as the aroma of eggs and peppers wafted up to my nose. As I ate, I kept one eye on the back of the café to see who emerged from the kitchen. But mostly I watched the traffic and pedestrians passing by outside the window.

By the time I'd finished my meal, the two young mothers had left with their kids and an elderly couple had entered the café, but I still hadn't identified Shelley. Leaving my table, I approached the back counter. Gina carried a load of dirty dishes into the kitchen and then came back to the cash register.

I handed her a ten dollar bill, and as she counted out change for me, I asked, "Is Shelley working today?"

"Shelley?" Gina handed me my change. "Sure, she's in the office."

I slipped the coins into my wallet. "Would it be possible to talk to her for a moment?"

Gina shrugged. "I don't think she's busy, so I don't see why not." She leaned through the door behind the counter. "Shelley! Someone here to see you!" Gina flashed a smile at me. "Have a nice day."

"You too," I said as I shoved my wallet into my purse.

She scooted around the counter and headed toward the elderly couple, now seated at a small table in the middle of the café. I remained where I was, waiting for Shelley to appear and wondering how she would react to my questions.

Chapter 8

I DIDN'T HAVE to wait long. While Gina was still discussing the menu with the elderly couple, a woman in her late twenties poked her head out from the kitchen, her wide eyes curious. Her highlighted chestnut hair was tied back in a ponytail and she wore plenty of mascara, black eyeliner, and shimmery pink lip gloss.

"Yeah?" she said when her eyes settled on me, the only person nearby.

"Shelley, I'm Midori. I knew Jeremy and I wanted to come by and say how sorry I am for your loss."

Shelley's big blue eyes welled with tears, and I immediately felt mean for upsetting her.

"You knew him? How?"

"We played in orchestras together from time to time."

"He did love music." Shelley sniffled and dabbed at her eyes with her sleeve.

Something glinted on her finger and caught my attention. "Were you two engaged?" I hoped I didn't sound as surprised as I felt.

Although her eyes still shimmered with tears, Shelley smiled and held up her left hand to admire the diamond ring on her finger. "Yes, he proposed earlier this week." Her smile faded and a tear finally escaped from one eye to trickle down her cheek. "Two days before he died."

"Shel!" Gina hustled over to join us. "What's wrong?"

Shelley sniffed and dabbed at her eyes again. "We're talking about Jeremy."

Gina put an arm around Shelley. "Maybe we should go in the back," she said, glancing toward the two patrons in the middle of the café.

I followed her line of sight. The man and woman watched us with curiosity, and I knew they could probably hear our conversation. When Gina ushered Shelley into a cramped back room with lockers along one wall, I followed, whether I was supposed to or not.

"I'll be okay, G," Shelley said, although another tear had tracked through her makeup.

"Are you sure?" Gina didn't sound convinced.

Shelley nodded. "I'm sure."

After casting an uncertain glance in my direction, the waitress left me alone with Shelley. Jeremy's fiancée sank down onto a scarred wooden bench, its blue paint chipped away to reveal older coats of red and green.

"It's still so hard to believe that he's gone." Shelley hiccuped. "And the police didn't even bother to notify me. I had to find out from Mrs. Landolfi."

"Mrs. Landolfi?"

"Jeremy's landlady. He lived in her basement." Shelley closed her eyes and let out a sob. "Oh, Jer. We were so happy!"

I was a bit alarmed by the fact that she was outright sobbing now. I sat next to her on the bench and patted her awkwardly on the back, but she didn't seem to notice.

"We were planning our honeymoon," she went on between sobs. "He was going to take me to Hawaii. He even brought me travel brochures so I could pick the resort."

She dropped her face into her hands and I patted her back again.

"I'm so sorry," I said, my guilt growing more intense with every minute. "I didn't mean to upset you by coming here."

With a hiccup and a whole lot of sniffling, Shelley raised her head and blinked her blue eyes. "Oh, no. It's okay. It's actually kind of nice to talk to someone who knew Jeremy, who knows how sweet he was."

Sweet? That wasn't a word I would have used to describe Jeremy, but I bit my tongue and simply nodded with what I hoped was a sympathetic expression.

Shelley twisted the ring on her finger. "I guess I'd better get back to the office. I have suppliers to call." She got to her feet.

"Shelley." When she turned back to me, I asked, "Did Jeremy have any enemies that you know of?"

Her big eyes widened. "No way. Not Jeremy. That's why it's so confusing. I don't get why anyone would want to hurt him."

I was afraid she would start to cry again, but she took a deep, shuddering breath and the welling in her eyes subsided.

"The police will find who did it," I said with far more confidence than I felt.

She gave me a tremulous smile. "Thanks for coming by. It was really nice of you."

Before I had a chance to feel too guilty about my ulterior motives, Shelley disappeared out into the hall.

I remained sitting on the bench, trying to absorb everything she'd told me. I didn't even have a chance to sort out my thoughts before a fortyish woman with dark hair and wrinkles at the corners of her eyes came into the small room.

"You the one who was talking to Shel about Jeremy?" the woman asked as she opened one of the lockers.

I couldn't tell from her tone if she was accusing me of something or simply asking a question. "Yes." I stood up, planning to make a quick exit if the woman became hostile. "I'm Midori."

"Lorelei," she offered, her voice less aggressive now. "So you knew Jeremy well?" She grabbed a pack of cigarettes and a lighter from the locker and banged it shut.

"Er . . . our paths crossed several times over the years."

"Hrm." Lorelei fished a cigarette out of the carton and stuck it in her mouth.

"Did you know him?" I asked.

She dropped the carton into the pocket of her apron and spoke around her unlit cigarette. "I knew more than I wanted to."

With that cryptic statement, she left the room. I followed after her, unable to leave things like that. She didn't seem to mind that I accompanied her, saying nothing as she pushed her way through a back door and descended three concrete steps into an alley.

I kept my distance as she lit up, having no desire to blacken my lungs with her secondhand smoke.

"So you didn't think much of Jeremy?"

Lorelei snorted. "I thought plenty of him. He was a cheating bastard, for starters."

I couldn't stop my eyebrows from going up. "He was cheating too?"

She gave me a sidelong look as she took a drag on her cigarette and let out a stream of smoke. "What do you mean by that?"

"I heard that Shelley might have been seeing someone else."

"Flipping malarkey." She paused to take another drag on her cigarette. After she exhaled, she jabbed her cigarette in my direction. "Shelley was devoted to that jerk. She might be naïve, but she's a good kid and she deserved much better than the likes of him."

All this new information was jumbled in my head, confusing me and threatening to trigger a headache. If Lorelei was right and Jeremy was the one having the affair, why had he told the reverend that he thought Shelley was cheating? Or had Jeremy for some reason mistakenly believed that she was unfaithful? If that were the case, why would he have proposed to her?

Or perhaps Estelle had misheard. Maybe Jeremy had gone to Reverend McAllister because he felt guilty about his own affair. Perhaps that's why the discussion had become heated. If McAllister had told Jeremy to come clean to Shelley, he might not have liked that advice. It certainly wouldn't have been out of character for Jeremy to start an argument.

I shook my head, unable to come up with any concrete conclusions. Even though I had come to the café for answers, I now had more questions than ever.

"Are you sure he was cheating?" I asked.

"Damn sure." Lorelei dropped her cigarette and ground it under her heel. "And I've got the picture to prove it." She extracted a cell phone from the pocket of her tight jeans. "I was going to show it to Shelley before she got hitched to the guy, to save her from making a huge mistake. But then when Jeremy kicked the bucket, I didn't have the heart to add to her misery."

She skimmed her finger across the screen of her phone, sorting through her pictures. The cigarette smoke now safely dispersed, I drew closer to her.

"He dropped by to see Shel one day, and not five minutes later he was out the back here kissing some chick in his car. How do you like that? Right under Shel's nose, just about." She found the right picture and held up her phone. "See for yourself."

The picture wasn't of the greatest quality, but I recognized Jeremy's blue car and there were definitely two people sitting inside of it, locked in an embrace. The woman flicked to a subsequent picture, one which provided a closer view of the vehicle's occupants.

"Definitely Jeremy," I said.

Lorelei gave a satisfied nod.

"Do you know who the girl was?" I couldn't see her

face in the picture, only the back of her head. I could tell that she had short dark hair but that was about it.

"No idea. But I've got a close-up of her face somewhere." She skimmed through a couple more pictures and held the phone up again.

I peered at the screen and nearly spluttered in surprise. The woman in the photograph was none other than Clover Delgado, bass player in the Pont Grey Philharmonic.

I HAD TO work hard to keep myself from grumbling under my breath like a crazy person as I rode a bus away from the Green Willow Café. Everyone had told me something different, and for the life of me I couldn't figure out how all the pieces of the puzzle fit together. If they did fit together. Some of the bits of information I'd gathered were at odds with each other, and I didn't know if that was because of mistakes, differing opinions, or lies.

The tidbit about Clover only confused things further. I supposed I could understand why she hadn't mentioned her relationship with Jeremy. I'd seen her hulk of a boyfriend waiting for her after rehearsals as recently as last week, so she too had been cheating on someone. But could she have wanted to harm Jeremy?

I didn't know, and I wasn't sure that she'd want to tell me. After all, she didn't volunteer anything about her relationship with Jeremy the last time we spoke. I might have to ask her nonetheless, because I wasn't a single step closer to proving Hans innocent, and that frustrated me to no end. I needed more pieces of the puzzle. At the moment, there were far too many gaping holes to get anything close to a clear picture of what had happened and who was involved.

Unfortunately, I didn't know where to turn to find more clues. My mind was going like a merry-go-round on super speed. As much as I wanted to keep investigating, I needed to take a breather, to give my brain a chance to calm down. I also had to teach three violin lessons in the afternoon and stock up on some groceries.

I got off the bus at a grocery store near my apartment and bought a few essentials. Once I got the groceries home and put them away, I gathered up my violin and hopped on another bus that took me to JT's neighborhood. I dropped in at a bakery on Dunbar Street and bought a dozen of JT's favorite cookies—chocolate chip macadamia nut.

Tucking the paper bag of cookies into my purse, I walked the remaining three blocks to JT's house. It was almost noon, my typical time to show up at my studio, so I didn't bother to notify him of my impending arrival.

As soon as I let myself in through the front door, Finnegan came bounding along the hallway, skittering across the hardwood floors before coming to a stop at my feet.

"Hi, buddy!" I knelt down and we went through our usual routine of doling out hugs (me) and sloppy kisses (Finnegan).

Once we had sufficiently expressed our mutual delight at seeing each other again, I left my violin in the foyer and headed along the hallway toward the back of the house.

"Where's JT?" I asked Finnegan.

His tongue lolling out of the side of his mouth, Finnegan grinned and trotted over to the basement door. I started down the stairs, Finnegan running down ahead of me.

"JT?"

His voice drifted up to me from below. "Nobody down here but the FBI's most unwanted."

I smiled and descended the last few steps, turning to the right of the stairway where JT sat on a chair, strumming on one of his acoustic guitars.

"Speaking of which," I said as I flopped down onto a beanbag chair, "we haven't had an *X-Files* marathon in ages."

"Too long," JT agreed, still strumming. "How about next Friday?"

"You're on." I took the paper bag of cookies out of my purse and held it out to him. "I brought you something."

JT set aside his guitar and accepted the bag, peering inside at the contents. "Dori, you know the way to my heart."

I grinned, already feeling calmer. No matter how much of a whirlwind my mind might be in, hanging out with JT always helped to relax me.

"What have you been up to today? Besides going to the bakery." JT fished a cookie out of the bag before holding it out to me.

I selected a cookie for myself. "You might not want to know."

He eyed me suspiciously as he chewed a big bite of his cookie. "You might be right," he said once he'd swallowed, "but now you've got me curious, so spill."

As I nibbled my own cookie, I told JT about my excursion to the Green Willow Café and my conversations with Shelley and Lorelei. After eating two cookies, JT set the paper bag on a table out of Finnegan's reach and picked up his guitar again. Instead of playing the instrument, he held it in his lap, listening carefully to everything I said.

I stroked Finnegan's silky head as I related my story, finishing up by saying, "It's all so muddled in my head. I can't figure out how it's all connected to Jeremy's death."

"Maybe it's not." JT played a couple of random chords. "Maybe his death had nothing to do with any of it."

"But there was so much going on beneath the surface!" I didn't want to think that all of my investigating had been for naught.

JT shrugged. "That's the way it is with a lot of people."

I slumped back into the beanbag chair, dejected.

"I'm not saying everything you found out means nothing, just that it isn't necessarily the reason for his murder."

"That only makes things even more confusing," I said. "How am I supposed to know what's significant and what isn't?"

"You're not. That's for the police to figure out."

"But it could take them forever." I slumped even deeper into the beanbag chair. "And in the meantime, I have to keep looking at the faces of people I know and wondering if they killed Jeremy. Not to mention, I have to keep things on hold with Hans."

Although JT had started strumming the opening to one of his compositions, he stopped mid-phrase. "Does he really mean so much to you?"

I tugged on my left ear. "I don't know. I mean, I don't know him that well yet, but . . . I really liked where things were going."

JT let out a breath. He didn't look happy.

"I know you don't approve," I said.

He shook his head before I could say more. "It's not that. I just wish you'd leave the investigating to the police. I don't want you getting yourself into trouble."

"I won't."

There was doubt in his eyes, but also concern.

I pushed myself up from the beanbag chair and stood behind JT, putting my arms around his neck and giving him an affectionate squeeze. "Don't worry."

I felt him relax and one corner of his mouth quirked upward. "Kind of hard not to when you're determined to play Nancy Drew."

I pressed my cheek against his and gave him another squeeze before letting go. "I could always use a sidekick, you know."

Finnegan sat in front of me and let out an enthusiastic bark.

"Looks like I've got competition for that position," JT said, ruffling the fur on Finn's head.

"You can both be sidekicks." I knelt down to give Finnegan a hug.

"And what does that entail?"

"For starters, going with me to talk to Jeremy's landlady." The thought had only just occurred to me, but I figured it was a good idea.

"His landlady?"

"She might know something."

"When are you going?"

"As soon as I'm done teaching today."

"Then you're on your own." JT stood up and hung his guitar on a hook on the wall. "My studio's booked all evening."

"So much for my sidekicks."

"Maybe another time." The smile on JT's face faded and he regarded me with a serious expression. "Be careful, Dori, okay? Don't go stirring up a hornets' nest."

"I'm not planning on it," I said. "All I'm going to do is ask a few questions."

"Questions can be dangerous when asked of the wrong person," he warned.

I waved off his concerns as I headed for the stairs. "I'll be fine, JT. I promise."

As I jogged up to the main floor, JT said from below, "Make sure that's a promise you keep."

Chapter 9

TEACHING MY STUDENTS that afternoon gave me more time to relax and focus on something other than the dozens of unanswered questions bouncing around in my head. I enjoyed teaching, helping my students improve and learn new pieces of music. It was satisfying work— most of the time—and I was glad for the few hours of normalcy before I launched myself back into my investigation.

I wasn't able to completely forget about Jeremy's death or Hans's issues with the police as I worked with my students, but I was at least able to tuck those thoughts away from the forefront of my mind. That, however, changed as soon as I finished teaching and checked my phone.

I'd received a text message from Hans less than half an hour earlier.

I miss you, the message read.

Although the text brought all of my doubts and questions back to the surface, it also brought a warm, fuzzy feeling to the center of my chest and a smile to my face. It was nice to know that he was thinking of me.

I miss you too, I wrote back.

I packed up my violin and tidied my studio, all the while hoping to hear more from Hans, but no more messages came through.

I was disappointed. If he missed me, why didn't he want to schedule another date? If he asked me out again, responding would be awkward, considering the promise I'd made to JT. But at the same time, it would be nice to know that he wanted to spend more time with me.

Maybe he was simply too busy to text me back and would ask me out again before too long. For now, I'd have to settle for him missing me, even if he didn't miss me enough to be desperate to see me.

Giving up on receiving any more messages, I used my phone to look up how many people with the surname Landolfi lived in Vancouver. I crossed my fingers that it wasn't too many. I smiled when only two results came up, especially since one address was for a unit in an apartment building. Since Jeremy had lived in Mrs. Landolfi's basement, the other listing had to be the one I wanted.

Gathering up my purse, I decided to leave my violin at the studio so I didn't have to carry it around with me or waste time by stopping off at my apartment. JT had already disappeared into his basement studio along with some people who had arrived an hour earlier, so I headed straight out of the house without disturbing him.

After two short bus rides and a few minutes of walking, I stopped before a house of pale blue stucco with a carefully tended front garden and rhododendrons in full bloom. I followed the cement pathway to the front steps and climbed up to the small porch. I hesitated, not knowing the type of reception I would receive, but then I pushed the doorbell before I could worry about it any further.

After four or five seconds I heard footsteps approaching and then a shadow flickered across one of the sidelights. The lock clicked and the door opened. A tiny woman with gray hair stood in the doorway. She was probably in her early eighties and wore a lavender cardigan over a flower print dress. Her cornflower blue eyes were sharp but kind, and focused on me with mild curiosity.

"Yes, dear?"

"Mrs. Landolfi?"

"Yes."

Her expression turned expectant and I rushed to explain my presence.

"I knew Jeremy Ralston. He lived in your basement, didn't he?"

Mrs. Landolfi's eyes clouded with sadness and she put a hand over her heart. "Yes, that's right. Such a dreadful thing, him getting killed like that." She shook her head. "A real shame."

"Yes, it was awful." I paused for a second before continuing. "Would it be all right if I talked to you about Jeremy for a few minutes?"

"Of course." She stepped back and opened the door wider. "Come on in."

"Thank you." I stepped into the foyer and she closed the door behind me.

"Come on back to the kitchen." Mrs. Landolfi led the way down a hallway to a white and yellow kitchen that probably hadn't been renovated in several decades. She gestured to the table and chairs by a window that looked out over the back garden, as carefully tended as the front one. "Sit yourself down, dear. Would you like a cup of tea? Or perhaps some lemonade?"

I pulled out a chair. "Lemonade would be lovely, thank you."

I sat down as Mrs. Landolfi removed a jug of lemonade from the refrigerator and two tall glasses from one of the kitchen cupboards. She filled the glasses and returned the jug to the fridge.

"So you were friends with young Jeremy, were you?" She joined me at the table.

"Thank you," I said as she placed one of the lemonade-filled glasses in front of me. "I'm a musician. We played together in the same orchestras from time to time over the years."

Mrs. Landolfi didn't seem to notice my lack of a direct answer to the friendship question. She shook her head sadly. "He was such a talented young man. He was about to be hired by a professional orchestra. Now he won't have that chance."

I took a sip of tart lemonade, homemade by the taste of it, to cover my surprise. Had Jeremy really believed he could bully Hans into giving him a permanent place in the orchestra? He must have been delusional.

"Things had been difficult for him. It would have been nice if he had a chance to improve his circumstances," Mrs. Landolfi continued.

"Difficult?" I asked with interest.

Jeremy's landlady took a sip of her own lemonade. "Well, he went through a bit of a rough patch. Money was tight, and he was late paying his rent a few times."

"When was this?"

"Oh, quite recently. This month was the first one of the year that he paid on time. Of course, I didn't worry about that too much on my behalf. He promised he would pay, and he always did eventually. Such a good, honest boy."

I wasn't sure I agreed with her description of Jeremy, particularly considering the fact that he'd cheated on Shelley, but I was far more interested in everything else she'd said. How could Jeremy have afforded to pay for an engagement ring and a trip to Hawaii if he didn't even have the money to pay his rent? Or had he foolishly spent several months' worth of rent on the ring?

I wanted to growl in frustration. With every person I talked to, I only ended up more confused.

"Did Jeremy have any recent troubles aside from money problems?" I asked, fishing for a clue that would point to a murder suspect.

"I don't believe so," Mrs. Landolfi replied. "He loved his music and he was seeing a lovely young lady." Her eyes grew damp.

"Shelley," I said with a nod, hoping she didn't mean Clover.

"That's right. Poor girl. It must have been such a shock

to her." Mrs. Landolfi dabbed at her eyes with a paper napkin. "The police asked me similar questions, but I'm afraid I have no idea who would have wanted to harm Jeremy. It must have been a random attack by someone quite deranged."

The more I learned about Jeremy, the more I doubted the random killing theory. Anyone who lied and cheated was bound to make some enemies along the way. But I didn't see any point in interfering with her rather rosy view of his character.

"It's all very hard to understand," I said. That much was the truth.

Mrs. Landolfi nodded and dabbed at her eyes once more. "His sister arrived from Halifax yesterday, but the police won't allow her to clear out his things yet. It will be hard to find another tenant as good as Jeremy. It was so nice to have a fellow musician around."

I perked up at her last words. "You're a musician too?"

"Oh, back in the day. Flute and piano. I stopped playing years ago because of my arthritis. My grandchildren have my instruments now, but it was nice to talk music with Jeremy now and then." The elderly woman got up from the table. "I'll show you some pictures."

"Of Jeremy?" I asked with surprise.

"No, no. My grandchildren."

I stifled a groan as Mrs. Landolfi shuffled off to another room. I liked the woman, but what was I in for now? It was already getting dark outside, and my stomach was clamoring for some dinner. I wasn't keen on spending hours oohing and aahing over photos of people I'd never met, but when Mrs. Landolfi returned with a photo album tucked under one arm, I tried my best to look interested. Maybe the woman was lonely. If that was the case, it was the least I could do to give her some of my time.

She set the album on the table in front of me and sat down. As she flipped through the pages one by one, pointing to the pictures and relating a story for each one, I made all the appropriate sounds and comments. I learned that Jeremy's landlady had four grandchildren—Amy, Kristie, Jordan, and Lily—all very sweet, apparently. They all played piano and Kristie also played the flute. Jordan and Amy excelled at soccer, and little Lily—scowling in almost every picture—was a darling six-year-old angel.

I fought back several yawns and didn't allow my eyes to stray to the clock above the kitchen sink, no matter how many times they wanted to. I wondered if Mrs. Landolfi was hard of hearing, because she didn't seem to notice that my stomach was rumbling like a giant beast ready to burst out of its dark cave and devour an entire village of screaming people.

After what felt like hours, Mrs. Landolfi flipped to the last page of the album and finished her narrative. I smiled with relief.

"Thank you for showing me your photos, Mrs. Landolfi. You have a beautiful family."

"Oh, thank you for listening, dear. I hope I didn't bore you."

"Not at all," I lied, pushing back my chair. "But I should be on my way now."

"Yes, yes, of course. It was lovely of you to stop by to talk about dear Jeremy."

We both stood up, but a thud from somewhere below the kitchen made me pause. The thud was followed by the tinkling of breaking glass. I glanced at Mrs. Landolfi, but she apparently hadn't heard a thing. Maybe she really was hard of hearing.

"Ah, Mrs. Landolfi? Is anyone supposed to be down in the basement?"

The elderly woman placed our two empty glasses in the kitchen sink. "No. Why do you ask?"

I strained to hear more sounds but all was quiet. "I'm not positive, but I think you could have an intruder."

Mrs. Landolfi's blue eyes widened. "Oh my. Goodness me. Should we call the police?"

I thought I detected another muffled thud from somewhere in the basement. I fished my cell phone out of my purse. "I think that would be a good idea." I eyed the door to the basement. "And maybe we should go out on the front porch." I didn't like the idea of a criminal deciding to join us in the kitchen.

"Yes, yes. Good idea." Mrs. Landolfi fingered the collar of her sweater as we made our way quietly to the front of the house.

I dialed 911 as I eased open the front door, trying to make as little noise as possible. We stood on the small porch in a pool of yellow light from the sconce by the door and I related my suspicion about an intruder to the dispatcher. I rattled off Mrs. Landolfi's address and explained that the last occupant of the basement suite had recently been murdered.

As the dispatcher instructed me to remain outside, I thought I heard something from around the corner of the house. With my phone still to my ear, I tiptoed down the front steps and along the narrow concrete path that led to the side gate.

"I think the intruder might be leaving," I hissed into my phone.

"Do not attempt to approach or intercept the suspect!" the dispatcher ordered.

"I won't," I whispered, not bothering to mention that I'd left the front porch to investigate. I didn't plan to confront the burglar—I knew that would be stupid—but I wanted to know if I was right, if there really was an intruder.

I leaned over the wooden gate and peered into the darkness. I could barely make out a stairwell and the side door to the house. A dark shadow moved in the stairwell and I froze, my heart fluttering in my throat like a trapped moth.

My free hand gripped the top of the gate. It rattled, and the shadow leapt out of the stairwell. It was a person. I had no doubt about that now. The burglar faced me for a split second, and then whipped around and sprinted away through the backyard.

"He's getting away!"

The dispatcher ordered me to stay put, and I retreated back to the front yard, my legs shaking. Moments later a police cruiser pulled up to the curb and I ran to meet the two officers who climbed out of it, informing the dispatcher of their arrival as I went.

"Someone just came out of the basement through the side door and took off through the back," I said, pointing toward the gate.

"We'll need you to remain here, ma'am," one of the officers told me as a second police cruiser arrived on the scene.

I rejoined Mrs. Landolfi on the front porch while two of the four police officers, their flashlights casting beams of light around the yard, proceeded through the side gate. The other two officers entered the house through the front door to take a look around.

I hugged myself and rubbed my arms, feeling the chill of the night air now that the immediate excitement had worn off. "How are you doing, Mrs. Landolfi?"

"It's rather frightening, having an intruder," she said. "And you, poor thing, standing out here in the night without a sweater."

"Don't worry about me." I peered through the open front door but saw no one. "Hopefully you'll be able to go inside and sit down soon."

"I think I'd like to call my son." Mrs. Landolfi fingered the collar of her sweater again.

"Does he live in Vancouver?"

"Oh, yes. He's a professor at UBC."

I held my cell phone out to her. "You can use my phone to call him."

"Thank you, dear. But I wouldn't have any idea how to use one of those newfangled contraptions."

I smiled. "That's okay. If you know his number, I can dial it for you."

"I'm afraid I haven't memorized a phone number in decades," Mrs. Landolfi confessed. "I have his number written in my address book, and he programmed it into my telephone."

The two officers who had disappeared into the house came back along the hallway toward the front door.

"Maybe the police will let you go inside and phone him now," I said.

"It's all clear, if you'd like to come in," a female officer said.

I followed Mrs. Landolfi into the living room. She settled herself in an armchair and picked up the receiver of the telephone set on a round side table. While she spoke to her son, the police officers conferred on the front porch. I tried to listen in on their conversation but couldn't make out their words.

I thought back to the figure I'd seen fleeing from the side of the house. Surely it wasn't a coincidence that someone had broken into Jeremy's suite mere days after his murder. But if it wasn't a coincidence, did that mean I had caught a glimpse of Jeremy's killer?

It had been too dark around the side of the house to see the intruder's face, so it wasn't as if I could identify the person, but the thought of being in such close proximity—yet again—to what might have been Jeremy's murderer creeped me out.

I thought about calling JT but remembered he was working in his studio all evening. I considered calling

Hans instead, but rejected that idea almost immediately. Even if I hadn't had any doubts about his innocence, I wasn't sure that our relationship was at the point where I could call him for comfort and reassurance.

Mrs. Landolfi said goodbye to her son and hung up the telephone. "He'll be here within the hour," she told me. "He wants me to stay with him for a few days."

"That's probably a good idea." I knew I wouldn't want to stay alone in a house that had just been broken into.

I heard new voices out in the foyer and my ears perked up. I thought I recognized Detective Bachman's voice. Yes, I decided after another moment, it was definitely him talking.

I wasn't surprised that Bachman had an interest in the break-in, but I hadn't expected him to show up quite so soon. I moved closer to the foyer so I could pick up some of his words.

" . . . know he was blackmailing Clausen . . . maybe . . . connection . . ."

Stunned by what I'd heard, I stepped out into the hallway. Bachman and Salnikova were both there with two of the uniformed officers. All four heads turned in my direction.

"Jeremy was blackmailing Hans?" I couldn't believe it.

Bachman cleared his throat. "Ms. Bishop. You seem to be turning up everywhere."

I narrowed my eyes, unsure of what, if anything, he was insinuating. "I came to talk to Mrs. Landolfi about Jeremy. I didn't realize there was anything wrong with that."

"We're not suggesting that there's anything wrong with it," Salnikova said in a placating tone.

I wasn't sure I believed her, but I was more interested in what I'd overheard. "Are you sure Jeremy was blackmailing Hans?" I wanted them to tell me that I'd misheard.

Neither detective answered my question, but I could tell from their expressions that they were certain. I was at a loss.

"Why?" I asked. "What reason would he have to blackmail Hans?"

"That," Detective Bachman said, "is something you'll have to ask him."

He and Salnikova passed by me to join Mrs. Landolfi in the living room while the two uniformed officers headed out the front door. I remained in the foyer, too stunned and confused to move.

Jeremy had blackmailed Hans.

Hans. Blackmailed.

Reality was sinking in, slowly but surely. But as it did, one question continued to repeat itself in my mind.

Why?

Chapter 10

I WAS STILL in the foyer when Salnikova emerged from the living room a moment later.

"Ms. Bishop, I'd like to ask you a few questions about what happened."

With effort, I forced myself to think of something other than Hans. "I don't really have much to tell, but all right."

"Shall we sit down somewhere?" the detective suggested.

I led her back to the kitchen and we settled in at the table, Salnikova with her notebook and pen out. I recounted how I'd heard noises from the basement and how I'd seen someone emerge from the stairwell at the side of the house.

"Did you get a good look at this person?" Salnikova asked.

I shook my head. "It was too dark. He was wearing a

dark colored hoodie, and I'm pretty sure there was white lettering on the hood, but that's all I could make out. I didn't even catch a glimpse of his face."

The detective made a notation in her notebook. "So it was a man?"

Her question made me pause. "Actually, I'm not sure." I replayed the memory in my head, focusing on the shadowy figure I'd seen. "It could have been a woman. If it was a man, he wasn't all that big." It was hard to form a precise mental picture of the person's size. I'd seen the intruder for less than five seconds, and for part of that time he or she had been standing down in the stairwell.

A thought struck me like a lightning bolt. "You don't think it was Hans, do you?"

Salnikova's face gave nothing away. "Do you?"

"Of course not!"

"Because the intruder wasn't the right size and build, or because you don't want to believe him capable of breaking and entering?"

Both! I wanted to yell. But was that the truth?

"This is ridiculous," I said. "Why would Hans break into Jeremy's place?"

Salnikova didn't reply, but I could see the answer in her eyes. Jeremy had blackmailed Hans. If Hans had killed Jeremy because of that, maybe he wanted to destroy some evidence.

Another thought struck me, this one giving me more hope. "If you already knew that Jeremy was blackmailing Hans, what would be the point of Hans trying to destroy evidence?"

Salnikova's expression was shuttered. She wasn't about to answer my questions.

My frustration level was on the rise, but I tried my best to quell it.

"You didn't answer my question," Salnikova reminded me.

It took me a second to realize which question she meant. I sighed, releasing some of my frustration. "I think the intruder was smaller than Hans. But," I added with reluctance, "I can't be sure." It was almost painful to admit that.

If only I'd seen the person's face. If only I could have identified him or her as someone other than Hans.

I slumped back in my chair, tired and hungry and more than a little grumpy.

Salnikova's pen moved across the page of her notebook. "Do you remember anything else?"

"No. Nothing." I paused for a split second before saying, "If you don't know who the person was, I take it they got away."

"Unfortunately," Salnikova said. "We brought in a dog and it tracked the suspect to the end of the alley, but we figure he or she must have retreated by car from that point."

That only added to my frustration. Mrs. Landolfi's neighborhood was a residential one. Without traffic cams or surveillance video from businesses, what was the chance that the police would be able to track the intruder? Slim to none, was my guess.

If the police had caught the intruder, they probably

would have been much closer to solving the murder. Now, however, the case was muddier than ever. At least, it was to me.

"Do you have any other suspects aside from Hans?" I asked, hoping for an affirmative response.

Salnikova shut her notebook. "I'm afraid I can't discuss that."

I gritted my teeth. "And you really won't tell me what the blackmail was about?"

The detective got to her feet. "I can't." For a second her expression softened with something close to sympathy. "I'm sorry." She pushed her chair back underneath the kitchen table. "That's all the questions we have for now, if you'd like to leave."

Disgruntled, I grabbed my purse and stopped by the living room to say goodbye to Mrs. Landolfi. One of the uniformed officers assured me that someone would stay with her until her son arrived, so I took my leave, hoofing it along the darkened street to the nearest bus stop.

I understood that the police couldn't discuss an open investigation, but their unwillingness to share even a shred of information still rankled. Although, if I were completely honest with myself, some of my annoyance stemmed from the fact that I had more doubts than ever about Hans.

I didn't want to believe that Jeremy had blackmailed him, but it was hard for me to have faith in him when he'd avoided my questions the last time I'd spoken to him. I was starting to wonder if he was worth the effort, if I should even bother trying to make sense of things.

But at the same time, I knew my mind wouldn't rest until I'd found the truth, and part of me still craved a chance to pursue our relationship. If he was innocent.

Yet, even if he hadn't killed Jeremy, he must have a secret. Otherwise, why would Jeremy have blackmailed him?

I arrived at a bus shelter and sat down on the bench, pulling out my phone to check the time. It was getting late, but I wanted answers and I wanted them that very night. So instead of going home, I decided to visit Hans.

HALF AN HOUR later I walked up the path to Hans's duplex. I hadn't forgotten about my promise to JT, and I paused outside the front door, wondering how to confront Hans without breaking my word. I didn't plan on going inside, but I wasn't sure that standing on the front porch on a dark, deserted street counted as not being alone with Hans. Actually, I was pretty sure it didn't. But I was determined to talk to him that night.

I decided on a compromise. Before knocking on the door, I pulled out my cell phone and sent a text message to JT.

I have to talk to Hans. I'm at his house. I'll text you again in 10 minutes. Don't freak out!

I raised my right hand to knock on the door but my phone chimed before my fist made contact with the wood. I glanced at the display. JT had responded already.

Dori, don't!

I have to, I wrote back.

What's his address?

I sighed, knowing that if I gave JT my location he'd probably hightail it over to meet me. I had to admit, however, that I'd feel safer if someone knew where I was. Just in case Hans really was capable of harming Jeremy. And me.

I tapped out Hans's address and then added, *Stay home. I'll be fine. Don't. Freak. Out.*

I didn't wait for any more messages, rapping hard on the door with my knuckles.

My phone chimed, but the door opened before I had a chance to read the latest text.

I stared at the woman standing in the doorway, her flawless ivory skin expertly highlighted along her cheekbones, her shiny blond hair cascading over her shoulders. "Elena?"

"What do you want?"

"I . . ." My tongue seemed to have stuck to the roof of my mouth. "Is Maestro in?"

"Sorry, no." She looked me over from head to toe. "Is there something I can help you with?"

With every passing second, my stomach sank lower. My throat had gone dry and I had to swallow before I could speak again. "No. I was hoping to speak to him about . . . something important."

"You'd better come in, then," she said with a sigh. "Hans should be back any moment."

Hans. Not Maestro. Hans.

She was on a first name basis with him and she was in his home, barefoot and with an unmistakable air of belonging. I wanted to turn around and flee, to pretend that I'd never run into her there. Yet, somehow I found myself stepping into the foyer. Numbness had taken over my body and I couldn't seem to process any thoughts.

"It's Dora, isn't it?" Elena asked as she closed the door.

"Midori," I corrected, my voice strained.

She didn't even seem to hear me. "You might as well have a glass of wine while you wait." She started toward the kitchen and, like a robot, I followed her. "Red or white?"

I shook off some of my numbness. "Neither." I hesitated in the kitchen entryway. "I should be going."

Again she gave no indication that she'd heard me. "I'm surprised Hans isn't back already. It doesn't take that long to buy a few groceries." She opened a bottle of red wine and took a glass down from one of the cupboards. "Are you sure you don't want some?"

I nodded, my stomach sinking even lower as I realized how familiar she was with Hans's kitchen. I took a step backward. "I should really go."

"Don't go on my account." Elena poured a generous amount of wine into her glass. "Don't you want a chance to confront Hans?"

"Confront him?" I still couldn't think clearly. My thoughts were scattered, racing helter-skelter in my mind, so I couldn't pin down a single one.

"About me." She leaned one hip against the kitchen counter and took a long sip of her wine. "I don't think you stopped by to chat about orchestra business." She regarded me over the rim of her wineglass. "You thought you were his only lover, didn't you?"

I nearly choked. "We aren't lovers," I said quickly.

"But things were headed that way." She swirled her wine and took another sip. "No doubt he found you quite . . . amusing."

My body flooded with humiliation. "You don't seem upset." I had to force the words out through my constricted throat.

"Why would I be? I know what Hans is like. He enjoys little diversions now and then, but he always comes back to me. It's been that way for years."

"Years?" I echoed her last word in a hollow voice.

"We met in Germany when he was working in Munich."

Germany. They really had been together a long time. My stomach churned and I had to blink back hot tears.

"It doesn't surprise me that he wasn't honest with you," she went on. "He does have a tendency to keep secrets."

Secrets.

The word resonated in my head.

"Jeremy was blackmailing him," I blurted out. Then I bit my lip, wishing I could take the words back.

"The dead guy, you mean? Yes, that's true."

My numb mind finally kicked back into gear. "Wait. You know about that?"

"Oh, yes." Elena refilled her wineglass. "He hadn't got around to telling me about you yet, but he did fill me in on the blackmail fiasco. I told him weeks ago that it was foolish to lie about his last job, but he's a typical man and always thinks he knows best."

Although finding out about Elena and Hans had

kept me off kilter, my desire for answers worked its way through my shock. "He lied about his job in Uppsala?"

"There was no job in Uppsala," Elena said by way of confirmation. "He last worked in Germany, but he was asked to resign due to certain indiscretions involving a very beautiful first violinist and an equally beautiful flautist." A superior smile flitted across her face. "Apparently, neither one was too pleased to find out that she wasn't his one and only."

My humiliation grew exponentially. I was one in a long line. His interest in me had probably been nothing more than a game, a distraction. My stupidity astounded me. I couldn't believe that I hadn't seen through him. And to make matters worse, Elena knew all about my foolishness.

"Of course, Hans didn't want that to affect the rest of his career, so he fabricated the position in Uppsala. Yet another one of his little diversions helped him out by acting as his reference."

"But how did Jeremy find out?" Despite my overwhelming emotions, I couldn't dampen my curiosity.

Elena drained her second glass of wine. "Apparently he knew someone in the Uppsala orchestra. They mentioned that they'd never heard of Hans and, well, I guess the guy saw an opportunity to get some extra money."

A car door slammed somewhere outside.

"Maybe that's Hans now," Elena said. "I'm sure you want to chat with him."

I shook my head, backing up into the hallway. "No." Hans was the last person I wanted to talk to right then. "I'll be on my way."

I turned and fled for the front door, careful not to look at the living room. I didn't want to see the spot where Hans and I had shared our last kiss.

As I wrenched open the door, my throat constricted. I was afraid I would come face-to-face with Hans. Luckily, the front stoop was deserted. I hurried down the pathway to the sidewalk. A shadowy figure stood by the street, and for a second I thought I was about to run into Hans after all.

"Dori?"

Intense relief washed over me. "JT?"

He came toward me. "I thought you weren't going inside."

His voice held an unusual edge of annoyance. It was catching.

"And I thought you were staying home." I didn't mean for my words to sound accusatory, but that's how they came out. "I told you I'd be fine."

"You don't look fine. You look . . . rattled." Concern replaced some of his annoyance. "What happened?"

I brushed past him and climbed into the passenger seat of his blue pickup truck. He remained standing by the curb for a second before circling around the truck to the driver's side. By the time he settled in behind the wheel, I regretted my reaction from moments earlier.

"I'm sorry," I said, clutching my purse in my lap. "You're right. I am rattled. I didn't mean to take it out on you."

"What happened?" JT asked again. "Did Clausen do something to upset you?" His hand went to the driver's door as if he were about to get out.

I put a hand on his arm to stop him. "Hans isn't even there."

"Then how did you get inside?"

I glanced up and down the street, not wanting to wait around until Hans arrived home. "Can we get out of here? I'll explain in a minute."

"Dori—"

"Please, JT."

He buckled his seat belt and started the engine. He pulled away from the curb and headed down the street, casting glances at me every few seconds. When we were three blocks away from Hans's place, some of my anxiety drained away. Unfortunately, that made room for my humiliation to resurface.

A minute later JT pulled into the parking lot of a 7-Eleven and shut off the truck's engine. "Now can you explain to me what you were doing in the house of a suspected murderer when he wasn't even home?"

"My plan was to talk to Hans out on the front porch."

"And when you realized he wasn't home, you broke in?"

"No! Of course not!" I exhaled a huff of air. I didn't want to tell him what had happened. It was too embarrassing. But his eyes were fixed on me, and I knew he wouldn't let me get away without explaining. "Hans wasn't home, but his girlfriend was."

There was a moment of stunned silence. I closed my eyes, waiting for JT's response. It came a couple of seconds later.

"His *girlfriend*?"

"I didn't know about her! I swear!"

"Of course you didn't." JT gripped the steering wheel so hard that I thought he might break it.

"And apparently . . ." I swallowed, finding it hard to get the words out. "Apparently I'm just one in a long line of women on the side." Tears pricked at my eyes as a fresh wave of hurt and humiliation crashed over me. "You were right. Getting involved with him was a huge mistake. What was I thinking? How could I have been so stupid? To think I actually believed that he . . ."

I choked back a sob and shut my eyes tight to keep my tears from escaping. I didn't want to cry, but the situation had truly sunk in now. I felt like the dumbest person alive. I'd thought I was special to Hans, that there was the possibility of something great between us. But I was nothing more than a temporary amusement.

How did I not see this coming? What signs did I miss?

"Hey." JT lifted the hair that had fallen across the side of my face and tucked it back over my shoulder. "You're not stupid. He's the idiot."

I shook my head. "You knew it was a mistake for me to get involved with him. So why didn't I?"

"I didn't know it was a mistake. I just had misgivings. But for entirely different reasons."

I wiped away the one tear that had managed to escape from my eyes and drew in a deep, shaky breath. "Hans Clausen is a lying, cheating bastard."

"I won't argue with you there."

"But, JT," I said, my voice strained by my overpowering emotions, "I think he might also be a burglar and a murderer."

Chapter 11

"YOU REALLY THINK he's the killer?" JT asked. "And what do you mean by a burglar? Did I miss something?"

I rested my head against the back of the seat and focused on his first question. "I don't know. I really don't. He's not the person I thought he was, and he's obviously deceitful, but I know that doesn't necessarily make him a murderer. Still, I can't help doubting everyone and everything, him included."

"Why would you say he might be a burglar?"

"Because of my adventurous time at Jeremy's landlady's house." I went on to explain about the basement intruder and the fact that Jeremy had blackmailed Hans.

"So Clausen had a motive to kill Jeremy," JT concluded.

"Yes," I said with a sigh. "He did. But even though I have doubts about him, I'm still not convinced he's guilty. Some things don't quite fit."

"Such as?"

"I can't say for certain that the intruder wasn't Hans, but my first impression was that the burglar was smaller than him. And the more I think about it, the more I'm convinced of that. Plus, if the police already knew about the blackmail, why would Hans need to break into Jeremy's place?"

JT tapped his fingers on the steering wheel, staring out through the windshield as he thought things over. "Maybe he wanted to hide or destroy evidence that would implicate him in something beyond the blackmail."

"Like murder?" A chill ran down my spine as I pictured Hans wrapping his hands around Jeremy's neck and squeezing tight.

"Maybe." JT dropped his hands from the steering wheel. "Then again, maybe he wasn't the burglar. Clausen could be innocent of everything except being a lying bastard, or the killer and intruder could be two different people."

"But that's the thing," I said, my frustration rising. "It's impossible to figure out!"

"It's not your job to figure it out," JT reminded me. "Leave it to the police. Please."

"But what if they never figure it out?" That was a scary thought. "I don't want to keep suspecting my fellow musicians, wondering if one of them is a killer." I let out a sound of frustration and unbuckled my seat belt, climbing out of the truck.

"Where are you going?" JT asked as he exited the vehicle through the driver's door.

"I need a Slurpee." I headed for the 7-Eleven, JT jogging to catch up with me.

He beat me to the door by half a step and held it open for me. "At this hour?"

He had a point. It was after ten o'clock, and that amount of sugar would wind me up further and keep me awake half the night. But all I'd eaten since breakfast was one cookie and my mood was crying out for junk food.

"I need *something*." I bypassed the Slurpee machine and snagged a bag of Doritos off a rack.

"Dori, I know it's been a crappy week, but things will get better." He grabbed a bag of potato chips for himself. "Give the police a chance to do their thing. I know it's hard, but I think you should try to focus on something else."

"You're probably right." I plunked my Doritos down on the cash counter and reached into my purse.

"I'll get that," JT said, pulling out his own wallet and handing the clerk enough cash to pay for both our purchases.

I gave him a smile of thanks and followed him out of the convenience store.

"Tomorrow is Jeremy's memorial service," I said once we were back in the truck. "Maybe once that's over with things will start to get better." I opened my bag of Doritos and reached in to grab a chip. "After all, I don't see how they could get much worse."

THE DORITOS DID little to assuage my hunger, so once JT dropped me off at my apartment, I fixed myself a peanut butter and jelly sandwich. Thank goodness I'd managed to buy some groceries earlier that day. I didn't need a growling stomach keeping me awake. I had enough other problems threatening to do that already.

As I munched on my sandwich, I tried not to feel morose, but it was hard to dispel the gloomy cloud that seemed to hang over my head. As sweet as it was for JT to say that I wasn't the stupid one, I sure felt like I was. I should have known better than to get involved with Hans. I didn't know if there were signs that I had missed, ones that would have alerted me to his deceit, but it didn't really matter now.

The fact was, I'd been fooled into thinking our relationship had real potential. Hans had hurt my pride, and even my heart. At least I hadn't fallen in love with him yet, but I had liked him. A lot.

I cringed at the thought of facing him again, and lost my appetite when I imagined Elena delighting in my stupidity and rubbing it in for the rest of my career. Despite the inevitable unpleasantness, I'd have to deal with the consequences of my less-than-wise decision to pursue a relationship with the man who held my professional fate in his hands. Would he be annoyed with me for finding out about Elena? Would it be too awkward to be in the same room together from now on?

If so, I could be in trouble. The orchestra meant so much to me, and I didn't want to lose my place in it. Sure, I now knew that Hans had lied about his past to get the job with the PGP, but I wasn't about to blackmail him into keeping me in the orchestra. I was upset with him, but I wasn't spiteful, and despite his indiscretions he was a good conductor.

I was relieved that a very limited number of people knew about our relationship. I wouldn't have to suffer my humiliation publicly, and that was something at least. But it wouldn't be easy to see Elena on a regular basis, to have her look down her nose at me with her smug superiority. Ugh.

I'd survive, though, even if it wouldn't always be a walk in the park.

As I got ready for bed, I thought over what JT had said earlier. I no longer had any real reason to try to prove Hans innocent. Even though I wanted to know who the murderer was, to feel safe and no longer suspect my fellow orchestra members, I could leave the investigating to the police.

It was time for me to focus on something other than murder and unwise relationships. As much as possible, I would put Hans and Elena out of my mind and keep my nose firmly out of other people's business. Things would get back to normal soon.

At least, that's what I hoped.

IN THE MORNING, I dressed in black pants and a blazer over a printed blouse. My dark clothing matched my mood. Despite my determination to forget about my relationship with Hans, a thunderous mixture of emotions hung over my head like a gloomy cloud. I hoped it would drift away in time, but for the moment I focused on fas-

tening my hair in a twist at the back of my head and pulling on black, high-heeled boots. After forcing myself to
eat a quick breakfast of toast and green tea, I rode the bus
to Jeremy's funeral service.

It was being held at the same church as our recent rehearsals, a fact I'd found surprising at first, considering
Jeremy had met his violent end there. However, our assistant conductor, who notified the orchestra of the service,
had explained that Jeremy's sister had chosen the location
because she and Jeremy had attended the church as children. I'm not sure that would have been enough reason
for me to hold a family member's funeral service at the
scene of their murder, but it was, of course, her decision.

When I arrived at the church, I found several familiar
faces in the small crowd milling about in the narthex.
Katie Urbina and Winston Chiu, two violinists from the
PGP, had gathered together with violist Evan Katz. Two
percussionists and a clarinet player from the orchestra
huddled together a few feet away, and Clover the bass
player stood near the stairway where I'd found Jeremy's
body. She rubbed her arms as if she were cold, her eyes
flitting over the crowd, never settling.

I wondered if she'd ever had any feelings for Jeremy, or
if their relationship had been purely physical. She certainly
didn't seem at ease at the moment, but whether that was
because she was upset about Jeremy or because funerals in
general made her uncomfortable, I didn't know.

Although my first instinct was to join Katie and Winston, I changed course and headed for Clover.

"Hey," I greeted as I stopped next to her.

Clover's eyes darted in my direction for only a fraction of a second. "Hey."

"How are you doing?"

"Fine," she said, the word clipped. "I mean, considering we're at a funeral."

"Right." I paused, trying to figure out how to broach the subject of her relationship with Jeremy. "I understand you and Jeremy were close."

Her head jerked my way, her eyes fearful. "What makes you say that?"

"Oh," I said, feigning confusion. "I thought you and he were . . . together."

"What?" The fear in her eyes had turned to panic.

"You were seen together. Kissing."

Clover's frightened gaze darted over the crowd in front of us. "We tried to keep it a secret," she said so quietly that I barely heard her.

I nodded with what I hoped would come across as understanding. "So his girlfriend wouldn't find out."

She seemed to relax a bit. A tinge of pink colored each of her cheeks. "And my boyfriend."

"Were you and Jeremy still . . . together when he was killed?"

"No. He got engaged to his girlfriend and said he wanted to be true to her."

Although she tried to hide it, I could tell the breakup had hurt her. A red flag went up in my mind.

"You must have been upset with him."

She looked at me sharply. "Of course I was upset. But I didn't kill him, if that's what you're suggesting."

That was what I was suggesting.

The fear returned to her eyes as she focused on something over my shoulder. "Please don't tell anyone about this."

Without another word, Clover hurried past me to join a big beefy man who had emerged from the hallway leading to the washrooms. She hooked her arm through his and led him away from me.

Her boyfriend had to be at least six-foot-five, and could probably bench-press a small car. He had a jagged scar on one cheek, and his dark, beady eyes didn't look the least bit friendly. I had no intention of saying anything to him that might tick him off.

However, the fact that Clover had a boyfriend who looked like he wrestled grizzly bears for fun made me wonder if he could be the one who killed Jeremy. If he found out about Clover and Jeremy's relationship, maybe he reacted violently. It wouldn't have surprised me.

Clover said that Jeremy had broken things off between them when he got engaged to Shelley, but the engagement had only occurred a few days before Jeremy's death. So it was possible that Mr. Grizzly Bear Wrestler had found out about the relationship while Clover and Jeremy were still together, and had simply taken a few days to act on his displeasure.

Clover's boyfriend didn't strike me as the patient type, but it was still possible he was the killer.

And what about Clover herself? Despite her denial, could she have been upset enough with Jeremy to kill him? She was present in the church that night. But then, so were dozens of others.

I sighed. Why weren't there any concrete clues?

It was only as the question ran through my head that I realized I was off to a bad start with regards to leaving the investigating to the police. I wasn't supposed to ask questions or come up with viable suspects. I wasn't sure if I could help myself, though. I didn't know how to switch off my curiosity. I didn't even know if that was possible.

Someone took hold of my arm, distracting me from my thoughts.

Mikayla.

"You still owe me details," she said, drawing me away into a quiet corner.

"We're at a funeral. I don't think this is the right time or place."

Mikayla ignored my objection and gave my shoulder a poke. "Spill."

I sighed and gave in. "It's over."

"What?" She gaped at me. "Since when?"

I glanced around to make sure no one could hear us. "Since last night, when I found out he's involved with Elena," I whispered.

"Elena?" Mikayla squawked. "He was carrying on with her at the same time?"

I shushed her. "Yes, and I don't want anyone to know there was ever anything between us."

She recovered from her initial surprise. "Of course not. Your secret's safe with me." Her eyes filled with sympathy. "But you poor thing. Are you okay?"

"I will be. As long as he doesn't kick me out of the orchestra."

Mikayla waved off my concern. "He won't do that. How would he explain it to the board of directors?"

She had a point. Maybe I didn't need to worry so much.

The crowd of people filtered into the nave, and Mikayla and I fell into step with everyone else. We slid into a pew about halfway down the aisle, Katie and Winston joining us soon after. Hans passed by our pew and I tensed. He didn't look in our direction, claiming a seat in a pew across the aisle and three rows ahead of us. I relaxed once he was seated. At least I wouldn't have to face him yet.

I searched the room for Elena's head of blond hair but didn't find it. That wasn't all that surprising, considering her views on Jeremy's death. No doubt she considered the funeral to be another waste of time.

I didn't know how many true friends Jeremy had during his life, but he certainly had a lot of acquaintances and colleagues in the music community. About two-thirds of the pews were occupied by the time the service started.

Reverend McAllister presided over the funeral, speaking about Jeremy's life and leading everyone in a few prayers. I only half listened to the reverend. The rest of my attention was focused on those present.

A tall, thin woman sat in the front row, flanked by two preteen children. I presumed she was Jeremy's sister. Directly behind her sat Shelley, crying quietly, with Gina and Lorelei sitting on either side of her.

There were several teenagers and young adults in attendance, and I figured they were probably Jeremy's cello students or members of the youth orchestra he had helped out with. A few of them looked bored, while others seemed sad but dry-eyed. One girl, however, rivaled Shelley with her quiet crying, fat tears rolling down her round cheeks. I guessed her age to be about fifteen. She wore a tight black dress and her straight brown hair reached down to the middle of her back. I wondered why she was so much more upset than all the other youngsters present. Perhaps Jeremy had been her cello teacher for a long time.

I turned my attention away from the girl and my eyes continued to wander over the attendees. Three rows back from the crying teenager, my gaze locked on two figures dressed in somber suits.

Detectives Bachman and Salnikova.

I wondered about their presence. Was it standard for detectives working on a murder case to attend the victim's funeral simply out of respect, or were they there for investigative purposes? Were they observing everyone's behavior in an attempt to identify more suspects, or were they watching Hans?

I didn't know if they were focused solely on him as the possible killer. I no longer even knew if they should bother searching for other suspects. I hadn't judged Hans's character well, so for all I knew the police had the right man in their sights. And yet, despite everything I'd discovered the night before, I found that I still hoped he was innocent.

Even though I couldn't be sure of the reason for the detectives' attendance at the funeral, I was willing to bet they were thinking along the same lines as me. Whoever the killer was, there was a good chance that he or she was in the room with us at that very moment.

Chapter 12

FOLLOWING THE SERVICE, everyone filed past Jeremy's sister in a receiving line before heading into a large room directly above the basement auditorium. Double doors along one wall stood open, revealing a kitchen, and two tables had been loaded with food and drinks for the reception. I led Mikayla over in the direction of the food tables, spotting several platters of tea sandwiches. I'd had a particular fancy for tea sandwiches my whole life.

We both loaded up plates with sandwiches, veggies, and other tasty tidbits before claiming some floor space near a potted fern. My eyes roamed over the crowd, searching for and finding Hans. Once I knew where he was, I angled my back to him, not wanting to draw his attention.

As I devoured my first sandwich, I realized that I hadn't asked Mikayla about her date the night before. "So, how did things go with Dave last night?"

She grinned as she licked some vegetable dip off one finger. "Fabulously. I'm seeing him again tomorrow night."

I smiled, happy for her. "He's not here today?"

"No, he plays in a soccer league and his team had a game. Besides, he knew Jeremy even less than we did." She selected a cherry tomato off her plate and waved at someone across the room as she swallowed it. "There's Bronwyn. I need to ask her if I left my favorite sunglasses at her place last week. I haven't been able to find them anywhere. See you in a bit!"

She left me alone by the potted fern, navigating her way through the crowd toward Bronwyn, one of the first violinists in the PGP. As I munched on a carrot stick, I spotted Mrs. Landolfi across the room. I made my way over to her as she filled a white mug with hot liquid from the coffee urn.

"Mrs. Landolfi," I greeted.

"Oh, hello, dear." She added a dollop of cream to her coffee.

"How are you today?"

"Still a little shaken up by last night's events," she said. "But I'm staying with my son for a few days, so that makes me feel better. Of course, today is a sad day. Poor Jeremy." Her eyes grew misty.

"I don't suppose the police have had any luck catching the intruder yet," I said, changing the subject in an attempt to prevent her from crying.

"No, not that I'm aware of." She took a sip of her coffee. "But those young men and women are so good at their job. I'm sure they'll catch the burglar eventually."

I wasn't sure that I shared her optimism, but I didn't say so.

"I'm going to talk to Jeremy's sister." Mrs. Landolfi patted me on the arm. "It was nice to see you again, dear."

"You too."

I looked down at my empty plate and decided I needed a refill. I was in the midst of selecting more tea sandwiches when someone came up behind me and stood by my right shoulder.

"Midori."

I tensed at the sound of Hans's voice in my ear. "Maestro." My tone was curt and I didn't bother to look at him, instead keeping my attention on the platter of sandwiches as I added two more to my plate. My hand shook and I cursed myself silently. I hoped he hadn't noticed the tremor.

He stood close enough that I heard his sigh. "Elena told me you came by last night."

"Did she." I moved along the table, adding a strawberry tart to my plate. I tried to stay relaxed but couldn't. Tension zinged through my muscles, leaving them taut, rigid.

Hans moved along with me. "I'd like a chance to explain."

I barely stopped myself from letting out a snort. "I think I understand the situation very well, thank you."

He followed me as I moved toward a relatively quiet corner of the room. "Midori, my feelings for you are real. Elena doesn't need to come between us."

"She already has. *You* already have. And I really don't

want to hear this." I chewed on a sandwich with more vigor than usual.

"Is there anything I can say to—?"

"No." I picked up another sandwich but set it down on my plate again, some of my ire draining away. "Can we forget about everything that happened between us? I'd like to go back to the way things were when you first arrived. A strictly professional relationship."

Hans regarded me with his blue eyes. "If that's what you want."

I thought I detected a hint of disappointment in his voice, but it didn't move me in the least. "That's what I want."

"All right, then. I'll see you at the next rehearsal."

If you haven't been arrested for murder first, I thought.

I watched him walk away and then turned my attention back to my sandwiches and strawberry tart. The food was delicious, but the recent company had drained away some of my enthusiasm for it.

As soon as I'd finished eating, I set my empty plate on a table near the kitchen door and wended my way through the crowd to join Mikayla and Bronwyn. Unsurprisingly, I found their company far more enjoyable than Hans's. We got so caught up in our conversation about our various students that we barely noticed the crowd dispersing around us. It was only when Mikayla glanced at the clock on the wall and said, "Sorry, girls, I've got to run," that I realized we were among the few remaining in the reception room.

After Mikayla and Bronwyn left, I helped two elderly church ladies carry used dishes and leftover food into the kitchen, snagging another mini sandwich as I went. By the time everything had been shifted into the kitchen, I was the only nonchurch lady left in the room.

Waving goodbye to the ladies, I headed down the hall to the narthex. I was relieved that all the other attendees had already taken their leave. I didn't want to run into Hans again. The few minutes during the reception earlier had been more than enough to deal with.

His feelings for me were real? Could he really expect me to believe that?

If he truly cared for me, he would have been honest from the start.

Pushing all thoughts of Hans aside, I pulled out my phone and sent a text message to JT.

Want to catch a movie?

He'd sent a reply by the time I reached the exit.

Sure. Still at the church? I'll pick you up.

Yep, I typed back with my thumbs. *Still here. See you soon.*

I paused inside the double doors leading outside. Did I want to wait inside or out?

Out, I quickly decided.

The spot where Jeremy met his end was only fifteen feet away, and its proximity still creeped me out. Besides, even though the skies had been overcast upon my arrival at the church that morning, the spring air had been fresh and scented with flowers. Much preferable to the creep-out vibes coming at me from the nearby stairway.

I pushed out the doors and onto the wide stone steps leading down to the sidewalk.

So much for flower-scented air.

Sometime during the past two hours the cloudy skies had opened up, and rain now poured down in sheets, pelting the poor flowers in the church's garden and obliterating all scents but that of the rain itself. Even so, outside was better than inside.

Apparently I wasn't the only one who thought so. The teenage girl I'd seen sobbing during the service was huddled on the top step, off to one side. The overhang protected her from the rain, but just barely. Even if the rain had drenched her, she probably wouldn't have noticed. She was too busy crying.

Still or again? I wasn't sure, but I felt a twinge of sympathy for her.

"Hey." I sat down beside her.

The girl sniffed and glanced at me with red-rimmed eyes. She wiped a tear with the back of her hand but another soon took its place.

"Were you one of Jeremy's students?" I asked.

The girl sniffed again and nodded. "I took cello lessons from him. He also helped out with my youth orchestra." She choked on a sob. "I can't believe he's dead. I can't believe somebody killed him."

Her whole body shook as sobs overcame her. She buried her face in her hands.

I gave her back an awkward pat. "I know it's been an awful shock. Is someone coming to pick you up?"

I didn't like the thought of leaving her there sobbing on her own.

The girl gulped and sniffled. "My mom. She should be here soon."

Phew. I hoped she was right about the soon part.

"What's your name?" I asked.

"Susannah."

"I'm Midori."

Susannah blinked back her tears, which, thankfully, were subsiding. "Like Midori Ito?"

"You know about her?" I was surprised. Ito was in the spotlight before my time, and therefore way before Susannah's time.

"I'm a figure skater."

Ah. That explained it. "Yes, like Midori Ito."

A tremulous smile pulled at the corners of her mouth but disappeared after only a second or two.

The wind had picked up during our conversation and a gust blew a wall of rain at us.

I winced as the drops pelted against me. "Why don't we wait for your mom inside?" I suggested. "Otherwise we'll get soaked."

Susannah didn't protest. With more sniffling but fortunately no more tears, she got up and followed me inside.

I pushed aside my former misgivings about hanging around near the scene of Jeremy's death and led her to the bench between the two staircases. I despised wet clothes even more than I despised the creepiness of the staircase where Jeremy died. Plus, hanging around the area wasn't quite so bad when I had company. At least if I had someone to talk to, I wouldn't keep picturing Jeremy's dead body.

Moments after we seated ourselves on the bench, Reverend McAllister emerged from the nave. When he spotted Susannah, his expression darkened, just for a second, until he noticed me sitting next to her.

"Oh . . . Hello, ladies." His eyes skittered away from us as if they didn't know where to settle. With a quick nod in our direction, he fled up the stairway to our left.

I stared after him, puzzled.

"That was weird," I remarked.

I glanced at Susannah, and grew even more puzzled. She was tense, staring at her hands clasped in her lap, her tear-streaked face pale.

"What's wrong?" I asked.

"Nothing." She pressed her lips together in a tight line and kept her eyes on her lap.

Obviously it wasn't nothing, but my thoughts had already strayed. I still had vague suspicions about the reverend and was curious to know how he would react if I dropped hints about everything I'd learned about Jeremy recently.

"I wonder if the reverend has a moment to spare." I shifted forward on the bench, ready to get up.

Susannah grabbed my arm. "Wait!"

Startled, I slid back on the bench.

"Please don't leave me alone here."

Now she had me downright perplexed. "What's wrong, Susannah?"

She chewed on her bottom lip and didn't respond.

I realized that her odd behavior had started after McAllister's appearance, and that sent my suspicion meter through the roof. "Susannah? Did Reverend McAllister do something to you?"

"No!" Her shoulders sagged. "I mean, nothing like that. Not what you're thinking. But he's not a good person."

"What do you mean?"

She bit her lower lip again. "I don't know if I should say anything." Her eyes filled with tears.

"If it's got you this upset, I think you should," I said.

She wiped at her fresh tears. "I don't want to get my uncle in trouble."

"Your uncle?" Now I was really confused.

Susannah sniffled. "Reverend McAllister and his wife are good friends with my uncle. They were all at my house for a dinner party a few weeks ago and . . ." She hesitated, but only briefly. "My uncle and Reverend McAllister had a lot to drink. They were playing pool in the basement after dinner and I overheard them talking."

"What about?"

"Reverend McAllister was making fun of people in his congregation, people I know, and my uncle wasn't exactly discouraging him. The things they said about some of the women were really awful. And then it got even worse." She glanced around as if to make sure we were still alone. "Then Reverend McAllister started saying terrible things about Bishop Maguire. He's a really nice man, but the reverend called him names that I can't even repeat."

I considered her words. I didn't know Bishop Maguire, but I doubted that he'd be pleased to hear what Susannah had just told me. Still, I thought I was missing something.

"Did McAllister realize you'd overheard him?" I

asked, wondering if that would explain the glare he'd sent in Susannah's direction.

She shifted on the bench. "I took a video of them on my phone."

"And McAllister knows that?"

Susannah nodded, fear flickering in her eyes. "I think Jeremy must have told him. But I don't know why he would do that to me." She sniffled, but fortunately no more tears spilled from her eyes.

"Jeremy?" My brain was on high alert now.

"I was here rehearsing with the youth orchestra one day when the reverend was around. Jeremy could tell that I didn't like the reverend and asked me why. I told him about the video and the things Reverend McAllister had said, but he thought I was exaggerating. So I sent him a copy of the video so he could see for himself. He believed me after that, but then he told me it would be best to keep quiet about the whole thing if I didn't want to make my uncle look bad. Except . . ."

"Except what?" I prompted, the gears turning in my head as I wondered if any of what she was telling me could be related to Jeremy's death.

Susannah clenched her hands together and took a deep breath. "Just before the funeral, Reverend McAllister cornered me and told me that if I ever showed the video to anyone else or posted it online, I'd be sorry." Her voice quavered when she continued. "So Jeremy must have told the reverend about the video, and then he got killed. What if his death is my fault? And now my mom's late picking me up, and I really don't want to be left alone when Reverend McAllister is around." Her last words came out in a rush.

So Susannah thought McAllister had killed Jeremy to keep him quiet about the video. That sounded like a good theory to me.

I reached over and gave her hand a quick squeeze. "Even if McAllister killed Jeremy, and even if it was because of the video, his death wasn't your fault."

"But what if the reverend wants to kill me too?"

That was a valid concern.

"I think you should tell your mom the whole story as soon as she gets here. Then you two can talk to the police."

Susannah nodded reluctantly. "I guess you're right."

A floorboard creaked. I leaned forward to see if anyone was nearby, but there was no one in sight.

Standing up, I turned my attention back to Susannah. "Do you want to go wash up? Hopefully your mom will be here any moment."

She got to her feet and I accompanied her to the small restroom down the hall. While she locked herself in a stall, I waited by the sinks, pulling my phone from my purse to check the time. JT would likely arrive in the next few minutes, and I was glad of that. As much as I sympathized with Susannah's predicament, passing her off to the care of her mother would be a relief.

I returned my phone to my purse and decided I might as well make use of the facilities while I was there. I locked myself in the stall next to Susannah's and hung my purse on the hook on the door.

Outside my stall, the washroom door opened with a creak of oil-thirsty hinges. I winced at the metallic screech I heard next. It sounded like someone had dragged the metal garbage can across the floor.

A maintenance worker?

I paused, listening.

I heard a splash of liquid, then a click and a loud whoosh.

I didn't like the sound of that whoosh.

The washroom door banged shut as Susannah's toilet flushed.

Abandoning my plan to use the facilities, I grabbed my purse and fumbled with the door latch.

The smell of smoke needled my nose. Alarm bells went off like crazy in my head.

"Midori?" Susannah's trembling voice came from her stall.

I pushed out of my own stall and froze.

Someone had moved the large trash can over to the door and lit its contents on fire. Flames danced in the air, dangerously close to the wooden door of Susannah's stall.

"Is there a fire?" Panic had sent the pitch of her voice up several notches. She undid the latch on her stall.

"Don't open the door!" I warned.

The wooden stall ignited and the flames grew bigger.

Susannah screamed. "Midori!"

"Crawl into the next stall!"

As soon as her head poked under the divider and into the stall I'd vacated, I took three cautious steps toward the burning trash can. I reached out with one foot and nudged the can away from the door. It only moved a few inches.

Heat blasted my skin. I couldn't get any closer to the can without getting burned.

Behind me, Susannah crawled out into the open and climbed to her feet. "What are we going to do?"

"Stay calm." I said it as much for my sake as hers as I inched my way around the fire. My heart skittering in my chest, I reached for the doorknob.

My hand seared with pain. I snatched it away with a cry. The knob was hot, heated by the flames before I'd moved the trash can.

"Midori! Are you okay?" Susannah hovered in the background.

I ignored her. I blinked back tears of pain and slid out of my blazer, careful not to let the fabric touch my burned hand. Shaking now, I wrapped the garment around my good hand and reach for the doorknob again. I turned it. Nothing happened. I rattled the door and tried the knob again. Still nothing.

The door was locked.

Chapter 13

I POUNDED ON the door. "Help! Somebody help us! We're trapped!"

I threw my bodyweight against the door, hitting it with my shoulder, but it barely even shook in its frame. I tried again, but it still didn't budge.

Choking on the thickening smoke, I shied away from the intensifying heat, stumbling backward into Susannah.

She clutched at my arm. "How can the door be locked? How can this be happening?" Tears streamed down her face from her wide, terrified eyes.

The acrid smoke grated at my throat and nostrils. I coughed and shoved Susannah toward the back corner of the cramped, windowless washroom, as far from the flames as possible. I pushed her down into a crouch. "Stay down. Below the smoke."

I huddled down next to her and fumbled around in my purse with my good hand until I found my cell phone.

My hands shook so much that I dropped the device. It clattered to the floor. With fear constricting my chest and my heart galloping at a frantic pace, I snatched it up and dialed 911.

"Help!" Susannah yelled next to me. "Someone help us, please!"

Despite Susannah's panicked calls for help, I heard the dispatcher on the other end of the line ask me to state the nature of my emergency.

"There's a fire and we're trapped!" I realized that I sounded as frantic as Susannah, but we both had reason to be freaked out.

Both bathroom stalls had caught fire, and the flames crept toward us, the heat intensifying with every passing moment. Dark gray smoke filled the room, choking us despite the fact that we were huddled down low on the floor.

I let out a harsh cough, but managed to relate the details of our location to the dispatcher before my hacking turned into a full out fit.

"We're going to die!" Susannah croaked between coughs of her own. She grabbed onto my arm and buried her face in my shoulder.

Somewhere out in the corridor an alarm sounded with a sustained, shrill ringing.

"Please hurry," I rasped into the phone. I knew we didn't have much time left.

Somebody shouted outside the washroom. I couldn't make out what they said, but I didn't care. There was someone there.

"Help!" Susannah and I yelled.

Our voices were hoarse, but whoever was out there must have heard us.

"Hold on!" the voice called to us. A male voice.

Susannah clung to me as we both succumbed to coughing fits again.

Seconds later something banged against the washroom door. It shuddered in its frame but held. A second bang splintered the wooden frame. With a third blow the door broke open.

The flames grew bigger, greedily consuming the new oxygen flowing in through the open door. I winced and Susannah screamed. The heat was so intense, the smoke so thick.

A large hand grabbed my arm and yanked me to my feet. I stumbled along with our rescuer, my good hand clutching Susannah close to me. I couldn't see anything but smoke and flames. I couldn't breathe.

We ducked past the hungry flames, heat blazing against my face. The rescuer pulled us out of the washroom and down the corridor to the narthex. I tripped and almost went down, but the hand on my arm tugged me upright and propelled Susannah and me out the double doors and onto the stone steps.

Somehow we made it down the stairs without falling. At the bottom, we collapsed together onto the wet grass next to a sodden flower bed. I cradled my burned hand against my chest and held onto Susannah with my other arm. We clung to each other, coughing and hacking, drawing fresh air into our lungs whenever we could.

I was only half aware of sirens piercing the air with their wails, of two fire trucks pulling up in front of the church. I hardly even noticed the dampness from the rain and wet grass seeping through my clothes. All I cared about right then was the fact that Susannah and I were safe. No flames were going to burn us to ashes, no smoke was going to suffocate us.

Still coughing on and off, I concentrated on moving beautiful, clean air in and out of my lungs. It was only when I'd had several breaths of damp air that I registered the sight of our rescuer.

"Ray?" I was more than a little surprised that the oboe player was the one who had saved us.

He was breathing heavily, but otherwise seemed fine. "You two okay?"

"Thanks to you," I said.

I didn't have a chance to say anything more to him. Two firemen approached, and Susannah and I quickly became separated as they—and soon, paramedics as well—looked us over, asked us questions, and assessed our health.

By the time a female paramedic led me over to an ambulance, my coughing had subsided to only the occasional hack. Fresh air was the best thing for me, the paramedic had told me, and she was right. I'd never been so grateful for clean, cool air. My throat felt sore and irritated, but I could breathe, and that was what mattered most.

Once I was seated in the back of the ambulance, the paramedic tended to the burn on my right hand, cleaning it gently. Despite the care she took, I winced with pain.

"I don't have to go to the hospital, do I?" The thought of spending hours in the emergency room didn't appeal to me in the least.

"No," the paramedic said. "You're lucky. This is just a minor burn. I'll get it cleaned and bandaged for you. Then you just need to look after it on your own. If it doesn't seem to be healing properly, go see your doctor."

She finished cleaning the burn, and the pain in my hand eased to a less excruciating level. As she wrapped my hand with gauze, my attention wandered. Outside the open back door of the ambulance, firemen moved back and forth between the church and their trucks. The sense of urgency about them had dwindled over the last several minutes, and I figured that the fire was probably out. Hopefully it had remained contained within the washroom and hadn't damaged any more of the church.

Several people, probably residents of the neighborhood, had gathered in a cluster nearby, watching the excitement outside the church. A blond woman pushed her way through the crowd and rushed toward the church's entrance. Cindy McAllister.

I lost sight of her, my view limited by my position within the ambulance.

The paramedic finished wrapping my hand. "There you go. Be sure to keep it clean."

"Thank you."

She helped me out of the ambulance, and I stepped up the curb to stand in the damp grass. The rain had stopped, but water still dripped from the branches of the trees planted along the street, and the sidewalk was dotted with puddles and earthworms.

The firemen had waylaid Cindy McAllister, preventing her from entering the church. She seemed distressed, but that wasn't surprising. I spotted the reverend talking to another fireman near one of the trucks. When he saw his wife, he excused himself and hastened across the lawn to join her.

"Dori!"

I spun around. JT jogged diagonally across the street toward me. Until then my emotions hadn't gone beyond relief at being safe, but somehow the sight of JT brought the enormity of the experience down on me. I could have died. A few more minutes in that room with the smoke and flames and I would have.

As soon as JT reached me, I wrapped my arms around him and pressed my cheek against his chest, my eyes closed. I was careful of my burned hand but still held on tightly. It was as if I'd been thrown a life preserver in the midst of a stormy sea. Tears pricked at my eyes, but I managed to hold them back.

JT's arms closed around me. "Midori, what's wrong? What happened?"

I didn't feel like talking right then, but I knew from the alarm in his voice that he needed an immediate explanation. I didn't relax my hold but I tilted my head up so I could speak to him. "There was a fire. I was trapped in the washroom with Susannah, but Ray broke down the door and got us out."

"Susannah? Ray?" He shook his head before I could explain. "Never mind. Are you okay?"

I nodded against his chest. His warmth and solid frame were so comforting that I didn't want to let go. But I did. I stepped back out of his arms and held up my bandaged hand.

"Just a minor burn on my hand. I don't think I'll be able to hold my bow for a few days." That was annoying and disappointing. I didn't like the idea of taking time off from playing the violin, but I wasn't about to complain too much. It was better than being dead or lying in the hospital with serious burns.

JT must have been thinking along the same lines, because he pulled me back into a tight hug. "Your violin will have to wait. I'm just glad you're okay."

"Me too." I drew back then, realizing that I reeked of acrid smoke. "Sorry about the smell."

"Believe me, that's the least of my worries right now."

His brown eyes were fixed on mine, and a fresh wave of intense emotion hit me. My breath caught in my irritated throat. That set off a coughing fit, and several seconds passed before I could stop hacking.

JT put a hand on my back. "You're sure you're okay?"

I nodded. "Promise." The coughing fit had distracted me enough to calm my emotions, but now exhaustion swept over me.

"Ma'am?"

I turned around. It was a uniformed policeman who had addressed me.

"Are you one of the ladies who was trapped?" the officer asked.

"Yes. Susannah and I." I pointed across the lawn toward Susannah. She was in the arms of a plump, middle-aged woman. Her mother, presumably.

The policeman followed my gaze and nodded. "What can you tell me about what happened?"

I closed my eyes briefly, fighting off the exhaustion that threatened to overwhelm me. JT kept his hand on my back, and his steady warmth helped to ground me. I related everything I could remember to the officer, including the sounds I'd heard as I stood inside the bathroom stall. I sensed JT tense next to me as I told my story to the officer, but he didn't speak until I finished my narrative.

"The fire was set deliberately?" JT asked with an edge to his voice.

"It must have been," I said. "Why else would someone have dragged the trash can over by the exit and locked the door on us? And the splashing sound I heard . . ." I directed my next question at the police officer. "Did the person who set the fire use an accelerant?"

The officer wrote something in his notebook as he answered my question. "That will be for the fire investigation team to determine." He jotted down another note before raising his head. "Do you remember anything else? Did you see anyone in the area before you went into the washroom?"

"Only Reverend McAllister. He came out of the nave and went upstairs."

"How long after that did you go into the washroom?"

"Not long," I replied. "A few minutes, maybe."

The officer made another notation in his book, but I barely noticed. Had Reverend McAllister overheard me and Susannah talking about him? Had he been so concerned about getting in trouble over his drunken comments that he'd deliberately set the fire, to . . . what? Frighten us into keeping quiet? Silence us forever?

I shivered at the thought and leaned into JT's side.

Although I wanted to share my suspicions about the reverend with the police officer, I decided to hold back for the moment. It would probably be better to go straight to Detectives Bachman and Salnikova.

JT put his arm around me. "Officer, can I take Midori home now? She's been through a lot."

"Of course. Ma'am, I just need your contact information in case we have any more questions."

I rattled off my address and phone number, and he copied them down into his notebook. Once he was done recording the information, the officer left us and headed in Susannah's direction.

I let out a tired sigh and leaned more of my weight against JT.

He gave me a quick squeeze. "Come on, let's get you home."

"There's nothing I want more than a shower and clean, dry clothes," I said, wrinkling my nose at the stench of smoke that clung to my hair and damp clothing like a harsh and pungent cloud.

JT returned his hand to my back to guide me toward his truck, but I stopped before we reached the street.

"Hold on a second." I left him standing by the curb

and turned back toward the church. I'd spotted Ray talking to a policewoman, but as I headed in his direction, the officer finished her conversation with him and went to speak to one of her fellow officers.

Ray started off down the street, his hands stuffed in the pockets of his pants. His hunched shoulders and brisk steps suggested an eagerness to get away from the scene.

"Ray, wait!" I jogged after him. "Ray!"

He stopped at the sound of my voice and turned back.

I had to slow my pace as I broke out into another fit of harsh coughs. "I wanted to thank you," I wheezed between coughs when I reached his side. "You saved my life. Susannah's too."

He shifted his feet and fixed his eyes on the sidewalk. "I'm just glad I could help."

I coughed again and took a second to catch my breath. "We're lucky you were still around. I thought all the other people from the funeral had already left."

Ray's eyes slid to the side. "I'd stepped out the back for a few minutes. I guess I was there for a while before I came back in and smelled the smoke. When I went to investigate, I heard screaming, so I kicked down the door and . . ." He shrugged. The rest we both already knew.

"Well, thank you. Thank you times a million."

Ray nodded, still not meeting my eyes. "See you next week."

He set off down the street again and disappeared through a small cluster of curious local residents who still had their eyes on the church and emergency personnel.

A hand touched my arm.

"Midori?"

Susannah had approached me from behind, her mother hanging back a short distance.

"Are you okay?" I asked her.

She nodded. "That was really scary, though."

"It was," I agreed. "Are you going home now?"

"Yes." She bit down on her lower lip. "Thank you for . . . you know, talking to me and everything."

"You're welcome. Are you going to tell your mom what you told me?"

Susannah glanced over her shoulder at her mother. "Yes. As soon as we get home."

"Good. It's for the best," I assured her. I opened my arms and she stepped into them. I gave her a quick hug, still taking care not to use my bandaged hand. "Listen, why don't I give you my number? That way if you ever want to talk about what happened today you can get in touch with me."

"I'll give you mine too."

We dug our phones out of our respective purses and exchanged numbers.

"Take care of yourself, okay?" I said once we were done.

She stepped back and gave me a tremulous smile. "You too."

She returned to her waiting mom, who put an arm around her and led her off down the street.

JT came over then. "Susannah, I take it?" he said, following my gaze as I watched the girl leave with her mother.

"Yes."

Once they were gone, I glanced around at the quieting scene. The ambulance and one of the fire trucks had already departed, and most of the onlookers had left now too. A fireman led McAllister and his wife inside the building. The sight of the reverend brought all my suspicions back to the surface.

I couldn't help but see him in a sinister light now. Had he strangled Jeremy and then tried to do away with me and Susannah?

Jeremy had blackmailed Hans, and I now believed that he had blackmailed McAllister as well. He'd told Susannah to keep quiet about the video, yet McAllister knew about it. I figured that meant Jeremy had threatened to make the video public, demanding money from the reverend in exchange for keeping the video a secret. Maybe I was wrong, but I didn't think so.

The question was, had blackmail and the threat of exposure driven Reverend McAllister to murder?

Chapter 14

"I THOUGHT YOU suspected Clausen," JT said when I told him about Susannah's story and my latest suspicions.

"I did. I do." I lowered the passenger window of JT's truck so the stench of smoke from my clothes and hair wouldn't overwhelm us. "I guess I suspect several people. McAllister just happens to be at the top of my list at the moment."

JT turned his truck off a tree-lined street and onto a busy road, heading toward my neighborhood. "So who else is on your list?"

"Well, there's Ray."

"The guy who just saved your life?"

"Maybe the whole rescue thing was meant to deflect suspicion away from him."

JT sent me a skeptical, sidelong glance.

"Why not?"

"I suppose it's a possibility," he conceded. "But setting

fire to a church and endangering people's lives seems a bit over the top if his sole purpose was to make himself look unsuspicious."

I tugged on my left earlobe and breathed in the fresh damp air blowing in through the open window. "Maybe he wanted to scare me because I'm getting too close to the truth."

"Are you?"

"Am I what?"

"Getting close to the truth."

"I have no idea." I rested my head against the back of the seat. "All I've got is a bunch of suspicions. But he might think that I know more than I do."

"What would make him think that?"

I searched my memory for anything I might have done to make Ray believe I could be a threat to him. "I was asking questions last rehearsal. About whether he'd seen Jeremy in the minutes before his death. But I don't think that would have been enough to worry him, even if he is the killer." I thought things over for a moment. "And I have no idea why he would want to kill Jeremy. But that's why he's lower down my list than McAllister, who had motive and opportunity for both Jeremy's murder and the fire. He probably wanted to get rid of me and Susannah so no one would find out about the video."

If I'd had a physical list of suspects, I would have underlined and circled McAllister's name. He seemed to me the most likely culprit.

"You said you suspected several people," JT reminded me. "Who else?"

"Clover seems pretty upset that Jeremy dumped her when he proposed to Shelley. And her boyfriend looks like a grizzly bear on steroids. If he found out about Clover and Jeremy, he might have decided to take Jeremy out of the picture, whether or not he knew that things were over between them."

"But what about the fire?"

"Clover knows I was asking questions the other night." I shook my head. "Nope. I still like the reverend for it." I tapped my fingers on the armrest. "I should tell the detectives about him."

"Really?" JT didn't sound too thrilled.

"Don't you think they should know? I bet they have no clue that Jeremy was blackmailing McAllister."

"*You* don't even know that he was blackmailing McAllister," JT pointed out.

I made a face. "Fine. But I strongly suspect that he was, given what Susannah told me. And if McAllister is the killer, isn't it my civic duty or something to put the police on the right track?"

JT let out a breath as he turned his pickup truck onto my street.

"What?" I could sense his exasperation, but I wasn't sure what had caused it.

"If you feel you should tell the police, then go ahead. But then can you please leave the investigation to them?"

I rolled my eyes as I raised the passenger window. "Haven't we had this conversation before?"

"Yes. Without effect, apparently." He pulled into a parking space across the street from my apartment building.

"You can't blame me for wanting to know who the murderer is. Especially since he or she was likely behind the fire that almost killed me and Susannah."

"I don't blame you for wanting to know who the killer is." JT shut off the engine and pulled his keys out of the ignition with more force than usual. A muscle in his jaw twitched. "But if the murderer set the fire to silence you, or to scare you into backing off, that means you could still be in danger. If you keep poking around and asking questions, the killer might try to harm you again."

"Possibly," I said. "But it's also possible that the fire was set by some random pyromaniac or maybe as a foolish prank. Or maybe it was aimed solely at Susannah for whatever reason, and I was simply in the wrong place at the wrong time."

"Do you really believe that?"

"I don't know what to believe," I confessed.

"Exactly." The muscle in JT's jaw twitched again. "So can we please err on the side of caution?"

I opened my mouth to argue but then shut it again. "I guess that would be the smart thing to do," I said after a moment.

"It would."

Even though the truck's engine was off, JT gripped the steering wheel. I wasn't used to seeing him so uptight.

"I'm sorry, JT. I didn't mean to exasperate you."

He relaxed his hold on the wheel. "I'm more worried than exasperated."

He unbuckled his seat belt and I followed suit. We climbed out of the truck and waited for a car to pass before crossing the street.

"I think you should go visit your parents for a few days," JT said as I dug my keys out of my purse.

I stopped and stared at him. "Why?" My parents lived out of town, four hours away by car.

"To get out of harm's way."

I shook my head and resumed my search for my keys. Once I had them in hand, I unlocked the front door of my apartment building. "I can't take off. I have to work."

JT held the door open for me. "A few days off won't kill you."

"No." I led the way across the lobby and up the stairs. "But they'd hurt my bank account. If I don't teach, I don't get paid."

Even though I earned some money from playing in the orchestra, I depended on my teaching income to keep me afloat. I'd already canceled my Saturday lessons to attend Jeremy's funeral. I didn't want to cancel any more if it weren't absolutely necessary. And in my mind, it wasn't.

"Then come stay with me for a few days. That way you can still work."

We reached the third floor and I unlocked the door to my apartment. "This isn't like you, JT."

"Caring about the safety of my best friend isn't like me?"

I sighed and opened the door. "Okay, so that is like you." I entered my apartment and tossed my keys and purse on the coffee table. "But I'm used to you being so calm. When you worry, I worry."

"Maybe you should be worried."

I put my hands on my hips. My burned hand protested vigorously. "Ow!" I cradled it against my stomach and frowned, partly at JT and partly at my painful injury. "Are you trying to scare me?"

"No, I'm trying to get you to take things seriously so you don't get hurt again." He nodded at my gauze-wrapped hand. "Things could have turned out a lot worse today, Dori."

"I *know* that. I'm the one who almost got charred." I sighed again, the tension that had been building in my shoulders now slipping away. "I'm not sure why I'm arguing about this. I'm as worried as you are. I just don't like to admit it because . . . because that makes it real. I mean, maybe the fire was random, but what if it really was aimed at me?" A quiver of fear jittered up my spine. "It's too scary to think about. So I'd rather not." JT was about to say something, but I cut him off before he had the chance. "I know, I know. Denial won't stop something like that happening again."

"So you'll stay at my place?"

"For a few days."

JT relaxed and rewarded me with a half smile. "Good."

I slipped out of my blazer and grimaced at the smell of it. "I don't think I can wait any longer for a shower." I headed for the closet in my bedroom and rummaged around for some clean clothes. "I guess I messed up our movie plans," I said when I emerged back into the living room. "Feel free to have a snack if you're hungry."

"What have you got?" JT asked, heading for the fridge.

"Some stuff for sandwiches. Not much else. Have a look while I de-smoke myself."

I grabbed some plastic wrap and a garbage bag from the kitchen and left JT with his head in the fridge. After I shut myself in the bathroom, I removed all my clothes and stuffed them into the garbage bag. I wasn't sure if they could be saved with washing or dry cleaning, but for the moment I didn't want them stinking up my apartment.

I wound the plastic wrap around my bandaged hand, careful not to hurt myself in the process. I didn't want to have to replace the bandage already, and I also didn't want any water pelting against my burn. Once I'd created what I hoped was a waterproof wrapping, I turned on the water and climbed into the shower.

As I scrubbed away the smell of smoke, I thought over everything JT and I had talked about since leaving the church. There were too many puzzle pieces to make much sense of the whole situation. Few of the pieces seemed to fit together, and for all I knew, the most important information could still be missing. Even so, I still had the reverend pegged as my prime suspect, and I felt sure that the detectives needed to know about Susannah's video and the fact the McAllister had threatened her.

With any luck, the police would tell me they were way ahead of me and about to make an arrest. I'd be more than happy to put this whole thing behind me. Jeremy's murder, my disastrous relationship with Hans, my brush with death—it was all getting to be a bit much. And I really didn't like the thought that I could still be in danger.

As I massaged shampoo into my hair with my uninjured hand, I decided to get in touch with the detectives that afternoon. If McAllister was indeed the murderer and the arsonist, the sooner the police took him into custody the better.

I wanted to stop worrying. I wanted JT to stop worrying. And for that to happen, Jeremy's killer needed to be safely locked away.

ONCE I WAS thoroughly scrubbed from head to toe and smelling pleasantly of citrus body wash rather than smoke, I dressed in jeans and a T-shirt and joined JT in the kitchen. While I showered, he'd made sandwiches using the deli meats, cheese, and tomatoes I'd purchased the day before. I was hungry despite the amount of food I'd eaten at the reception, maybe because of the stress I'd been through since then. As we ate, we chatted about JT's latest music projects and a couple of our mutual friends. It was nice to talk about something other than murder and arson, but those subjects were never far from the forefront of my mind.

JT needed to be back at his studio by late in the afternoon to work with a trio of musicians, so we didn't hang around my place long after we finished eating. On his way home he dropped me off at the police station, and I waved to him as he pulled back out into the Saturday afternoon traffic.

I hesitated before entering the station, wondering if I should have called first. Maybe Detectives Bachman and Salnikova weren't even in. But since I was already there, I figured I might as well try my luck.

I entered the reception area and approached the

woman behind the glassed-in reception desk. When I asked to speak with either Bachman or Salnikova, she directed me to take a seat. I did so, staring at the gray walls adorned with crime prevention posters as I waited.

Several minutes ticked by. When I finished reading all of the posters on the closest wall, I pulled out my phone to check for text messages. I had none. I opened a game of solitaire on my phone and was halfway through it when a female voice spoke my name.

"Ms. Bishop?"

I looked up. Detective Salnikova stood near a corridor leading away from the reception area.

I shoved my phone into my purse and stood up. "Hi. Thanks for seeing me."

Salnikova nodded. "Come this way." She led me down the corridor to a small room with a table and four chairs. "Take a seat."

I settled into one of the chairs, a rickety old wooden contraption that creaked beneath my weight. I hoped it wouldn't break on me. A burned hand was enough injury for one day.

Salnikova chose a seat to my right, at the head of the table, and set a notebook out in front of her. She rested her pen on top of it and sat back, regarding me with her blue eyes. "I hear you were involved in a scary incident earlier today."

"So you did hear about that. Do you think the arsonist and the murderer are the same person?"

"Is that why you're here? Because you think there's a connection?"

I didn't miss the fact that she answered my question with more questions. I tried not to let it annoy me. "Kind of. I thought you should know what I learned right before the fire."

"Which is?"

Once again I related the story about meeting Susannah and learning about her connection to Jeremy, as well as the incident with Reverend McAllister. "I think blackmail could be the reason for Jeremy's death," I said once I'd finished my narrative. "I would have told the officers at the scene of the fire, but I figured it would be easier to explain everything to you."

Salnikova made no verbal comment, but wrote something down in her notebook. I tried to read her notes without being obvious about it, but her writing was too small for me to make out from my position.

"Susannah didn't say she was aware that Mr. Ralston was blackmailing Reverend McAllister?" the detective asked after she finished writing.

"No. But it makes sense, doesn't it? We already know that Jeremy was blackmailing Ha—Maestro Clausen. Surely once he knew about the video, he'd have seen dollar signs in front of his eyes." I sat forward as I got into the groove of sharing my theory. "And it's possible that McAllister overheard me and Susannah talking. If he did, he had motive to set the fire. Even if he didn't overhear us, maybe he was afraid that Susannah would post the video online, or at least tell someone else about it, which she did. The purpose of the fire could have been to get rid of both of us, or just Susannah, depending on what was going on in McAllister's head."

I sat back and waited for the detective's response, feeling quite pleased with myself.

Salnikova's bland expression didn't change. "Do you know Susannah's last name?"

I suppressed a growl of frustration. The detective obviously wasn't about to discuss the possibilities with me. I understood that and probably should have expected it, but it annoyed me nonetheless. I'd hoped she'd be more enthusiastic, if not impressed, with my ideas.

"No," I said after swallowing my frustration. "But I have her cell number. And the officers that were at the scene of the fire probably have her contact information."

"I'll get in touch with them." The detective made another short notation with her pen. "What can you tell me about the person who started the fire? Anything?"

I slumped back in my seat. "No, nothing. I didn't see him. Or her. Not even a glimpse. No telltale scent of perfume or anything like that either." A thought struck me. "And no smell of marijuana," I said more to myself than the detective.

"Marijuana?" Salnikova's expertly plucked eyebrows rose slightly.

"Yes. Um. Hmm." I tried to figure out how to explain. "Ray. He plays the oboe in the orchestra. The Point Grey Philharmonic, not the youth orchestra," I clarified. "He often smells of marijuana, and I thought he could possibly be the arsonist too, but I didn't smell any marijuana when the fire was started. But I did smell it on him after he rescued us." I paused for a second. "Then again, he could have set the fire and then gone out back to smoke. That's where he said he was before he realized there was something wrong. If he hadn't smoked any marijuana for a while before that, maybe I wouldn't have smelled anything, even if he was the one who started the fire."

I was talking more to myself than Salnikova by then, and it took me a second to remember that I was sharing my thoughts. I hoped I hadn't rambled too much.

"Does that make sense?" I asked the detective.

Once again she didn't bother to answer my question. "Does this oboe player have any connection to Mr. Ralston that you know of?"

"Aside from the fact that they played in the same orchestra, at least temporarily?" I thought that over. "Not that I know of. Except . . ."

"Except?" Salnikova prompted.

My mind went back to the conversation I'd had with Ray before our last rehearsal. "I was talking to him the other night, and he asked me if I knew whether the police had searched Jeremy's place. It struck me as an odd question, and now I can't help but wonder if he had a sinister motivation for asking it."

I watched the detective's face, but she still gave nothing away. I couldn't even tell if she was the least bit interested in what I'd said.

She pulled a cell phone out of her pocket. "Excuse me one moment."

I waited in my seat as she tapped out a text message. When she was done, she set the phone on the table and jotted down a quick line in her notebook. As she set down her pen, somebody knocked on the door. It opened, and Detective Bachman stuck his head in the room.

He nodded at me but said nothing.

Salnikova rose to her feet and joined him at the door. "I'll just be another moment," she said to me, before following Bachman out into the hallway and closing the door behind her.

I couldn't help myself. I wanted to know what they were talking about. I wanted to know if Salnikova was more interested in what I'd told her than she'd let on.

As quietly as possible, I got up from my rickety chair and crept over to the door. I pressed my ear against the minuscule crack between the door and its frame and held still, listening. Fortunately for me, the detectives were conversing right on the other side of the door. What wasn't so fortunate was the fact that I could only make out the odd phrase.

" . . . marijuana . . . searched Mr. Ralston's . . ." That was Salnikova's voice.

Bachman's deeper voice rumbled in response. " . . . amount was only consistent with personal use . . . if the oboe player . . . dealer . . . possible connection."

I wanted to pump my fist in the air but refrained. So they did think my information was valuable. Even though I couldn't hear everything said on the other side of the door, I could hear enough to get some new ideas to add to my theory.

Maybe the police had found some marijuana in Jeremy's basement suite, and maybe Ray had been Jeremy's drug dealer, or vice versa. That might explain Ray's concern about a potential search of Jeremy's quarters, especially if he believed there might be something in Jeremy's suite that would lead the police to him in the context of a drug investigation.

I didn't have time to think much more about it right then. Bachman said something unintelligible and then footsteps headed away from the room. I dashed back over to the table and plunked myself back down in the rickety wooden chair a mere second or two before Salnikova opened the door and came back inside.

"Sorry about that," she said as she rejoined me at the table.

"No problem." I hoped the creaking of my chair hadn't given away the fact that I hadn't remained at the table while she was out of the room.

"Now, was there anything else you wanted to tell me?"

I was so distracted by the new potential angle to the case that it took me a moment to be sure of my response. "No, I can't think of anything else."

Salnikova shut her notebook, signaling the end of our meeting. "Thank you for coming in, Ms. Bishop. We appreciate the information."

She got to her feet and I did the same.

"If you catch whoever set the fire, will you let me know?"

The detective nodded. "You'll be informed."

"Thank you."

"Ms. Bishop," Salnikova said, stopping me as I made for the door.

I turned back.

"I understand your interest in the recent events, but I must advise you to leave the investigating to the professionals." She nodded at my bandaged hand. "We don't want you coming to any more harm."

"Neither do I, believe me," I said. "And I have every intention of leaving the investigating to you guys."

"That's good to hear." She walked with me out to the reception area, where we parted ways.

Once outside the station, I stood for a minute on the sidewalk, pondering everything that had happened inside.

I hadn't lied when I said I planned to leave the investigating to the police. Now that I'd imparted all my information and suspicions to them, I really did intend to keep my nose out of things. It wasn't that I was no longer curious or anxious to see the criminal or criminals brought to justice—I simply didn't want my curiosity to get me killed.

Chapter 15

Before leaving my apartment earlier that day, I'd packed a bag with enough clothes and belongings to last me a few days. JT had taken it with him in his pickup truck, and when I arrived at his house, I found it waiting for me upstairs in the guest room. That night, I snuggled into bed and listened to the spring rain that had recently started tapping out a staccato rhythm against the roof.

Whenever I actually stopped to think about what had happened at the church, my nerves felt frazzled. If there really was someone out to get me, I didn't much like the idea of giving them an easy opportunity to do whatever they might want to try next. Just because my best friend happened to be a strong, six-foot-two guy didn't mean I was a damsel in distress for taking him up on his offer to stay with him. Independence was well and good when it didn't brush shoulders with foolishness, and I couldn't help but feel that staying at home alone would have been a foolish move.

Comforted by the sound of the falling rain and the knowledge that both JT and Finnegan were within shouting distance, I fell into a deep sleep. I didn't wake up until nearly eight in the morning, and when I rolled out of bed and opened the curtains, sunlight streamed in through the window.

The rain clouds had dispersed during the night, and the outside world looked green and fresh. I opened the window and stuck my head out, taking a deep breath. The air smelled springlike and delicious. I took another deep breath and smiled. Things would get better from here on out. No more foul play to deal with, no more brushes with danger. In that moment, I felt certain of it.

After closing the window, I took a quick shower, dressed, and brushed out my hair. I disposed of my old bandage and carefully rewrapped my hand with fresh gauze. The burn already looked incrementally better, and I hoped it wouldn't take too many days to heal completely. I didn't want it to interfere with my violin playing for long.

My throat was still scratchy and irritated from all the smoke I'd inhaled, but not as much as the day before. Things were definitely looking up.

I headed downstairs and into the kitchen. Finnegan was curled up on the floor by the back door, but he jumped up as soon as he saw me, his tail wagging with great enthusiasm.

"Morning, guys," I said to both Finnegan and JT, who was seated at the breakfast bar, drinking coffee and reading news stories on his tablet. I crouched down to give Finnegan a hug.

"Morning," JT replied.

Finnegan responded by giving me a sloppy kiss on the cheek.

"Sleep well?" JT asked as I left Finnegan for the fancy coffeemaker.

"Very well." I set about making myself a mocha latte.

"Help yourself to whatever you want for breakfast."

I glanced around the kitchen and my eyes settled on a bowl of fruit. I grabbed a banana and peeled it. I paused before taking a bite. "Oh, shoot."

JT looked up from his tablet. "What?"

"I should have brought some of the stuff from my fridge. I have milk and some vegetables I don't want to spoil."

"I can drive you home to pick up whatever you want," JT said.

"I can take the bus."

"It's no bother."

"All right, then. Thanks." I took a bite of my banana and chewed.

"I was going to take Finnegan for a walk in Pacific Spirit Park. You want to come with us? We can go by your place a little later on."

"A walk sounds good." I looked down at Finnegan. "Right, Finn?"

He gave a sharp, happy bark in response.

After I finished off my banana and my latte, the three of us walked a few blocks to Pacific Spirit Park, a large tract of forest that sat between JT's neighborhood and the University of British Columbia. A network of walking trails traversed the forest, and we met several other people out enjoying the spring morning, most with dogs accompanying them.

We walked for over an hour before returning to JT's place. I grabbed my purse from the guest room and then the two of us headed off to my apartment in JT's truck. When we arrived, he parked in a free space at the curb outside my building, and moments later we were up on the third floor.

"This shouldn't take long," I said as we approached the door to my apartment. "I —" I cut myself off when I saw my apartment door.

It stood open a crack.

I froze. "JT," I said in a strangled voice.

JT's whole body went tense when he saw what had frightened me. "Stay here." He brushed past me and approached the door, pushing it open slowly.

Despite his instruction, I followed him and stood on tiptoe to peer over his shoulder. My heart hammered in my chest and my already irritated throat went dry. I swallowed in an attempt to quell a threatening coughing fit.

When JT had the door fully open, I gasped, which allowed my coughing fit to win out. Several seconds passed before I could focus on what lay inside.

Through the open door, most of my living room was visible. Except I barely recognized it as my living room. Picture frames had been ripped from the walls and shattered on the floor. The lamps had also been smashed, including the beautiful art glass lamp I'd picked up at an antiques fair a few weeks earlier.

The destruction didn't end there.

My couch and armchair had been attacked with a sharp implement of some sort, the backs slashed and oozing stuffing, the cushions shredded on the floor along with more foam filling.

My stunned eyes moved from the floor to the far wall. Someone had taken the squeeze bottle of ketchup from my fridge and used it to scrawl in big letters: *Back Off!*

The ketchup had dribbled down the wall like trickling blood. The messy, dripping letters only made the message seem more vicious.

At first I was at a loss for words, my mouth gaping open in shock. A wave of nausea swept over me, quickly replaced with burning anger.

"Who would do such a thing?" I demanded.

Fury bubbling in my bloodstream, I stepped inside my apartment.

JT grabbed my arm and pulled me back out into the hallway. "I don't think you should go in there."

"JT!" I was too angry to get any more words out.

He produced his phone from his pocket. "You're not going inside until the police have been in there."

I knew he was right, but I wanted nothing more than to march inside and scrub away the ugly letters, to clean up the terrible mess. I couldn't stand the thought that someone had broken into my private space, had destroyed my home, but the evidence was right there in front of me. It had happened. There was no doubt about that.

As JT spoke with an emergency dispatcher over the phone, a prick of fear wormed its way into my anger.

Who had done this? The same person who set the fire? The same person who killed Jeremy?

What if I'd been home at the time? Would I have been harmed?

I shivered and retreated two steps down the hallway so I could no longer see the disarray. Staying with JT had clearly been a wise decision. I didn't have a shred of doubt about that. But I didn't want the threat of danger hanging over my head forever. I wanted to reclaim my home, my security.

That wouldn't happen until the guilty party had been identified and apprehended.

I returned to JT and put a hand on his arm to get his attention. "I'll go downstairs and let the police in when they arrive."

He nodded and walked with me down the hall, his phone still to his ear.

"You're coming too?" I asked.

He stopped at the top of the stairwell and lowered his phone for a second. "They don't want us waiting right outside the door, in case someone's still inside."

My eyes widened at the thought of somebody lurking in my apartment, waiting to . . . do what? Nothing good, that was certain.

I hesitated, no longer wanting to leave JT alone.

He must have read the concern on my face. "You go on," he said with a nod at the stairway. "I'll be fine here."

I jogged down the stairs, only a hint of fear creeping up on me whenever I turned a corner. I didn't really expect somebody to be waiting to jump out and attack me, but my nerves were frazzled. The thought of someone breaking into a place where I'd always felt safe and secure had rattled me. That was my home. My sanctuary. I didn't like the idea of somebody with bad intentions getting inside uninvited, standing amidst all my belongings and leaving me a threatening message.

Back Off!

I couldn't see how the message could be related to anything other than Jeremy's murder, or the fire, or both. I wasn't in the habit of hanging out with questionable characters or making enemies. No, it was definitely related to at least one of the other events, and I was more convinced than ever that *all* of the events were related.

When I reached the lobby, I stood by the glass front door, shifting from foot to foot as I waited for the cops to arrive. Within minutes a police car pulled up outside the building, without a siren or flashing lights. Two uniformed officers climbed out and approached the building. I opened the door for them.

"We received a report of a break-in," the taller of the two said, his name tag revealing his name to be Jones.

"My apartment, up on the third floor."

"Your name?"

"Midori Bishop," I said as I led the way to the elevator, deciding to bypass the stairs this time.

When we stepped off the elevator, JT stuck his phone in the pocket of his jeans and greeted the officers.

I pointed down the hall at the door to my apartment. "That's my unit there. The door was open a crack when we arrived."

"Remain here, please," Jones said.

He and his partner proceeded down the hallway and cautiously entered my apartment.

I leaned against the wall, my muscles taut, and glanced at JT. He was more relaxed, but I detected some tension in his jaw and shoulders. We didn't speak, instead waiting in silence, our eyes focused on the open door to my apartment.

After several minutes the two officers emerged from my unit.

"You said this is your apartment, ma'am?" the shorter, stockier officer asked me.

I glanced at his name tag. His last name was Chong.

"Yes," I replied.

"Would you mind coming inside? I'll have to ask you not to touch anything quite yet, but if you could take a look around and see if anything is missing or out of place or otherwise disturbed, we'd appreciate that."

"Aside from the fact that someone decided to redecorate my living room?"

"Yes, ma'am."

I followed Officer Chong into my apartment and made a slow circuit of the kitchen and living room. Aside from the threatening ketchup paint job and the destroyed furniture and decorations, nothing seemed different. I moved on to the bedroom and bathroom, but nothing had been disturbed in either room.

I returned to the living room and shook my head. "It doesn't look like anything else was touched."

I angled my back to the ketchup message so I didn't

have to see it and glanced through the still-open door of my apartment. The other officer was in conversation with JT out in the hallway.

"You arrived home shortly before your friend called 911?" Chong asked.

"Yes. He made the call as soon as we saw the state of things."

"And did you enter the apartment or touch anything before we arrived?"

"No," I said. "Well, JT pushed open the door but that's it. And he didn't touch the doorknob. Only the middle of the door."

"When was the last time you were home?"

"Yesterday, in the middle of the afternoon. I think I left around three o'clock."

"Have you noticed anything unusual around the building of late? Strangers loitering about or anything like that?"

"No."

Officer Chong's eyes went straight to the ketchup lettering, and I knew what was coming next. "Do you have any idea why someone would leave such a message for you?" His dark eyes studied me sharply as he waited for a response.

"Kind of. Maybe." I sighed and tried to figure out how to explain. "I think someone believes I've been too involved in a murder investigation. Or that I know too much. Or something along those lines."

"And what murder investigation would that be?"

"Jeremy Ralston was the victim. He was killed on

Tuesday evening. Detectives Bachman and Salnikova have been investigating."

Chong continued to study me for a moment before saying anything more. "All right, Ms. Bishop. I'll inform the detectives of what occurred here. They may wish to speak with you at some point."

"Yes," I said, resigned to the thought of spending even more of my time with the police. "But for the moment?"

"We'll dust the door and a few other places for fingerprints and have a chat with your neighbors to see if anyone heard any sort of disturbance." He paused. "I didn't notice any security cameras in the building."

"No, we don't have any." That had never bothered me before, but right then I wished there were cameras. An image of the intruder could have helped to crack the case. I gestured at my kitchen chairs, thankfully left untouched. "Do I have to wait outside, or can I sit down?"

"You can take a seat. Excuse me." Officer Chong retreated out into the hallway and conversed with his partner while JT came inside and joined me at the table.

"I guess I should call Harry," I said, referring to the manager of my building.

"Probably a good idea," JT agreed.

I placed the call and explained the situation. After Harry assured me that he was on his way over, I disconnected the call and sat back, letting out a deep breath.

"What a mess. I hope Harry doesn't think I'm a bad tenant now."

"I doubt he will," JT said. "This is only one incident and . . ." He didn't finish his sentence. He didn't have to.

"You were going to say that this wasn't my fault, but then you had second thoughts, right?" Somehow I kept the annoyance out of my voice.

"It wasn't your fault that somebody broke into your apartment, but it's possible your actions triggered this." He gestured at the sloppy red letters on the wall.

"What actions?" This time I couldn't suppress my annoyance. "I haven't done anything!"

"You've talked to people, asked questions."

"I didn't realize that was a crime. And besides, I hardly asked any questions at all."

"I didn't say it was a crime, but it might only take one question to scare someone into thinking that you know too much, or that you're at least trying to find out more than they'd like."

I let out a growl of frustration, but I knew JT was right. Obviously I had someone worried. I took in a calming breath and let it out slowly. "Okay. So what have I done recently that could have scared Jeremy's murderer? Because I'm sure that's what this is all about."

"Who have you talked to about Jeremy since the murder?"

I thought back over the past week. "Hans and I talked about it briefly over dinner." I cringed at the memory. I'd enjoyed that evening with him so much. Now I felt like a fool for that. I moved on quickly, trying to remember whom else I'd spoken to on the subject. "I asked Mikayla what she knew of Hans's whereabouts in the minutes before I found Jeremy's body. But I know she didn't have anything to do with all of this."

"How do you know?"

I glared at JT. "She's my friend. I *know* her. She doesn't have any more to do with this than you do."

He held up his hands in surrender. "I'm just trying to cover all our bases here."

I relaxed and tried to get back on track. "Anyway, asking her about Hans wouldn't have concerned her unless the two of them were in cahoots, which is totally ridiculous."

"But could Clausen have found out that you asked about him?"

I considered that. "Doubtful. Besides, even though it's possible that Hans was still at the church after the funeral, would he really have tried to burn me to a crisp?"

"If he killed Jeremy, why not you?"

I frowned. That made sense, but I didn't want to admit it.

"You just don't want to believe him capable," JT said. "Do you still have feelings for him?"

"No! Of course not." I saw the skepticism in JT's eyes and realized that it mirrored my own. I wanted to shake myself. How could I have any residual feelings for Hans? He was a lying, cheating bastard.

But I'd been so into him.

I tipped my head back to stare at the ceiling. "Maybe I'm a bit sad about losing out on what could have been. If he'd been the guy I thought he was. But you're right. If he killed Jeremy, he probably wouldn't have any problem killing me too."

"Okay, so he's on the list. Who else did you talk to?"

"Ray. Clover. Jeremy's girlfriend, Shelley—make that his fiancée," I amended. "His landlady." I gave my left earlobe a single tug. "And there's still a possibility that Reverend McAllister—or someone else, for that matter—overheard me talking with Susannah about McAllister's drunken, inappropriate remarks."

"All right. So we know McAllister might have had a motive to kill Jeremy if he was blackmailing him about the video."

"Right," I said. "And there's something shifty about Ray. Plus, there's a possible connection between him and Jeremy involving drugs."

"Is there?"

"Oh, right. I haven't told you about that yet." I explained about what I'd overheard at the police station the day before. "As for Clover, Jeremy hurt her when he put an end to things between them, and she seemed awfully scared when I talked to her."

"And you mentioned the other day that her boyfriend might have found out about her and Jeremy," JT reminded me.

"Yes, that's a possibility." I got to my feet and put my uninjured hand to my hip, glaring at the defaced wall. "This is so frustrating! The killer could be any one of a long list of suspects. The only people I talked to about Jeremy who I don't suspect are Mikayla and Mrs. Landolfi." I closed my eyes for a moment, attempting to quell my growing frustration. When I opened them again, I looked at JT with a sense of helplessness. "How will this ever end if I can't figure out who's responsible?"

"You don't have to figure it out," JT said firmly. "The police will."

I wished I could be as confident as he was.

Chapter 16

JT AND I waited out in the stairwell while the police dusted for fingerprints and searched for other possible clues inside my apartment. I engaged in another spot of eavesdropping when Officer Chong and his partner knocked on my neighbors' doors, but I didn't learn anything of interest. Nobody was home at two of the units on my floor, and those residents who were at home hadn't heard any sort of disturbance over the past twenty hours. Whoever had broken into my apartment had done so quietly, even if the destruction they'd left behind practically screamed of their vehement anger.

Harry stopped by for several minutes, standing in the doorway to my unit to get a glimpse of the destruction within. Without touching anything, he examined the jimmied lock on my door and assured me that he'd have a locksmith sent over that day to fix me up with a new lock.

I thanked him and he went on his way after I'd assured him that his presence was no longer needed. At least he seemed concerned and sympathetic rather than annoyed. Hopefully that meant he didn't blame me for what had occurred.

After Harry left, the waiting continued. I got up and paced back and forth across the top of the stairway until JT got annoyed and ordered me to sit back down. I did so with a heavy sigh. I was restless, jittery. It was as if I'd had too many cups of coffee that morning, even though I'd only had the one latte. My mixed emotions were getting to me, my nerves jangling like triangles played out of sync by a dozen different musicians.

Fortunately, Detective Bachman arrived a short time later. He spoke to the other police officers, but then came over to ask me some questions. At least that provided me with a distraction from the activities in my apartment.

"We meet again, Ms. Bishop," Bachman said as JT and I stood up to face him.

I frowned at him. "It's not as if I enjoy spending a good chunk of my time with the police, you know."

JT shot me a look of warning, but I couldn't help it if my words came out sharply. The detective's tone had implied that all this was somehow my fault. To say that rubbed me the wrong way would have been an enormous understatement. Maybe the distraction of his arrival wasn't such a good thing after all.

Bachman cleared his throat. I couldn't tell if he was annoyed with me or taken aback by my response to his greeting. I didn't much care either way.

"Are you any closer to catching Jeremy's killer?" I

asked. "Because I'd rather not get stabbed in my sleep while waiting for you guys to figure out whodunit."

"Midori," JT said, trying to warn me off again.

Bachman and I both ignored him.

The detective's gray eyes regarded me with a hint of cool condescension. "I assure you that we're conducting a thorough investigation, Ms. Bishop. Perhaps you could assist us by telling me why you think this incident is related to Ralston's murder."

"Don't you think it's connected? I mean, you're here, aren't you?"

JT rested a hand on my shoulder.

I let out a deep breath, exhaling some of my frustration with it. I rubbed my forehead with my left hand and gathered myself together. Once I had my emotions under control, I related to Detective Bachman everything that JT and I talked about a short while earlier. I told him about everyone I'd spoken to about Jeremy, and all of my suspicions.

After I finished, I felt drained, as if all of my energy had dripped out of me, through all the floors below me, right down to the basement. I was tempted to lean against JT for support but I didn't want Bachman to view me as weak. He probably already had me pegged as overly emotional, and that was bad enough.

"If this incident is indeed connected to the murder, you've clearly got someone feeling threatened," Bachman said.

"*If?*" I echoed, incredulous. "What else would it be connected to? I'm not in the habit of instilling violent impulses in random people."

The skepticism in Bachman's eyes threatened to rile me up again.

"I suggest you take extra caution until we can figure out who's behind this," the detective went on.

"She can continue to stay at my place," JT said.

Bachman nodded his approval.

"What about Susannah?" I asked. "She could be in danger too."

"We'll suggest to her parents that they exercise caution," Bachman said.

That relieved some of my anxiety, but not by much. "When can I clean up my apartment?"

I wanted to get rid of all signs of violence as soon as possible.

"The officers should be done in a few minutes." Bachman nodded at JT and me, and proceeded toward the elevator.

"What a mess," I said as Bachman stepped onto the elevator.

"Your apartment, or the general situation?" JT asked.

"Both."

Officer Chong stepped out of my unit and raised a hand to get my attention. "Ma'am, we're done here. Feel free to clean up now if you'd like."

"Thank you."

JT and I waited as the investigators filed out of my apartment. When the way was clear, I entered my apartment and stood in the middle of the living room, staring around me at all the destruction and disorder. So much had been displaced and damaged. I didn't even know where to start the cleanup.

Perhaps JT sensed that the situation had me over-whelmed, because he took charge, deciding on a plan of action. "All the cushions are toast," he said, nodding at the shredded couch and armchair. "Why don't we stack them all by the door? Once we get all the big stuff out of the way we can start with sweeping and vacuuming."

I forced myself into action, gathering up the remains of the cushions and tossing them all in the entranceway. I collected some plastic garbage bags from a cupboard in the kitchen and filled one up with the larger pieces of stuffing scattered across the floor.

While I did that, JT carefully shifted pieces of broken glass from the smashed lamps and picture frames into another garbage bag. Next, I vacuumed up all the smaller debris, and while I did that JT used a damp cloth to wipe away the ketchup and fingerprint dust.

As bad as the mess was, I was relieved that the in-truder hadn't continued with his or her destruction in my bedroom. Somehow, that would have made the viola-tion of my privacy and security even worse. It also would have made for an even longer cleanup. As it was, nearly two hours passed before JT and I had everything tidied and free of debris.

During that time, Harry's locksmith made an appear-ance and took care of my apartment door. I wasn't sure that a new lock would be enough to make me feel safe in my apartment again. After all, the old one hadn't kept the intruder out. But my door needed a new lock in any event, and I was glad to have the installation taken care of.

After the locksmith left, I stashed the vacuum cleaner

away in the closet and sank down onto the arm of my cushionless couch. "I guess I'm going to need a new couch and chair." I surveyed my living space. "And lamps. And picture frames."

"If you want to keep the couch, you could always get it reupholstered and get new cushions made to match," JT said.

I shrugged. "It was secondhand anyway. Maybe I can use this as an excuse to splurge on a new one."

JT's attention shifted to the garbage bags and destroyed cushions piled by the door. "Why don't we take this junk down to the Dumpster?"

"Good idea." I got up to help him. "Thanks, JT. This would have been way more difficult without you. How about I buy you lunch when we're done?"

He grinned. "I won't say no to that."

My stomach gave a loud growl. "Then I say let's get moving, because after the morning I've had, I could sure use a good meal."

JT hefted up the garbage bags and I gathered up the remains of the cushions. After locking up my apartment and pocketing my new key, we set off, leaving my altered living space behind us.

AFTER WE DISPOSED of our load of trash in the Dumpster behind my apartment building, JT and I walked the two blocks to our favorite sushi restaurant. We took our time over the meal, and finished it off with some Matcha ice cream. Yet, even with the good food and good company, I couldn't forget the invasion and destruction of my home. I was unsettled, vacillating back and forth between anger and anxiety. I tried my best to hide my mood, not wanting to put a damper on the meal, but I wasn't sure if I was successful.

After eating, JT and I made a quick stop at my apartment to collect some perishable food items, and then we returned to his place. He headed out into the backyard with Finnegan, and I wandered into my studio after stashing the food in the fridge. Whoever was behind all of the recent crimes, I didn't want to let them get to me. I wanted to calm down, to put my mind and my nerves at ease. The best way for me to do that was always to play some music.

I snapped open the clasps on my violin case and picked up my bow in my left hand. I tightened it and then shifted it to my right hand. My burn protested, but not too badly. I lifted my violin out of its case and rested it against my left shoulder. I closed my eyes and played the opening notes of the first movement of Mozart's Eine Kleine Nachtmusik.

I only made it a few bars into the piece before I stopped. My burn now protested more fiercely. I could have played through the pain, but I wasn't sure if it was a good idea. Besides, the unpleasant sensation wasn't exactly helping me to relax.

I placed my violin back in its case and loosened my bow before putting it away as well. I drifted out into the hall and into the living room. JT's baby grand piano sat near the bay window, natural light pouring in through the panes of glass, making the room bright and welcoming. I plunked myself down on the piano bench and stared at the keys. Maybe playing the piano wouldn't hurt as much as playing the violin.

I placed my hands over the keyboard and my foot on the pedal. I played the opening bars of the first and best known movement of Beethoven's Moonlight Sonata, one of my all-time favorite pieces. Again my burn put up a fuss, and I broke off soon after starting. I dropped my hands into my lap.

I hadn't done a very good job of improving my mood. In fact, I felt worse than ever. I'd always relied on music to soothe me and cheer me up whenever I felt out of sorts, and having my burn interfere with that left me with a sense of frustration and loss. I knew the injury was minor and temporary, but at the moment it only added to my sense of being off-kilter.

I didn't know what to do with myself. I could listen to music, but I wanted to *do* something, to *create* the music. I used my left hand to play a few random chords. When the hardwood floors creaked behind me, I stopped and looked over my shoulder.

JT stood in the doorway to the living room, watching me. "You look like you could use some cheering up."

I glanced down at my right hand. "Stupid burn. It hurts to use it." I sounded as morose as I felt.

He crossed the room to join me. I scootched over so he could sit next to me on the piano bench.

He nudged me with his shoulder. "I think you need a little ragtime." He put his hands to the keys and played the introduction to Scott Joplin's "The Entertainer."

When he reached the end of the introduction, he

dropped his left hand off the keys and nudged me with his shoulder again.

A hint of a grin tugged at my mouth. I lifted my left hand and we played together, JT handling the melody and me the bass. It didn't take long for me to get into the lively two-step. With each note, my spirits rose and my smile grew bigger. All thoughts of murder, arson, and breaking and entering retreated to the back of my mind, and I lived only in the present, in the music.

Until JT's phone rang.

I broke off playing first. Once I stopped, he did too. He fished his phone out of the pocket of his jeans.

I caught sight of the display. "Shauna?"

The name showed on the screen along with a picture of a pretty, smiling brunette. I knew most of JT's friends and a lot of his colleagues. I'd never heard him mention a Shauna.

"I met her a couple weeks ago," JT explained as his phone stopped ringing.

"You could have answered it," I said. "Call her back, if you want. I don't mind."

"You're sure?"

"Of course." I forced a grin and nudged him with my shoulder as he'd done to me. "Thanks for cheering me up."

I slid off the bench and whistled for Finnegan. He came running from the back of the house.

"Come on, Finn. Let's go upstairs for a bit."

He raced up the stairs ahead of me, and I followed at a more sedate pace. JT's voice floated up toward me through the stairwell as he greeted the mysterious Shauna over the phone. I could tell from the sound of his voice that he was happy to talk to her. As his best friend, I should have been pleased for him, and in a way I was. His last girlfriend had cheated on him and hurt him badly. I wanted him to move on and leave her well in the past. But my lightened mood had slipped away in a flash, like a slithering snake darting away into a dark hidey-hole.

It seemed as though everyone's love life was on a better track than mine. Mikayla and Dave Cyders had sparks flying between them, and I sensed that might be the case with JT and Shauna too. My relationship with Hans, on the other hand, had received a liberal dousing of cold, harsh reality.

I didn't know why I couldn't find Mr. Right. It wasn't as if I was in a rush to get married or anything, but I did want to meet the One, and preferably before I hit middle age. But I had to wonder if that would happen.

Was I doing something wrong? Was I looking in the wrong places?

I sank down onto the edge of the bed in the guest room, my shoulders slumped. Finnegan sat at my feet and looked up at me. He whined and thumped his tail against the floor. He probably sensed my melancholy thoughts.

I scratched his ears to reassure him. "I'm okay, boy. I'm feeling a little down, that's all."

Finnegan rested his head on my knee, his brown eyes gazing up at me.

I couldn't help but smile, even if it was tinged with sadness. "Maybe things will look better tomorrow, right, Finnegan?"

It was worth hoping for, at least.

Chapter 17

THAT NIGHT MY sleep was troubled by bad dreams. Reverend McAllister chased me through a burning building, the ceiling collapsing in our wake as I ran along corridor after corridor. I slammed through a wooden door and found myself in my apartment. For a brief moment I thought I was safe, the fire and the reverend locked away on the other side of the door. But then I realized I wasn't alone. Half the orchestra was in my apartment, smashing and slashing at all of my belongings. They cackled at me as they carried out their destruction, their eyes wild.

Shelley and Susannah sat on the floor, rocking back and forth, sobbing loudly. Their tears flooded the room, the water level rising and rising until the windows burst outward. The water cascaded out of the new openings, sweeping the demonic orchestra members away.

Again I thought I was safe. But then the water turned to a rushing river of blood. It lifted me off my feet and carried me away. I struggled to stay afloat, but a hand grabbed my ankle and pulled me under. Blood filled my mouth, my nose.

I gasped and jolted awake.

It took me a moment to realize I'd been dreaming. There was no fire, no river of blood. Reverend McAllister wasn't chasing me, and my fellow musicians hadn't all gone psychotic.

My breathing and heart rate eventually slowed, but I was shaken up and wide awake. I switched on the bedside lamp and shoved back the blankets. I swung my legs over the edge of the bed and slid off the mattress until my feet hit the floor.

I considered getting a drink of water but decided that what I really wanted was company. I eased opened the bedroom door and crept out into the hallway. Finnegan was curled up on his bed outside JT's door. He lifted his head when I emerged from the guest room, going from asleep to alert in a split second.

"Finnegan," I whispered. "Come here, boy."

He got up off his bed and trotted over to see me. I knelt down and buried my face in his fur. After several seconds Finnegan wiggled free and licked my face. Our snuggle session left me feeling better, but I still wanted his reassuring company.

I made a clicking sound with my tongue as I turned back to the guest bedroom, and Finnegan followed. I left the door open a crack in case he wanted to leave the room later on and then climbed back into bed. Finnegan jumped up beside me and settled down on top of the covers.

I switched off the lamp and snuggled deeper beneath the blankets, comforted by Finnegan's weight pressed against my left side. The horrors of my nightmare weren't real, but they were triggered by the events of the past few days. The murder, the fire, the break-in at my apartment—they were all far too real for my liking. They were also too unsolved for my liking. But at least with Finnegan by my side, I was able to drift off back to sleep, this time without nightmares.

MONDAY BROUGHT A welcome distraction from all my worries—work. Although I couldn't play my violin during my lessons as I usually did, that wasn't much of a hindrance, and the day passed without me spending too much time dwelling on the macabre or my lack of luck in the love department.

After the last student left my studio, I checked my phone and found a text message from Mikayla, asking if I wanted to go out for dinner with her that night. I sent back an affirmative reply. A girls' night out was probably what I needed. We arranged to meet at a restaurant downtown and I ran upstairs to change and freshen up my makeup before heading out.

JT was downstairs in his recording studio, Finnegan keeping him company, so I sent him a quick text message to let him know that I was going out and set off for the bus stop.

When I met up with Mikayla, I had to explain how I'd injured my hand, and she was suitably shocked by my story. But as soon as we settled in at a table in the restaurant, our conversation drifted to other topics. I knew I'd been right to accept her invitation. She was a good talker and so upbeat that I didn't have to worry about my thoughts straying into territory that I wanted to avoid. At least, that was the case until we started in on our dessert of hot fudge brownie sundaes.

"I saw you talking with the maestro after Jeremy's funeral," Mikayla said, putting an end to my distraction from all the things I didn't want to think about.

I jabbed my spoon into the mound of brownie, fudge, and ice cream. "He tried to give me that whole 'my feelings for you are real' speech."

Mikayla rolled her eyes. "Don't they always."

I swallowed a delicious spoonful of my dessert, the heavenly taste a stark contrast to my sour thoughts. "Is there something wrong with me? I mean, do I have 'fool' written across my forehead or something?"

"Of course not. You're not the only one who's been lied to by a man. Not by a long shot. Believe me."

"I know. But sometimes I wonder if I'm destined to be alone, to never find the right guy."

"Oh, please." Mikayla jabbed the air with her spoon. "Don't you start thinking like that. You're younger than I am, for crying out loud, and it's not like I'm all settled down."

"I guess." I put another piece of brownie in my mouth and savored it. "But what if all the good guys are already taken?"

"They aren't. They're just a lot harder to find than the not so good ones."

I sat back and finished off the last sip of my cocktail. "I hope you're right."

"I am," Mikayla said before swallowing the remainder of her dessert. "Take JT, for example. He's not in any sort of long-term relationship, is he?"

"Not at the moment," I said, thinking of Shauna and wondering where that would end up going.

"And he's one of the good ones, isn't he?"

"Yes."

"So . . . any chance there could be anything between the two of you?"

"Mikayla!"

"What?" Her dark eyes were innocent.

"It's not like that with us. We're friends."

"I thought you once said you had a crush on him when you first met."

"Sure, but that was years ago." I'd only been nineteen to JT's twenty-one when I met him. At the time, I was smitten by his easygoing personality and good looks. Especially those root-beer-colored eyes of his. "I got over it. Now he's my best friend."

"Doesn't mean things can't evolve."

"Mikayla!"

She raised her hands in surrender. "Fine. But if you ask me, you're missing out on a keeper there."

I didn't respond. What was I supposed to say to that? I knew JT was a great guy. That's why he was my best friend. And sure, any woman would be lucky to have him as their significant other, but it simply wasn't like that between us. So it was End of Story, as far as I was concerned.

Still, I decided to hold onto one thing Mikayla had said. Maybe there still were some good guys out there who weren't already spoken for. Maybe there was even one out there for me. I just needed to keep looking, and not let myself get too jaded because of jerks like Hans.

I felt more hopeful about the future as I parted ways with Mikayla and rode the bus back to JT's house. I even had a bit of a spring in my step as I trotted up the stairs to the front door. I used my key to let myself in and pushed open the door. I stopped just over the threshold.

Finnegan scrabbled across the hardwood floors to greet me, but that wasn't what caught my attention. JT was on the couch in the living room, and he wasn't alone. A brunette sat next to him, and even though there was no physical contact between them at the moment, I got the distinct feeling that my entrance had interrupted a make-out session.

"Hi," I said, still standing in the foyer with the door open. I absently reached out with one hand to pet Finnegan on the head.

JT cleared his throat. "Hey, Dori. This is Shauna. Shauna, my friend Midori."

Shauna wiggled her fingers at me. "Hi."

"Hi," I said again.

A draft of cool evening air wafted against my back, reminding me that I'd left the door open. I pushed it closed and shoved my keys in my purse.

"Did you have a good time?" JT asked me.

"Yes, thanks." I shifted my weight from one foot to the other, awkwardness filling the foyer around me. "But I'm tired, so I'm going to call it a night." I smiled at Shauna. "Nice to meet you."

"You too," she said.

I dashed up the stairs, Finnegan racing along with me.

"Good night!" I heard JT call from below.

I headed straight for the guest room and plopped down on the bed. Encouraged by his invitation to join me the night before, Finnegan hopped up beside me.

I kicked off my boots, relieved to have escaped the stifling, uncomfortable feeling that had taken over me downstairs. "Talk about a third wheel, huh, Finnegan?"

My canine pal sat down at my side and licked my cheek. He gave me his best doggie grin, his tongue rolling out the side of his mouth.

I smiled. "You're right, buddy. I'm never out of place with you." I slung an arm around him and gave him a hug.

But even though I had Finnegan to keep me company, my temporarily raised spirits had taken a nosedive. I changed into my pajamas and climbed into bed, hoping once again that things would look up in the morning.

AT LEAST I managed to sleep through the night without any disturbing dreams. I awoke slowly, curled up beneath the warm covers. Finnegan was still beside me, somehow taking up two-thirds of the queen bed even though he wasn't a huge dog. I only had my eyes open for a few minutes when I heard a tap on the half-closed bedroom door. Finnegan jumped up and bounced off the bed.

I rolled over so I could see JT opening the door the rest of the way. "Morning," I mumbled in a sleepy voice.

JT crouched down to greet Finnegan. "Morning. Looks like you found yourself a roommate."

"Sorry about letting him on the bed. He keeps the nightmares away."

A flicker of concern showed in JT's eyes. "That's all right. But he probably needs to visit the backyard now." He got to his feet and Finnegan brushed past him, heading for the stairs. "You getting up?"

"Mmm." I snuggled against the pillows. "Soon."

JT leaned against the door frame. "I was thinking of cooking up some bacon and eggs. You want some?"

The prospect of a home-cooked breakfast perked me up. "Please."

"I'll start cooking in a few minutes, then." JT followed Finnegan downstairs.

I rolled out of bed and grabbed some clean clothes out of the bag I'd brought from home. After a quick shower, I padded downstairs in my bare feet, the smells of brewing coffee and frying bacon wafting toward me. I breathed in with deep appreciation as I arrived in the kitchen, slipping onto one of the stools at the granite breakfast bar.

JT poured a cup of black coffee for himself and set a vanilla latte in front of me. A plate of bacon and two sunny-side-up eggs followed shortly after.

"Yum," I said as I dug in.

JT joined me at the breakfast bar, and Finnegan settled at our feet. We ate in silence for a few minutes until I decided to raise the subject that had been on my mind the night before as I drifted off to sleep.

"I think I'll move back home today."

JT stopped with his fork halfway to his mouth. He lowered it back to his plate. "Do you know something I don't? Has the intruder been caught?"

I snapped a piece off a strip of bacon and put it in my mouth. "No," I said after chewing and swallowing.

"Then it's not safe for you to go back there." He resumed eating.

"But I can't let this person—whoever they are—keep me out of my home forever."

"It won't be forever. Give the cops a chance to do their job."

I chomped on another piece of bacon. The truth was, I didn't feel comfortable with the idea of going back home yet, but I wasn't sure that I wanted to stay at JT's any longer either.

I decided to address the heart of the issue. "I'm cramping your style. I'll be all right at home."

JT had picked up his coffee mug, but set it back down on the counter with a clack. "Cramping my style? What are you talking about?"

"Shauna, of course."

JT stared at me for a second and then picked up his mug again. "I barely know her, and it's not serious yet." He took a sip of his coffee. "You are not cramping my style, okay? I like having you here."

"You do?"

"Of course I do. Besides, if you go home, I'll have to camp out on your couch so I don't worry about you."

"My couch is toast," I reminded him.

"On your living room floor, then. And, so you know, I get grouchy when I have a sore back."

I smiled. "All right. I'll stay a while longer."

I munched on the last of my bacon, thoughts turning in my head. As sweet as it was of JT to let me stay at his place, I couldn't remain there forever. I needed to reclaim my home at some point. I couldn't let some shadowy figure keep me away from it and my normal life much longer.

But who knew how long it would take the police to catch the culprit?

There was even a chance that they'd never catch them. It wasn't as if unsolved cases were a rarity.

As I sipped my latte, I decided the only way to ensure that I could return home safely before too much more time passed was to figure out who the guilty party was myself.

Chapter 18

AFTER BREAKFAST I accompanied JT and Finnegan to the local park. A few joggers and other dog walkers were out, and kids loaded down with bulging backpacks were on their way to school. The morning air was sweet and refreshing.

JT and I stopped to wait as Finnegan conducted a thorough sniffing investigation at the base of a tree. My phone buzzed in my pocket and I fished it out to see who was calling.

Susannah.

I put the phone to my ear. "Hi, Susannah. How are you?"

"Okay." Somehow she managed to make that one word sound incredibly timid and fragile.

"What's wrong?" I asked, concerned.

"I just got an e-mail. I think it's from Reverend McAllister."

I frowned, not liking the sound of that. "What does it say?"

"He threatened me again." She sniffled.

"Susannah, you need to tell your mom right away."

"I can't."

"Why not? She already knows that McAllister threatened you before, doesn't she?"

Her silence spoke to me as loudly as a stereo playing at top volume.

I closed my eyes. "Susannah . . ."

"I couldn't tell her! Not after . . ."

"After what?"

She sniffled again. "After I told the police that nothing happened."

I closed my eyes again.

"I don't know what to do." She was crying now.

I let out a quiet sigh. "Why don't I meet you so we can talk some more?" I suggested. "Are you at school?"

"Yes."

"How much time is there before your first class?"

"Not much. But I don't mind skipping. I'd rather talk to you."

I wasn't in the habit of encouraging kids to skip school, but I couldn't ignore the fact that she was distraught. "Which school do you go to?"

"West Hill."

West Hill was my old high school. It wasn't far away. "I can be there in about twenty minutes. I'll meet you out front, okay?"

"Okay," Susannah agreed.

I hung up. JT and Finnegan had moved on to another tree.

When I caught up to them, JT asked, "Everything all right?"

"I'm not so sure. Susannah's really upset. I'm going to go meet her and try to sort things out."

"You're not going to do anything dangerous, are you?"

I rolled my eyes. "I'm going to talk to a fifteen-year-old girl. How dangerous could that be?" I raised a hand in a wave. "See you later."

I crossed the park to the nearest bus stop and only had to wait a minute or two before the right bus arrived. I climbed aboard and disembarked less than fifteen minutes later. The bus had dropped me off almost directly in front of the school, and I spotted Susannah right away. She sat at one of the picnic tables on the front lawn, facing outward. She waved when she spotted me.

Aside from a couple of straggling students making their way into the building without either haste or enthusiasm, Susannah and I were alone. I sat down next to her, noting that she wasn't currently crying. I wondered how long that would last.

"Did you tell the police what I told you about Reverend McAllister?" Susannah's tone wasn't accusatory but she looked at her hands in her lap rather than at me.

"I did," I admitted. "It was important. It's possible that the incident gave McAllister motive to kill Jeremy. You know that, so why did you tell the police nothing happened?"

Susannah chewed on her bottom lip. "I was going to tell my mom, but I was just waiting for the right time. Then a detective showed up at our house and I got scared."

"The police want to help, Susannah."

"But then this e-mail came in, and . . ." Tears welled in her eyes.

"What exactly did the message say?" I asked.

"It said if I told anyone about the video or made it public, the whole world would know I was a thief and I'd stolen money from the church." A tear escaped and trickled down her cheek. "I'm not a thief!"

I put a hand on her arm. "Of course you're not." I recalled what she'd told me over the phone. "You said you thought the e-mail was sent by Reverend McAllister."

She nodded.

"But you're not sure?"

"It wasn't signed, and there was no name in the e-mail address."

That was unfortunate, but since McAllister had threatened Susannah before, it was reasonable to assume he was behind the e-mail. Most likely the account was created solely for the purpose of sending Susannah the message. I was no computer expert, but I wondered if the police could link the message to an IP address and then to McAllister, or at least a specific Internet account connected to him.

"Did you delete the message?"

Susannah cringed. "Yes."

Darn. Maybe it was still in her account's trash folder. If not, maybe it was possible for a computer whiz to retrieve it somehow. Then again, maybe not.

"It was so awful. I just wanted to get rid of it," Susannah said.

I could tell she was worried that I was angry with her. I wasn't. Frustrated, but not angry. "I understand," I assured her. "But the police need to know about this, Susannah. All of it."

Her shoulders slumped. "I know. I guess I should call my mom," she said without a shred of enthusiasm.

"You should. Will she be at home?"

Susannah shook her head. "At work. She might have time to talk, if I tell her what it's about. But what if she's mad at me for lying?"

"I'm sure she'll understand why you lied. But it's time to come clean."

Susannah swallowed. "Will you stay here while I call her?"

She looked and sounded so young that my heart clenched with compassion for her. "Sure."

She moved a few feet away and put her phone to her ear. I could hear her voice but not her words. After minute or two her tears flowed again and the occasional hiccup interrupted her. I'd never known anyone who cried quite as much as Susannah, but in her defense, she'd been through a lot lately.

I watched the branches of a nearby ornamental cherry tree bow and sway in the morning breeze. The front door of the school banged open, and two boys in their midteens raced down the stairs and off around the corner of the building, laughing as they went.

To pass the time, I checked my own phone for messages. I had a text from JT which read, *You're staying out of trouble, right?*

You really have to ask? I wrote back.

Yes. Yes, I do, came his reply a moment later.

All I sent back in response was an emoticon with its tongue sticking out.

Susannah returned to the picnic table. I slipped my phone into my purse and waited for her to speak.

She clutched her phone in her hand. "My mom wants me to go to the police station and talk to Detective Salnikova. She's the detective that came to our house. My mom will meet me there as soon as she can."

"It's for the best."

She sucked on the inside of her cheek for a second. "Will you come with me? Just until my mom gets there?"

I grabbed my purse off the bench and stood up. "Of course."

I still had a couple of hours before I started teaching, and I could understand why she wouldn't want to walk into the police station on her own. Going there and talking to a detective would be overwhelming and intimidating enough for her with company. Doing it alone would probably be downright terrifying. Besides, I wouldn't mind an opportunity to speak with Bachman or Salnikova myself. I wanted to know if they'd made any progress with their investigation. They might not want to tell me much, but I still wanted to try to get some information out of them, even if it was only a scrap or two.

Susannah and I didn't talk much during the bus ride to the police station. She fidgeted the entire way, and chewed on her bottom lip so much I worried it would bleed. I hoped things wouldn't get any harder for her. She'd already been through so much.

At shortly past nine-thirty I accompanied her through the main doors of the police station. There was a different woman at the glassed-in reception desk this time. I explained to her who we were and why we were there and she directed us to sit in the molded plastic chairs in the waiting area.

We sat in silence, Susannah still fidgeting, her face pale. After about five minutes her mother bustled into the station. Susannah jumped up from her seat and catapulted herself into her mother's arms. Relief trickled through my body. I didn't mind keeping Susannah company and providing her with moral support, but her mother really was the best person for the job.

Mother and daughter were still hugging when Detective Salnikova emerged into the reception area from a door on the left. Her eyes focused on Susannah, but I jumped up from my uncomfortable seat and intercepted her.

"Ms. Bishop," Salnikova acknowledged when she saw me. "Are you here to share more information too?"

"No, I came along with Susannah. But I was wondering if there was any news, any progress with the investigation?"

"The murder investigation or the break-in at your apartment?"

"Both. They're connected, aren't they?"

"We haven't yet confirmed whether they are or aren't. However, we have a man in custody for another break-in, and we're looking at him as a possibility in your case too."

That was a surprise, but a pleasant one. "Where did the other break-in take place?" I was eager for information that might help me connect all the dots spattered crazily around in my mind.

Salnikova's eyes shifted to Susannah and her mother before returning to me. It wasn't hard to figure out that she was more interested in talking to them than to me. "Mr. Ralston's basement suite."

"Oh, so you caught the guy from the night I was there." Did that mean they'd also caught Jeremy's killer?

"Not from that night." The detective interrupted my thoughts. "This was another break-in. He was caught climbing in through a broken window last night."

Another break-in? Last night?

I tried to rein in my wildly galloping thoughts. "Who is it? Is it someone I know?"

"Sorry," Salnikova said, not sounding very sorry at all. "I'm not at liberty to disclose that information. When we have something to share with you about your particular case, you'll be informed." She gave me a curt nod. "If you'll excuse me."

She left me standing there in the middle of the reception area, a hundred different thoughts clashing together in my head like cymbals played by unruly children. One thought clamored more loudly than the others, about the identity of the man in custody.

I wanted to know who he was, so much so that I was tempted to chase after Salnikova and plead with her to tell me. But I knew that would be pointless. She wouldn't tell me any more than she'd go out and shout it in the street.

I made a face, fortunately only witnessed by a dusty

potted plant in one corner of the reception area. I stepped back as Salnikova ushered Susannah and her mother past me and through a door. Susannah glanced over her shoulder at me before disappearing. I sent her a quick wave and what I hoped was a reassuring smile before the door closed behind her.

I pulled my phone from my purse and glanced at the time. It was still fairly early, but it would probably be a good idea for me to head to my studio. It wasn't as if hanging around the police station would do me any good. I'd have to be happy with what little information I'd gleaned from Salnikova, even if it wasn't nearly as much as I wanted.

I pushed through the station doors and out onto the sidewalk, pointing myself in the direction of the nearest bus stop. As I walked to the shelter and sat down on its bench, I turned all the new information over in my mind. I didn't know the name of the person the police had caught breaking into Jeremy's suite, but I did know from what Salnikova had said that he was a man. Unfortunately, most of the people on my list of suspects were men.

I couldn't even cross Clover off my list of suspects for Jeremy's murder, because I didn't know if all of the events were related. I believed they were, but I didn't know for certain. Hopefully the police would come up with some answers soon. But even if they didn't, I planned to come up with some of my own.

Chapter 19

I SPENT THE afternoon teaching my students, and didn't have much time to think about murderers or break-and-enter suspects. My burn didn't hurt quite as much as the day before, and that pleased me. Any progress was more than welcome. I still avoided playing my violin with my students, wanting to save any use I might get out of my injured hand for that night's rehearsal, but I could move my hand more easily, and I'd done away with my bandages. A red mark still marred my palm, but not as angrily as before.

After my last student of the day left the studio, I chomped my way through an apple, said a quick goodbye to JT and Finnegan, and set off for orchestra rehearsal. I wondered how much damage the fire and smoke had done to the church. Hopefully not too much, although I was quite certain the women's washroom would need gutting and a complete do-over. That wasn't all bad, considering that the room probably hadn't been updated for at least thirty years, but I didn't know how much money the church had for such endeavors.

If funds were scarce, perhaps they could hold a fundraiser. If they did, I'd be willing to contribute. Even though I hadn't set the fire, I felt a bit guilty about the damage it had caused. Maybe that was silly, but the possibility that the arsonist had directed the fire at me was at the source of my guilt.

I entered the church through the same door as usual, the door through which Susannah and I had fled the fire with Ray's assistance three days earlier. As soon as I stepped inside, I detected the smell of smoke, dulled now but still clinging to the walls. For a second, panic threatened to well up inside me, to send me crashing back out the door and into the fresh air. But I was safe, I reminded myself. The fire was in the past, the lingering smell of smoke nothing more than an acrid but harmless memento of Saturday's terrifying experience.

I took in a deep breath to steady my nerves and sever my remaining threads of panic. The hallway leading to the washrooms was cordoned off with red tape, so I continued forward, passing the doors leading to the nave on my left and the bench where Susannah and I had spoken on my right. I followed the far hallway down to the basement auditorium, the clashing sounds of the instruments of the few early birds already on stage helping to calm me.

I stopped in the backstage room and barely had a chance to set down my violin and shoulder bag before Bronwyn and Katie closed in on me from either side.

"Midori! Is it true you were caught in the fire?" Katie asked, her eyes wide.

Bronwyn didn't give me a chance to respond. "Oh my God. Look at your hand. Can you even play tonight?"

Katie took my right hand in both of hers and gently turned it palm up to get a look at my burn. "Oh no. Does it hurt?"

"Yes, I think so, and not as much as before," I said, answering all three questions at once. "How did you find out that I was here when it happened?"

"Mikayla," Bronwyn replied, flicking a lock of her thick, crinkly brown hair over her shoulder.

"She's here?"

"Not yet. I ran into her yesterday."

Katie gave me a quick hug around my waist. She was so petite that she only came up to my shoulder. "We're glad you're okay."

"Thanks." I glanced around the room. Three more orchestra members had arrived behind me, and the time for rehearsal to begin drew nearer. I knew there was something I needed to do, as much as I didn't want to do it. "I'd better go talk to the maestro."

I excused myself from my fellow violinists and navigated my way out onto the stage. My steps faltered as I emerged from the wings. Hans was in conversation with Elena, both of them speaking in low voices. My stomach clenched at the sight of them together, but as Elena said one last word and turned away, I drew in a deep breath and forced myself onward, catching Hans's eye.

I steeled myself for our encounter as he wended his

way through the chairs and music stands to meet me. Talking to him at the reception hadn't been easy, but I needed to be able to hold a normal, civil conversation with him if I was to keep up my end of our agreement to maintain a professional relationship.

"Midori, I heard what happened. Are you all right?" His blue eyes searched me, as if checking for injuries.

I thought I detected genuine concern in his face and voice but quickly put up a wall to fend off any ghostly flutterings of my old feelings. "I'm fine. Except for a minor burn." I held my hand out, palm up, for him to see.

He moved to take my hand in his. I jerked it away before we made contact and cradled it against my stomach, more as a form of protection from him than because of any pain.

Hans sighed but dropped his hand. "I'm glad you weren't hurt any worse."

Again he seemed sincere, but that sincerity only wedged my throat with hurt and disappointment.

We could have had something good, a voice deep inside of me cried. *Why did you have to turn out to be a lying jerk?*

I swallowed hard and silenced my inner voice. I was better off without Hans. I knew that.

"Can you play tonight?" His question helped me refocus on the present.

"I'm not sure, but I want to try."

"Do what you can, but don't push it." He gave me one last, searching look before turning away.

I put my unburned hand on his arm to stop him,

snatching it away again as soon as I had his attention. "Have the police questioned you again?"

His blue eyes clouded with anger or annoyance. I didn't think it was directed at me. I hoped it wasn't.

"They wanted to know my whereabouts on Saturday at the time of the fire."

So the police did believe the fire and the murder could be connected. "And?" I asked, my throat dry. "What did you tell them?"

"The truth. I'd already left the church and met up with Elena for a late lunch. She confirmed that."

My stomach clenched for the second time in the last few minutes. I didn't want to hear about him having lunch with Elena.

Hans narrowed his eyes. "You don't really think I was involved in any of this, do you?"

"No."

He didn't miss the hint of uncertainty in my voice. His features hardened and he lowered his voice to a whisper. "Midori, failing to tell you about Elena and committing crimes are wildly different things. I didn't kill Jeremy. I didn't set the fire. And I certainly never would have harmed you."

"You already did."

Hans held his tongue and forced his face into a neutral expression as two violists passed by. "That's not the same thing," he said once they were out of earshot.

Easy for him to say. "Can you blame me for having a hard time trusting you?"

He let out a frustrated sigh but kept his voice low. "I'm

not a criminal, Midori. Hopefully, the police will figure that out and get busy tracking down the real killer. And I hope you'll come to believe I'm innocent too." He was about to turn away again but he stopped, his face softening. "Take care of your hand, all right?"

I nodded, and he returned to the stage.

I wandered toward the backstage room where I'd left my belongings, an internal battle brewing in my mind. As much as I knew I was better off without Hans, I still wanted to believe his claim to innocence. I didn't want to think him capable of even attempting to physically harm me, even if he didn't seem to care much about hurting my heart.

But he'd fooled me before. I had to remember that.

A whole week had passed since Jeremy's murder, and I was no closer to knowing who was responsible. I still didn't know if one of my fellow musicians was a dangerous criminal. Worst of all, I didn't know if the person who had broken into my apartment still wanted to harm me.

I didn't have time to dwell on those thoughts, which was probably for the best. I had to answer several more questions about the fire from my fellow musicians while I fetched my violin and bow. Within minutes of settling in on the stage, the rehearsal began.

Although my burn protested about holding my bow, the pain wasn't too bad, and I was able to play through it at first. We started rehearsing the Brahms pieces, and the familiar act of creating music helped to soothe me and ease the tension that had crept into my shoulders during my conversation with Hans.

All of the combined sounds of the various instruments knitted together into beautiful strains that washed over me and made my brain and body hum with a gentle peacefulness. This was why I loved playing in the orchestra. Making music on my own was wonderful, but working together with so many others to create something with so much depth and so many layers, that was something else altogether.

I was so happy to be doing what I loved and so into the music that it took me until the break midway through the rehearsal to realize that the pain in my hand had gone from easily ignored to more insistent. I considered whether I should continue playing after the break or give my hand a rest. I was distracted before I came to a decision.

Hans had only signaled that we should take a break seconds before, and while I thought about my hand, my eyes roved over the orchestra. People stood up from their seats to stretch or head for the washroom, but not before I made note of who was there and who wasn't.

Clover was present, over in the bass section, and of course Hans was accounted for as well. But one person of note was absent.

Ray.

I tried not to jump to any conclusions, but I was already getting air time.

Was Ray missing from rehearsal because the police had him in custody?

Maybe he was sick, or maybe there was some other perfectly innocent explanation for his absence, though that seemed too coincidental.

First the oboe player had shown an odd interest in whether Jeremy's place had been searched by the police. Then someone had broken into Jeremy's basement suite, not once, but twice, and the person responsible—for the second break-in, if not the first as well—was currently enjoying the accommodations Chez Police. And that would make him or her unavailable to attend any sort of function or event, including an orchestra rehearsal.

Way too coincidental for my liking.

And since the person in custody had been caught in the act of breaking into Jeremy's suite, there wasn't much in the way of doubt with respect to his guilt for that crime. But that didn't necessarily mean he'd killed Jeremy or set the fire.

Sure he had the opportunity to set the fire, and possibly even to murder Jeremy, but I still couldn't come up with a solid motive for him to commit those crimes. As JT had pointed out, simply because someone might be involved in drug trafficking to some degree, that didn't mean they had a reason to kill anyone.

I remained in my chair, holding my violin propped on my leg with my bow set on the rim of the music stand. I stared off into space, unable to reconcile what Ray's absence indicated with my deep suspicions of Reverend McAllister.

I was missing something. Probably more than one something.

I needed to find out more about McAllister.

Mikayla, already on her feet, poked me in the ribs with her bow. "Earth to Midori."

I blinked and realized I was one of the few people still in my seat.

"What's up?" Mikayla asked. "You were a million miles away there."

I retrieved my bow from the music stand and got to my feet. "My hand hurts. I'm not sure I can play through the rest of rehearsal."

She nodded in Hans's direction. "You'd better let the maestro know. Unless you're trying to avoid him."

I shook my head. "I'll talk to him."

Avoiding Hans would have been easier than dealing with him, but that option wasn't really available to me. As soon as I'd taken the first step down the nonprofessional path with him, I'd known there were risks involved. I'd accepted those risks, and now I would deal with the consequences, because he certainly wasn't worth giving up my place in the orchestra. It was awkward talking to him now, but it would get easier as time eased the pain he'd caused me. At least, I hoped it would.

As it turned out, I didn't need to have another conversation with him. I caught his eye when I was still more than ten feet away from him and simply held up my injured hand. He nodded in understanding and I took that as permission to leave. I could have remained for the rest of the rehearsal, listening to his comments and any discussions within my section about bowing changes or other details, but I decided not to. There was something else I wanted to do with my time.

I packed up my instrument as everyone else trickled back onto the stage. Then, with my bag over my shoulder and my instrument case held in my left hand, I set off in the opposite direction from my peers. When I reached the narthex on the main floor, I paused.

Several people milled about outside the nave. Three men of varying ages and a teenage girl hung off the edges of the group. The men looked as though they wanted to be anywhere but at the church, boredom hunching their shoulders and pulling at their faces. The teenage girl was oblivious to everything going on around her, her face hidden by a cascade of dark hair as she texted away on her phone.

A grandmotherly figure and two middle-aged women were busy attempting to calm a woman in her mid-twenties with her hair dyed a garish shade of red.

"Where *are* they? They should have been here ten minutes ago!" the redhead screeched.

"I'm sure they'll be here any minute," one of the middle-aged women said in a soothing voice.

Red didn't even seem to hear. "If they don't show up they're going to ruin *everything*!" She dug a phone out of her purse. "I'm texting them again. And they'd better respond or I swear . . ."

She didn't finish her threat, at least not verbally. Judging by her scowl and the way her eyes flashed, I doubted that she was holding back in her text message.

She started in with her verbal complaints again mere seconds later, but I tuned her out as I spotted Reverend McAllister descending the stairway to my left.

I intercepted him at the bottom of the stairs. "Evening, Reverend."

He seemed surprised to see me. Possibly nervous as well, although I wasn't positive about that.

"Evening. Ms. Bishop, isn't it?"

"That's right." I nodded in the direction of the cordoned-off hallway. "Is the damage extensive?"

"Oh, well, yes and no. The washroom was completely destroyed, but aside from some minor smoke damage out in the hallway, the rest of the church is fine." He flicked his eyes heavenward. "Thank the Lord." He refocused on me. "Weren't you one of the women trapped in the fire?"

"Yes. Along with a cellist from the youth orchestra."

I watched closely for his reaction to my mention of Susannah, but the small crowd outside the nave had drawn his attention away from me.

"Hmm. Yes. I'm glad you're all right," he said, his distraction leeching any sincerity out of his words.

"Reverend." I stopped him as he moved to abandon me for the redhead and what I guessed was her extended family.

His eyes slid back to me, but not without a good deal of reluctance.

"Were you aware that Jeremy Ralston was a blackmailer?"

McAllister's eyes nearly popped out of his head and he sputtered for a moment before echoing my last word. "Blackmailer?"

"That's right." I watched him closely, noting the flush rising up his neck and into his cheeks. "You weren't aware of that?"

McAllister swallowed hard. "Of course I wasn't aware

of that." He tugged at his clerical collar as if he couldn't get enough air. "Now, if you'll excuse me, I have a wedding rehearsal to attend to."

He hurried off toward the nave with what I thought was far too much eagerness, considering the way the redhead was throwing her hands about and squawking at everyone around her. He didn't enjoy talking to me. That much was clear.

Something else was clear too.

Reverend McAllister had lied to me.

Chapter 20

I WOULD BET my beloved violin that McAllister knew full well that Jeremy was a blackmailer. Although I was less certain about how he'd come to know that, I was still fairly sure he'd found out by falling victim to one of Jeremy's blackmailing schemes. I would bet my bow on that one.

I needed to find proof, though. If I could find some evidence that Jeremy had demanded money from McAllister in exchange for keeping Susannah's video a secret, I'd be able to establish the reverend's motive for committing both the murder and the arson. Maybe for one or more of the break-ins as well. After all, it was possible that the reverend had hoped to find and destroy any evidence of the fact that Jeremy had blackmailed him.

I knew that my theory about the reverend didn't take into account that the police had caught Ray red-handed trying to break into Jeremy's basement suite. If, in fact, it was Ray who was in custody. But I had to focus on one thing at a time, or I'd never get anywhere.

A man and woman in their early thirties burst into the church, two little kids with tearstained faces in tow.

The woman with the garish red hair threw up her hands and exclaimed, "Finally!"

She raved on at the harried couple, but somehow McAllister managed to usher everyone into the nave. The doors closed behind them, cutting off the redhead's rant, and all I could hear then were the far-off strains from the orchestra.

I tugged at my earlobe. I knew what I wanted to do but I wasn't sure if I should actually go through with it. In the end, I didn't hesitate for long. With a quick glance around me, I scooted up the stairs in a light-footed dash, the red carpeting helping to muffle my footfalls.

At the top of the stairway I paused and peeked around the corner into the hallway. Aside from me, it appeared that there was nothing on the second story but dust motes drifting in a lazy pattern through a shaft of evening sunlight in an open doorway. I could no longer hear the orchestra playing below, and thick silence was hanging in the air around me.

I left the red-carpeted stairs behind and crept along the hardwood floors of the hallway. I cringed as a floorboard creaked beneath my feet but kept moving. When I reached the half-open door of McAllister's office, I peered around the door frame. The room was empty except for more dust motes moving in a slow swirl through the sunlight. The door to the office across the hall was closed, but a quick glimpse through the small window near the top of the door revealed that the second room was as empty as the first.

So far the coast was clear.

I backtracked down the hallway and checked out the two meeting rooms. Both empty. I had the second floor to myself.

I didn't let myself hesitate again. I knew if I did I might chicken out. And if I chickened out, I had no chance of finding out more about McAllister. That wasn't an option. I wanted answers. I needed answers. Otherwise I might never feel safe in my own home again.

Still careful to walk quietly, even though I was alone, I returned to McAllister's office and eased the door open a few more inches. When I stepped over the threshold, the thick silence pressed down around me and I found myself even trying to breathe quietly.

After a mental shake, I forced myself to move with less care. If I didn't want to get caught snooping I needed to hurry, and holding my breath and tiptoeing around wouldn't help me with that.

I targeted McAllister's desk first. I set down my belongings, lowered myself into his aging, black leather swivel chair, and surveyed the scene in front of me. The jar of candies on his desk tempted me, but I wasn't there for snacking and resisted the urge to help myself. Besides, taking a candy would somehow make me feel even guiltier than I already did for poking around the office uninvited. The candies were there for visitors but, I guessed, not clandestine visitors like me. I might be a snoop, but I wasn't a thief. Not even a candy thief.

Now that I was at the desk, I heard something besides ringing silence—the hum of McAllister's computer. I switched on the flat-screen monitor and wiggled the mouse. The computer chugged for a second and then woke from its slumber. The reverend had left his desk in the midst of composing an e-mail. The address and subject lines were empty but the message box contained a partial message.

I glanced at the open office door to ensure that I was still alone and then riveted my eyes on the screen. As I read the message, my eyebrows rose and my eyes widened.

Adam, I appreciate your discretion in this matter. As I'm sure you understand, the missing funds concern me deeply. Honesty and trust are such important facets of our community that a breach of those virtues would have repercussions far beyond the financial. As much as I don't want to believe that someone I trust and care for could betray not only me but the church as well, I must. . .

That's where the message ended.

I sat back in the chair, staring at the highlighted dust motes without seeing them. Missing funds. Missing from where? The church bank account? The donation box? Somewhere else?

I didn't know and the unfinished message didn't provide me with any clues.

Did the threat to frame Susannah as a thief have to do with these same missing funds?

That was highly possible.

I wondered if McAllister knew who was responsible for the missing money. Clearly he was aware that it was someone from within the church community, and that made sense if the funds were connected to the church. But did he know exactly who was responsible, and did any of this have any bearing on the other recent crimes?

I had no idea.

I wondered if he were responsible for the theft himself. How else could he hope to frame Susannah? Unless the threat was an empty one, or someone other than the reverend had sent Susannah the message.

I returned my attention to the computer and accessed McAllister's Internet browsing history. Over the past week he'd visited various sites related to charities, Christianity, and fly fishing, but none that would in any way link him to Jeremy's murder.

I didn't really expect to find that he'd checked out Web sites on how to murder someone, or how to start a fire in a church washroom, but that would have helped me tie things together. Even if McAllister—or whoever the murderer was—lacked enough sense to leave evidence of such searches on his computer, I suspected that the murder and arson were more crimes of opportunity than crimes that had been carefully planned beforehand.

I shut off the computer monitor and used one foot to propel the swivel chair in a slow circle, checking out the entire office. Books lined the built-in shelves, and the few knickknacks present were free of dust. Two potted plants that I had no hope of identifying brought some life to the room, thriving under someone's careful care.

A crucifix hung on one wall, and the opposite wall featured a framed oil painting of baby Jesus in the arms of the Virgin Mary. Aside from the jar of candies and the computer, the surface of McAllister's desk was home to a tray filled with three pieces of snail mail, a pencil holder containing several writing implements, a stapler, a sharp letter opener shaped like a miniature sword, and a framed family photo.

I leaned forward to peer more closely at the letter opener, but didn't give it more than a second or two of attention. If Jeremy had been stabbed and the murder weapon had been missing from the scene of the crime, the item would have held my interest. But as he had died by strangulation, I moved on.

I picked up the family photo and studied it. It showed McAllister with one arm around his wife, Cindy, and his free hand resting on the shoulder of a young man I presumed was their son. Cindy had her free hand on the shoulder of a second son, slightly younger than the first. I estimated both young men to be in their early twenties. The photograph suggested they were a perfect, happy family. Perhaps that was even the case, but I had my doubts.

Approaching footsteps put an abrupt end to my musings. Alarm charged through my bloodstream like a locomotive racing at full speed. My heart pounding out an overzealous beat, I swept my shoulder bag and violin case up off the floor and dashed toward the office door. I halted as I reached the threshold, almost skidding to a stop.

Whoever was out there had already reached the top of the stairs and entered the hallway. I didn't have a chance of slipping out of the office unseen, so I scurried behind the open door and pressed my back against the wall, hugging my bag and instrument case to my chest. I all but held my breath, straining to follow the movement of the footsteps over the almost-deafening beat of my freaking out heart.

The creator of the footsteps drew closer to the office, each clunk of shoe against wooden floorboard increasing my dread.

I closed my eyes.

Please don't come in here. Please don't come in here.

I had no idea how to explain my presence if someone caught me in McAllister's office. I could say I'd dropped by to see if the reverend was present, but that would only hold up if the person who found me didn't check with him and discover that I knew full well he was tied up with the wedding rehearsal. Besides, whoever found me was bound to be suspicious, what with me hiding behind the office door, guilt written across my face.

The footsteps paused just short of McAllister's office, and I opened my eyes, cautious hope lowering my heart rate a notch or two. Across the hall a doorknob turned and then hinges squeaked with a quiet protest. Four more footfalls sounded against the aging hardwood and the door closed.

I held my breath. I detected a few more footsteps, but they were muffled now. Whoever had been out in the hallway had entered the other office.

I exhaled and nearly went light-headed with relief. Or perhaps the light-headed sensation was from holding my breath. Either way, I didn't let it slow me down. I slipped out of the office and made a rushed but near-silent escape down the stairs. I didn't pause even for a second, continuing on through the narthex and straight out the church's main doors.

I made a beeline for the nearest bus stop, my heart still lub-dubbing in my chest with greater speed and force than normal. It wasn't so much that someone had nearly caught me where I didn't belong that had me worked up and on edge.

No, it was more the result of what I'd seen as I fled from my hiding spot.

Hanging on a hook on the back of Reverend McAllister's office door was a black hoodie sweatshirt with white lettering on the hood.

"JT!"

I burst into the house through the front door, nearly tripping myself in my haste. I staggered to one side but managed to avoid falling flat on my face in the foyer.

JT's voice floated along the hallway toward me. "I'm out back."

I dumped my violin and bag in my studio and rushed toward the back of the house, Finnegan trotting up to meet me. I gave him a quick scratch on the head but kept moving. As I reached the kitchen, the rumble of additional male voices alerted me to the fact that JT wasn't alone out in the yard. I stepped out onto the porch and stopped.

Right. It was Tuesday night. Band night.

Every Tuesday, JT and the three other members of his band got together to practice and enjoy a beer afterward. I'd caught them in the midst of the latter ritual.

"Hey, Midori." Hamish, a guitarist, grinned at me from his Adirondack chair. "You sound kinda anxious to see JT. Miss him or something?"

I was used to Hamish's teasing and ignored him, aside from sending a glare his way.

"Everything okay?" JT asked. He too lounged in an Adirondack chair, a can of beer in one hand.

I squelched my impatience. I wanted to talk to him about what I'd found during my spot of snooping at the church, but I didn't want an audience. Especially one that included Hamish. I knew I'd have to wait until the guys left, even though I didn't want to.

"Everything's fine." I focused on the only person who hadn't yet spoken, a smile overtaking my impatient scowl. "Hi, Aaron."

The drummer saluted me with his beer can. "All right?"

My smile broadened at the sound of his British accent. It sounded as dreamy as he looked, with his rich brown skin and dimples that always made an appearance when he smiled.

"Yes, thanks."

He flashed that dimpled smile at me then, and I forgot my annoyance at having to wait to speak to JT alone. Aaron was the newest member of the band, and this was only the third time I'd met him. Whenever he spoke to me or brought out that smile of his, my stomach flip-flopped in a giddy, pleasant way.

"Why don't you grab yourself something to drink and join us?" JT suggested.

I did just that, fetching a can of root beer from the fridge. My choice of beverage earned me a comment from Hamish about not being able to handle the real thing, but I simply said, "Shut up, Hamish," and settled into the empty chair next to Aaron.

"Rafael's not here tonight?" I asked, noting the absence of the fourth band member.

"And good thing," Hamish said.

"He's got the flu," JT explained.

I made a face. "Poor guy."

After taking a long drink of my root beer, I asked about the songs the guys had worked on that night. We talked about their music for a half hour or so as darkness took a stronger hold around us. Moths danced in the yellow glow of the porch light, and crickets chirped in the shadows. The air cooled and I was ready to go inside to seek some warmth when the guys broke up the gathering.

I lingered in the kitchen while JT walked to the front door with his bandmates. At least, I thought all three of them had gone down the hall, but Aaron surprised me by popping his head back into the kitchen.

"Midori?"

I tossed my empty root beer can in the recycling bin and faced him.

"Do you want to grab a bite to eat next weekend?"

My heart danced a little jig in my chest. Despite that, I opened my mouth to turn him down, to tell him I was already seeing someone. But then I remembered that I wasn't. Hans and I were finished.

I smiled. "Sure. That would be great."

"Brilliant." I caught a flash of his dimples before he said, "Cheers," and disappeared down the hall.

I stood in the middle of the kitchen, processing what had happened.

I had a date. With a really cute guy.

My smile morphed into a goofy grin.

Maybe my love life wasn't on such a bad track after all.

The front door shut with a thud and the dead bolt locked with a clunk. JT and Finnegan returned to the kitchen without Aaron and Hamish.

"What's up with you?" JT asked when he saw my goofy expression.

"Nothing." I busied myself with shutting and locking the back door, doing my best to replace my grin with a neutral expression.

"So what was it you were so worked up about?"

I slapped my hands on top of my head. "I can't believe I forgot about that."

A trace of amusement lit up JT's eyes. "Aaron did seem to distract you."

My hands went from my head to my hips. "Don't tease. I have something important to tell you."

He settled himself on a stool at the breakfast bar. "I'm listening . . ."

Excitement tingled up my spine as I prepared to share my news. "I found evidence that Reverend McAllister is guilty."

Chapter 21

"Guilty of what?"

I nearly rolled my eyes right out of my head. "JT, where have you been for the past week?"

"I mean in relation to which crime. The murder? The arson? One of the break-ins? All of the above?"

"All of them." I rethought my answer. "Or at least some of them."

JT didn't look nearly as impressed as I thought he should.

"The intruder who broke into Mrs. Landolfi's basement the night I was there wore a dark hooded sweatshirt with white writing on the hood."

"Okay. So?"

"*So*, Reverend McAllister has a black hoodie with white writing on the hood. I saw it with my own eyes. It was hanging on the back of his office door."

"And you think that means McAllister was the intruder?"

"Well, duh!"

"Dori, how many people in Vancouver alone do you think own a black or dark hoodie with white writing on the hood?"

I opened my mouth to respond and shut it again. Some of my excitement fizzled away, leaving me feeling like a can of root beer left standing open for too long.

"Exactly," JT said to my silence.

I slumped onto the stool next to him, but a second later I perked up. "Okay, but how many people connected to the crimes have a sweatshirt like that? McAllister had a motive to kill Jeremy, the murder happened right in his church, *and* he owns a sweatshirt like the one the intruder wore."

"All right, so it's another connection," JT conceded. "But don't be surprised if the police don't jump up and down with excitement when you tell them."

"Hmm. I guess I should tell them, huh?" That hadn't yet occurred to me, even though it probably should have. "And I won't be surprised if they're not excited. I don't think Bachman and Salnikova would jump up and down with excitement even if they won the Lotto Max jackpot." I glanced at the clock on the wall above the kitchen sink. "I'll call them in the morning."

I tapped my fingers on the granite countertop. I had to admit that pegging McAllister as the guilty party didn't explain why Ray (assuming it was Ray in custody) had broken into Jeremy's basement suite. But that incident wasn't necessarily related to the others. McAllister could still be guilty of killing Jeremy, setting the fire, and committing the first break-in at Mrs. Landolfi's and the one at my apartment.

Whether my information about the hoodie would help lead the police to arrest the reverend, I didn't know. I only knew that I believed the information was important. I'd share it with the detectives, and what they did with it from there was up to them. I hoped they'd take the tip seriously, though. If McAllister was guilty of even half of what I suspected, he needed to be behind bars before he had the chance to commit any more crimes.

"Did Aaron ask you out?"

I didn't expect JT's question or the change in subject, so it took me a few ticks of the clock's second hand to steer my mind in the new direction.

"Yes, he did."

"And did you say yes?"

I sat up straighter as worry gnawed at me. "Is that okay?"

JT gave me an odd look. "Why wouldn't it be?"

"I don't know. Maybe you don't want me to date a member of your band."

"That's not an issue."

He said nothing more, but I knew that wasn't the end of it. I didn't know if it was something in his eyes or a vibe he emitted, but I could tell he wasn't happy for me.

"Then what's wrong?" My recent experience with Hans flashed through my mind. "Aaron *is* single, isn't he?"

"As far as I know."

"No secret wife or girlfriend hidden away back in England?"

A grin tugged at one corner of JT's mouth. "If she were a secret, I wouldn't know about her, would I?"

I checked my pockets for my phone but they were empty. "I should Google him." I slipped off my stool and dashed down the hall to my studio.

"Seriously?" JT called after me.

It only took me three seconds to retrieve my phone from my bag. As soon as I had it in hand, I skedaddled back to the kitchen and resumed my perch at the breakfast bar.

I accessed the Internet and paused, thumbs hovering over the touch screen. "What's his last name?"

JT shook his head as if he thought I'd lost mine but he answered my question. "Howsham."

"Oh, good. Not too common."

I typed Aaron's name into the search bar and pressed enter. I blinked and the search results appeared. I scanned through them. Aside from a couple links to social media profiles and an article about his previous band, the Web didn't have much to say about him. I gave the article and the profiles a quick glance but nothing set red flags waving in my head.

"Anything?"

"Nope. Thank God." I added the word 'girlfriend' to his name for another search. When that brought nothing to light, I tried one last search, this time replacing 'girlfriend' with 'married.'

JT watched from his seat at my elbow. "Again, seriously?"

"Can you blame me for wanting to be careful this

time?" When my latest search yielded no relevant results, a small puff of relief wafted through my body.

"No, I don't blame you."

A note of solemnity had entered his voice. It grabbed my attention, and I remembered what had put me on this track in the first place.

"What's wrong? Why don't you want me going out with Aaron?"

JT shifted on his stool and his eyes strayed down to Finnegan. "I just don't want you rushing into anything if you still need time to get over the fiasco with Clausen."

I leaned toward him and hugged his upper arm, resting my head on his shoulder. "You're a good friend, JT." I straightened up but kept one arm looped around his. "I can't say that Hans didn't hurt me, but I'm working on getting over it. And Aaron might even help me get over it."

"So he'll be your rebound guy?"

I released my loose grip on his arm and swatted his biceps. "I'm not saying he'll be my anything guy. All I've agreed to so far is one date. If that goes well and he's still interested . . ." I sighed, my thoughts drifting in a slightly different direction. "I just want someone in my life, you know? The right someone."

"Yes. I know the feeling."

Something in his voice told me that he really did understand, and I wondered if he had some of the same concerns about his life as I had about mine. I considered asking him about it, even though I wasn't sure it was a topic a guy would want to get into in depth, but he didn't give me a chance.

He got up from his stool. "I'm going to watch some news. How about you?"

"No. I think I'll head straight to bed."

"Come on, Finnegan."

Finn jumped to his feet and anticipated JT's next move, trotting off down the hall.

"Good night," JT called over his shoulder as he followed his canine companion.

"Night."

I remained at the breakfast bar for another minute or two after JT and Finnegan retired to the living room. Considering the sincerity behind JT's words moments earlier, I had to question how he felt about Shauna. I knew that they'd only met recently, but something told me he hadn't yet found what he was looking for in his relationship with her.

For some reason that filled me with little bubbles of something I couldn't quite identify. Hope? Happiness?

Whatever the feeling was, I squashed it before it could take on its full shape.

I didn't even know Shauna. I shouldn't want JT to break up with her. I should only want him to do whatever made him happiest.

I swallowed back the fear that I was a bad friend and refused to examine the source of my sudden confusion of thoughts and feelings. I was tired and had a lot on my mind. Most likely Mikayla's comments from the night before were playing tricks on my sleep-hungry brain.

The best thing for me to do was to get to bed. In the

morning I would talk to the police and tell them about McAllister and his black hooded sweatshirt.

WHEN I MADE my way downstairs the following morning, the house was silent. JT and Finnegan were both absent, as was Finn's leash, so I figured they'd gone off on an early morning walk or run. I munched my way through an apple and sipped at a cappuccino while I checked e-mail on my phone.

I had a message from one of my adult students letting me know she was sick and wouldn't be at her lesson that day. I sent off a quick reply to tell her I'd received her message and I hoped she'd feel better soon. As I hit send, a phone call came through from my mom. Even though my parents lived out of town, they'd read about Jeremy's murder, and were alarmed that someone who played in the same orchestra as I did had been killed in such a violent manner. I did my best to reassure my mom that I was safe, even though I didn't know if that was the case. I omitted any mention of the fire, the break-in at my apartment, or the fact that I was camped out at JT's place for fear that someone might try to harm me again.

Once I'd put my mom's mind at ease and ended the phone call, I dialed the number on the card Salnikova had given me on the night of Jeremy's murder. The detective's phone rang four times and went to voice mail. I paced the kitchen as I listened to detective Salnikova's recorded voice, pausing by the sink when a beep sounded in my ear. I left a brief message, stating that I had some information to share and asking her to contact me.

I hung up and put my cappuccino cup in the dishwasher before heading to the foyer to pull on my black high-heeled boots. It was frustrating that I couldn't talk to Salnikova right then, but I decided to focus on what I could do—visit the church again and try to find more evidence to link McAllister to Jeremy's death and the other crimes.

I was certain JT wouldn't approve of my plan, so I hoped to slip out of the house before he and Finnegan returned from their morning outing. I only made it as far as the front porch before I realized that the clear sky of the day before had clouded over. A cool breeze rustled the leaves of the rhododendron bush next to the front steps, and the thick gray clouds held a promise of rain.

I ducked back inside the house and dashed up the stairs to retrieve a light jacket from the guest room. Then I was back down, out the door, and on my way to the church, still with no sign of JT or Finnegan.

The bus dropped me off two blocks from the church, the closest it was possible to get by public transportation. Despite the disappearance of the spring sunshine, I enjoyed the short walk to my destination. The cool air was fresh, and the light wind only helped to waft the sweet smells of spring toward my appreciative nose.

When the church came into view, I spotted a woman jogging toward me from the opposite direction. As we drew closer to each other, I recognized her as Estelle, McAllister's sister. It was strange to see her in running gear rather than her conservative, officelike attire, but for all I knew, athletic clothing could have been more of a norm for her than pencil skirts and pantsuits.

I was about to call out a cheery greeting when I nearly choked. Along with her black leggings and running shoes, she wore a black hoodie sweatshirt. From my vantage point I couldn't tell if the hood had white writing on it, but I was determined to find out if it did.

Recovering my voice, I raised a hand in a wave and called out, "Good morning!"

Estelle slowed to a walk and returned my wave. "It's a lovely, refreshing day, don't you think?" she said when we were within a few feet of each other.

"Absolutely," I replied.

As Estelle grabbed one foot behind her to stretch out her quads, I slid my eyes to the hood of her sweatshirt. My heart thudded in my chest.

UNITED IN FAITH was written in white lettering along the edge of the hood.

I swallowed, wondering what this meant. Should Estelle be on my suspect list too?

Her sweatshirt was smaller than McAllister's, so she hadn't borrowed his. How many other people had the same one?

"Reverend McAllister has the same sweatshirt," I said, trying my best to sound casual and not overly interested.

Estelle dropped her left foot and kicked up her right one for the same stretch. "That's right. We sold them as part of a fund-raiser last fall. I should think half the congregation has one."

Great. So much for my valuable piece of information. Now I'd feel like a fool when Salnikova returned my phone call. I'd known all along that the sweatshirt clue wasn't the strongest piece of evidence to link McAllister to the break-in at Mrs. Landolfi's place, but now it was weaker than ever. It still suggested that the intruder was somebody with a connection to the church, but if Estelle was right, that left a long list of possible suspects.

I maintained my belief that McAllister was guilty, but I now doubted that Detectives Salnikova and Bachman would find my information the least bit compelling. Heck, even I didn't find it compelling anymore. That only left me more determined than ever to find more evidence to support my theory of McAllister's guilt.

"Are you heading to the church?" Estelle inclined her head in that direction.

"Yes, actually," I said.

Estelle seemed puzzled. "You don't have rehearsal today, do you?"

"Um, no." I scrambled around in my mind for a believable excuse for my presence. "But I'm thinking of joining the church."

The words came out before I could stop them, and right away I wanted to kick myself.

Estelle, on the other hand, brightened. "That's wonderful. Why don't you come upstairs and I'll see if Cindy is free to tell you more about our congregation and services?"

"Great," I said, trying my best to infuse the word with some enthusiasm. "Thanks."

With a bounce in her step, the reverend's sister led me into the church. Although I pasted a smile on my face as I followed along behind her, I couldn't help but wonder what I was getting myself into.

what Jeremy . . . had . . .

Chapter 22

WHY OH WHY *didn't I come up with a different excuse for
being at the church?*

That was the thought that ran through my head as I
traipsed up the church's interior stairway behind Estelle.
Guilt gnawed at my stomach because of my lie. I really had
no interest in joining any church, let alone the one where
Jeremy had met his violent demise and where Susannah
and I had nearly become charred remains. Not to mention
the fact that I suspected the resident reverend of murder.

At least I had told my lie outside the church this time,
but that didn't make me feel a whole lot better. Even
though I wasn't a religious person, I liked to be respect-
ful. Three years of my parents sending me to Sunday
school at a tender young age had probably had an effect
on me as well. I didn't much like to lie under any circumstances, and the church setting only made the deed seem
more sinful.

Still, I didn't want to draw suspicion on myself, and I wasn't sure that I could have come up with a better excuse for my presence on a nonrehearsal day even if I'd had more time to think. Whether I'd have a chance to dig around for more clues now remained to be seen. Sneaking away might not be so easy if Cindy McAllister was indeed available to give me the run-through on the church and its community.

I crossed my fingers behind my back as we ascended the final stairs, hoping Cindy would be absent from her office or otherwise occupied. We left the stairwell for the corridor and approached the office across the hall from Reverend McAllister's. The door stood open and Cindy sat at the desk, eyes riveted on the computer screen before her.

Estelle tapped her knuckles against the door frame. "Cindy?"

The reverend's wife snapped her head toward us, startled. She made a hurried move with the mouse, giving it a quick click before folding her hands in her lap and fixing a smile on her face. Although the computer monitor was angled away from me, I was certain she had just minimized or exited a program. Straight away I wondered why she would do that. What was it she didn't want us to see?

I longed to get a look at her computer, to have a chance to see which program she had minimized or take a quick gander at her Internet browsing history. Maybe she simply didn't want to get caught shopping online for frivolous items when she was supposed to be focused on church business, but I had to wonder if she was up to something more sinister. It wouldn't have surprised me, considering all the other suspect behavior of late.

Checking out Cindy's computer wasn't in the cards for me at the moment, however. Instead, I was about to pay for the lie I'd told Estelle.

"Cindy, this young lady is interested in joining the church." Estelle gave me an apologetic smile. "I'm sorry. I know my brother told me your name . . ."

"Midori Bishop," I supplied.

Cindy stood up and gestured at a seat in front of her desk. "How lovely. Please, sit down."

I fought the urge to hightail it out of the church and instead did as invited, setting my purse on the floor next to the chair.

"Do you need me for anything?" Estelle asked her sister-in-law. "Otherwise I'll go shower and change."

Cindy held up a finger. "Actually, would you mind taking Midori to Peter's office to show her our pamphlets?"

"Sure." Estelle's response was agreeable enough but the smile that went with it was strained.

I reached down to pick up my purse again.

Cindy fluttered a hand in the air. "Oh, you can leave your things here. It'll just take a moment to get the pamphlets, and when you come back we can have a nice chat."

I almost gulped, already wondering how I could get myself out of the upcoming chat. But I did as instructed, leaving my bag next to the chair as I followed Estelle out of the office. When we entered McAllister's office across the hall, I glanced at the woman's profile. The strain had gone from her expression but I was certain that I hadn't imagined it moments earlier.

Was there some ill will between the sisters-in-law? If so, why?

Although I was curious about the McAllister family dynamics, I doubted I'd ever get answers to my questions. Besides, it really wasn't any of my business. Unless it had to do with the recent crimes, some of which had been directed at me. I couldn't think how the women's relationship would be relevant, though. I wasn't even sure that the reverend's relationship with his wife was relevant.

My mind went back to the e-mail I'd surreptitiously read the last time I was in McAllister's office. Did the reverend know who had betrayed him and the church by misappropriating funds? It would be a betrayal for anyone in the church community to be the thief, but it would be even more scandalous and treacherous if the reverend's own wife or sister were involved.

I gave myself a mental shake. The missing money probably had nothing to do with Jeremy's death or the other crimes. I was getting too suspicious, reading too much into everything. I needed to stay focused on my mission. McAllister was still my prime suspect, and I needed more evidence to link him to one or more of the recent nefarious acts. If I didn't have something more than my next-to-useless information about the hooded sweatshirt by the time Salnikova got back to me, I'd feel like a fool.

Exactly how I was going to search for clues if I couldn't shake my well-meaning church ladies, I had no idea. Maybe once I made it through Cindy's sales pitch I'd be able to slip away. But even that wouldn't really solve my problem. The upstairs offices were the places I wanted to explore, and I couldn't do that unless both Cindy and Estelle went elsewhere.

I decided to take things one step at a time. Perhaps an opportunity for a spot of in-depth snooping would arise down the line.

"Here you are." Estelle's voice drew me out of my thoughts. She snagged a glossy pamphlet and a slim, magazinelike brochure from a shelf behind McAllister's desk and handed them to me. "These should give you a good idea of what we do within the church and the community, but I'm sure Cindy will be happy to answer any questions you might have."

I opened the pamphlet for a quick peek, feigning interest. "Thank you. I appreciate your time."

Estelle's smile was less strained this time. "I'll leave you in Cindy's capable hands. I hope to see you around more in the future."

I forced a smile and followed Estelle's lead as she left the office. While the reverend's sister jogged off down the stairs, I returned to the office across the hall.

Cindy was in the midst of hurrying around her desk to retake her seat. She appeared flustered, but as soon as she saw me she tucked an errant strand of hair behind her ear and smoothed her expression into a welcoming but rather bland one.

"Did Estelle find everything for you?"

I held up the brochures. "Yes, thanks."

The phone on Cindy's desk let out a shrill ring, and I recognized a chance to escape.

"I can see you're busy," I said as the phone rang a second time and Cindy's eyes flicked in its direction. I waved the brochures. "Why don't I go take a look at these on my own and get back to you later if I have any questions?"

"Yes, of course. Feel free to get in touch with me anytime."

I snatched my purse up from the floor and pasted another smile on my face as I backed toward the door. "Thanks again."

As Cindy reached for the telephone, I slipped out into the hallway with a great sense of relief. I stuffed the church brochures into my purse and descended the stairs to the main floor. I paused next to a large potted plant, sucking on the inside of my left cheek as I considered my options. I could call it quits and head back to JT's, or I could poke around other parts of the church, perhaps asking anyone I found a few questions under the pretense of my interest in joining the church. Neither plan was my original one, but the second was better than the first. I didn't want to give up. Not without at least attempting to gather more clues and evidence.

I heard voices coming from inside the nave. Female voices. I couldn't make out what they were saying, but I wondered if I should push through the doors and speak to whoever stood on the other side. I doubted the owners of the voices would be able to provide me with the information I sought, but one never knew. Perhaps some members of the congregation were observant enough to have noticed some suspicious, or at least unusual, behavior on McAllister's part recently. It was worth a try.

I took a step toward the nave but then paused. Cindy McAllister came down the stairs behind me. She flashed me a quick, distracted smile as she breezed past me.

"Ladies, how is everyone today?" she greeted as she swept into the nave.

The doors shut behind her, muffling the responses from the other women.

I hesitated for only a split second. This was my chance. With Cindy down on the main floor, her office—and the entire second story—would be unoccupied.

I pivoted on my heel and flew up the stairs. I spared only the most cursory of glances for the second floor hallway—empty, as I expected it would be—before darting into Cindy's office.

Even though Reverend McAllister was my primary suspect and target, I didn't want to leave any potentially slimy stone unturned by skipping over the second office. Besides, I wanted to know what Cindy had been in such a hurry to hide from Estelle and me upon our arrival.

I skittered around the desk and slid into the vacant swivel chair. A quick glance at the computer monitor told me that Cindy had left no programs open. Perhaps there were some interesting files on the hard drive, but I didn't know if I'd have time to browse through who-knew-how-many folders searching for who-knew-what. So I zeroed in on the Internet browser.

A double-click on the Firefox icon brought the browser

to life, and from there I accessed the browsing history. As my eyes ran over the list of sites recently visited, my eyebrows crept up toward my hairline. While the visits to Gmail and the church's Web site were unsuspicious and uninteresting, I couldn't say the same about another page.

Although the name of the site gave me a good idea of its contents, I clicked on the link anyhow, seeking confirmation. Less than five seconds later I had it.

Somebody had used the computer to visit a gambling Web site. Although I couldn't be certain that Cindy McAllister was the person who had done so, I felt in my gut that she was. Without stopping to think about what that meant, I delved deeper into the browsing history. Someone had visited the same gambling Web site the day before, along with another gambling site. I scrolled through the site visits for the past week and spotted the same two sites again, along with a few other similar ones.

I sat back and shook my head. What did this mean? Did it mean anything?

Even assuming that Cindy was the gambler, that didn't mean she had a gambling problem. However, the frequency with which the sites had been visited, and the number of sites visited, suggested otherwise. Cindy—or perhaps somebody else—had far more than a casual interest in gambling.

I reached up and tugged at my ear. As interesting as it was that the reverend's wife might have a gambling addiction, that didn't help me link McAllister—or anyone else for that matter—to Jeremy's death, the fire, or any of the break-ins.

Or did it?

Numerous scraps of information shifted around in my head, trying to fit together but not quite managing it. I wasn't sure if I still needed more pieces to complete the picture or if I had everything I needed and simply couldn't see how to put it all together.

I returned my attention to the computer and scrolled through the browsing history once more, checking for sites other than those related to gambling. Nothing else of interest popped out at me. I exited the browser and considered going through the files on the hard drive. I didn't know if it would be worth my time, and I'd already been in the office several minutes. The last thing I wanted was to get caught using the computer.

After considering my options for another second or two, I decided to wrap up my snooping for the day. I needed time to let the new information percolate in my brain, to see if I could make sense of the jumbled information in my head. Maybe I could talk things over with JT. He wouldn't be pleased that I'd poked my nose in other people's business again, but he might be able to see something I couldn't, make a connection that had so far eluded me.

I shifted my purse from my lap to my shoulder and crept out of the office. I took a direct route to the stairway, still moving with stealthy steps. As I reached the landing and started down the second set of stairs, a floorboard creaked somewhere not too far off. I froze, but only for a second. I didn't want to wait around to find out if someone was coming up the other stairway. My fictitious interest in joining the church might have saved my skin earlier, but I doubted that Cindy and company would continue to buy that explanation a second time, especially if someone caught me sneaking around where I didn't belong.

Keeping my steps as light as possible, I slipped away down the stairs. I let out a relieved breath when I reached the narthex and found it empty. Determined not to run into Cindy or Estelle again, I hurried to the main doors and pushed through them out into the fresh air.

With brisk steps, I set off down the street. I glanced back at the church as I went, my eyes darting up to the second story windows. I thought I caught a flicker of movement in the window of the office I'd just left, but when I slowed my pace for a better look I saw nothing. Continuing on down the street in the direction of the bus stop, I told myself that my eyes had played a trick on me. I didn't really believe that, though. In fact, I was almost certain I'd seen a figure in the window.

A figure looking down at me.

A shiver tickled up my spine like a spider shimmying up its dangling silk thread. As I turned a corner and passed out of sight from the church, the first raindrops of the day pattered down from the sky.

Chapter 23

BY THE TIME I reached JT's house, my hair was soaked from the rain. Inside the front door, I kicked off my boots and peeled off my sodden jacket, hanging it up before setting off in search of my best friend. There was no sign of him on the main floor, but the door to the basement stood open in the kitchen. I peeked down the stairway. Finnegan stood at the bottom of the steps, looking up at me with a big doggie grin on his face, his fluffy tail wagging behind him.

"Hi, Finnie boy." I padded my way down to greet him with a quick hug and a pat on the head.

JT stood across the room, lifting an acoustic guitar down from its hook on the wall. "Hey," he said when he saw me. "What have you been up to?"

"I went to the church."

The suspicion in his eyes was impossible to miss. "What for?"

"To look for more clues, obviously." I flopped down in the nearest beanbag chair, dropping my purse on the floor beside me.

JT held his guitar by the neck and looked at me with more than a little exasperation. "Dori . . ."

I waved off his unspoken admonition. "I know, I know. You think I should leave it to the police. But forget about that for a second."

His expression only grew more exasperated.

"Please, JT? I have such a jumble of thoughts in my head, and I can't make sense of any of them. I need a sounding board."

He sighed, a little more dramatically than necessary, I thought, but he relented. "Fine. What dirty secrets have you uncovered now?"

I smiled, unable to quell a spark of excitement at the thought of sharing the account of my latest sleuthing excursion. As JT grabbed a new guitar string from a shelf and unwrapped it from its packaging, I told him about my discovery of the numerous gambling Web sites in the browsing history on the church computer.

JT crumpled the packaging in his fist and tossed it in a nearby wastepaper basket. "Seriously, Dori? You snooped on a computer? In a church?"

"That's not the point."

"No, the point is that you're going to get yourself in serious trouble if you keep this up."

"I thought we were going to skip the lecture."

He heaved out another exasperated sigh and sat down in a ladder-back chair, resting his guitar across his lap so he could add the new string. "All right, no lecture. But what do gambling Web sites have to do with the murder?"

"That's the thing. I don't know. Maybe nothing. Unless . . ."

A few thoughts clicked together in my head, forming a new theory. Before all the pieces could adhere in my mind to create a clear picture, my phone chimed from the depths of my purse.

"Unless what?" JT asked, but I only half heard him.

I scrounged around in my purse until I came up with my phone and checked the screen. I paused when I saw the new text message from Susannah.

Can you meet me at the church? Please. I really need to talk to you.

What was Susannah doing at the church? She should have been in school. Besides, I would have expected her to avoid the church whenever possible, considering her fear of Reverend McAllister.

What's wrong? I texted back, my thumbs moving swiftly across the touch screen. *Why are you at the church?*

"Dori?"

I opened my mouth to speak to JT, but shut it again when my phone chimed in my hands.

Long story. Will you come? Please?

I glanced at the time. I still had three hours before I had to teach.

Okay, I wrote back. *I'll be there soon.*

I dropped my phone back in my purse and wiggled my way out of the beanbag chair. "I have to go back to the church."

JT eyed me with a mixture of disbelief and suspicion. "I don't think that's such a good idea."

Finnegan danced around my legs, probably hoping for a trip outside.

I scratched his head with one hand and hitched my purse up over my shoulder with the other. "I'm not going there to snoop. Susannah wants to talk to me."

"Why is she at the church? Shouldn't she be in school?"

"I have the same questions," I said as I did some fancy footwork to make my way around Finnegan and toward the staircase. "But I guess I'll find out when I see her."

JT shook his head but went back to stringing his guitar. "Just don't do anything stupid."

"*Moi?*" I said with as much innocence as I could muster.

Without giving him a chance to respond, I darted up the stairs with Finnegan at my heels. I let him out in the backyard for a moment, waiting without much patience while he sniffed at a bush by the fence before lifting his leg and relieving himself. Once he was back in the house, I pulled my boots back on and donned my damp jacket with a grimace before setting off into the rain once again.

ALTHOUGH I WAS happy to get out of the rain, I was less than thrilled to be back at the church. Sitting on the bus had given me a chance to firm up the connections that had tried to form in my mind back at JT's place. My new theory still had a few holes in it, but I figured it was as good as the one featuring McAllister as the murderer.

No matter which of my two theories was correct—if

either of them—I knew JT was right. Even if I wasn't snooping, the church probably wasn't the best place for me to be. If the wrong person became suspicious of my repeated presence, I could be in danger.

I remembered the figure in the upstairs window and shivered. Maybe the wrong person already was suspicious.

I paused inside the church doors, my eyes scanning the narthex for any sign of Susannah. Thick silence settled around me. I didn't see Susannah or anyone else. A sense of unease seeped its way through my body.

I gave my wet hair a twist and tossed it over my shoulder before pulling out my cell phone. I sent Susannah another text message, asking for her exact location. Searching the whole building for her didn't appeal to me, especially with the new edginess that had taken hold of me.

As I waited for a response, I remained near the exit. I fidgeted, fingering the zipper on my purse and shifting my weight from foot to foot. When my phone rang in my hand, I nearly jumped sky high. I thought I recognized the number as the one I'd dialed to reach Salnikova, so I answered the call, hoping to hear the detective's voice on the other end of the line.

I did.

"Ms. Bishop, I got your message," Salnikova said. "You said you had some information to share?"

Straight to the point. I didn't mind that.

"I did. I mean, I do." I paused, trying to gather my thoughts so I could sound more coherent. As I did so, I slipped outside the church, huddling beneath the overhang to keep myself out of the pouring rain. Even though there was no one around to overhear me, I lowered my voice. "I discovered that Reverend McAllister has a hoodie sweatshirt like the one the intruder at Mrs. Landolfi's house wore," I explained. "Well, I can't be sure that it's the exact same hoodie, but it looks very similar. I thought that was a good clue until I found out that half the congregation has the same sweatshirt."

"I see." Salnikova's voice provided me with no hint as to whether or not she was interested.

I continued on in a rush. "But if the intruder really was wearing one of those sweatshirts, that suggests that he or she was someone connected to the church, even if it wasn't Reverend McAllister." I lowered my voice even further. "I was pretty confident that McAllister was guilty, but now I have reason to suspect that his wife might have a gambling problem. And if that's the case, she could be responsible for the missing church funds."

I took a breath, intending to explain the rest of my new theory, but Salnikova cut me off.

"Hold on a second. Missing funds?"

So I did know something the police didn't. I couldn't help but feel a hint of glee at that. "Someone's been stealing from the church, and McAllister suspects it's someone close to him."

"And how is it that you know this?"

I gulped. I doubted the detective would be impressed if she found out about my snooping. "Long story," I said, hoping Salnikova wouldn't press the matter. "The point is, what if Cindy McAllister is the thief? Maybe she took the money to support her gambling habit. And what if Jeremy found out? He spent a lot of time at the church. It's possible that he got wind of the missing funds." It was also possible that he'd snooped around like I had. But I didn't mention that part. "Do you know if Jeremy was blackmailing her too?"

"We have no evidence of that."

"But that doesn't mean it wasn't happening."

"No, it doesn't. But, Ms. Bishop, I'm concerned about how you came by all this information."

Oh, darn. I really didn't want to explain that. "Like I said —"

"Long story," Salnikova finished for me. She didn't sound too impressed. "Where are you now?"

"At the church."

"Why?" The detective's voice was sharp with suspicion.

"I came to meet Susannah."

"Ms. Bishop, if you suspect one or more of the McAllisters of murder, as you say you do, the church is the very last place you should be."

I jumped on what I thought was the implication behind her scolding. "So you think I could be right?"

A heavy sigh came down the line. "I'm not saying that. We will, of course, look into the information you've provided, but in the meantime, you should stick to music and let us detectives do the police work."

JT would love Salnikova.

"I have no intention of doing any more detective work." At least, I didn't right at the moment. "But I thought I should pass along what could be pertinent information." My words came out sounding miffed. I couldn't help it. I was tired of being told to keep my nose out of other people's business. Partly because I knew it was good advice.

"And I appreciate that," Salnikova said. "But please take your meeting with Susannah elsewhere. I think that would be best for both of you."

I sniffed, still nettled. "I happen to agree. As soon as I find her, we'll leave."

"Thank you." Somehow she made those two simple words sound long-suffering. "I'll be in touch."

She hung up. I stood staring at my phone for a moment, wondering if her last words meant she would update me on the investigation or that she would check in on me to see if I was up to something she disapproved of. I didn't come up with a definite answer and I didn't much care because a new text from Susannah soon distracted me.

I'm downstairs. Backstage. Are you coming?

I'll be right there, I wrote back.

When I returned to the narthex, I passed by the smoke-damaged corridor, still cordoned off, and aimed myself in the direction of the parallel corridor on the far side of the building. Although silence in a church could often be comforting, this time it wasn't. Instead it felt eerie. The sooner I could find Susannah and get out of there, the better.

As I followed the hallway and the stairs down to the basement, floorboards creaked beneath my feet, the sound unnaturally loud to my ears. I paused outside the door to the backstage room where the orchestra kept our belongings during rehearsals. The door was ajar but I could hear no noises beyond it. I touched my fingers to it and pushed it open.

"Susannah?"

The room was empty. Perhaps I'd misinterpreted her message. Maybe she meant she was in the narrow area behind the back curtains on the stage. Why she would be there, I didn't know. But I didn't know why she would be anywhere in the church.

I took a step backward, intending to turn around and check the stage. I hit something solid, and a strong arm locked into place around my throat. I choked and grabbed at the arm.

Panic burned through me like a rapidly spreading wildfire. When the arm didn't loosen its grip, a gargling sound escaped my throat. I struggled both to free myself and to draw air into my lungs.

"Unless you want your windpipe crushed, I suggest you stop struggling," a man's voice said in my ear.

It was a voice I recognized.

It belonged to Reverend McAllister.

Chapter 24

I FROZE, STILL gripping McAllister's arm. His hold across my throat loosened just enough to allow me to breathe. I welcomed the oxygen that flowed into my lungs, but it did nothing to ease my heart-squeezing fear.

I'd walked into a trap. How dumb was that?

Was Susannah even here? Was she okay?

What was about to happen?

All of those questions ran through my head with the speed of a piece of music played prestissimo.

I voiced another thought aloud.

"So it was you." My voice was strained but clear. "You killed Jeremy."

His arm still across my throat, McAllister nudged me forward. "Move."

I stumbled and let out a garbled gasp as the pressure against my throat increased again. I steadied myself and was rewarded with a less restricted airway. I walked forward as well as I could with McAllister still holding me in his grip. I didn't know why he wanted me to enter the backstage room, and I was quite sure I didn't want to know. My eyes darted around, searching for a way out of my predicament, but I came up empty.

Then I remembered my phone. It was in my purse, which was still hooked in the crook of my left elbow. I inched my right hand toward it.

"I didn't kill anyone," McAllister said when we reached the middle of the room. "I'm a man of God."

"That didn't stop you from threatening a teenage girl or trying to strangle me."

Perhaps I shouldn't have provoked him, but I couldn't help it. I was ticked off, both at him and myself. Besides, I needed to keep him distracted so I could reach my phone.

"I'm not without sin," McAllister said, prodding me forward again. "But I do have my limits. And I certainly draw the line at murder."

"That's very noble of you." My voice dripped with acidic sarcasm. "But excuse me for thinking you're acting rather guilty at the moment."

We'd arrived at the far side of the room, and I stood facing a white paneled wall. I wondered why the heck he had forced me there until I saw the door cut into the paneling. I'd never noticed it before, but I never had a reason to look carefully at the wall.

As McAllister reached around me with his free hand, my fingers made contact with my purse. As quietly and discreetly as possible, I worked the zipper open. As he pressed his hand against the door and it popped open, I slid my hand into my purse and closed my fingers around my phone. Anxiety and hope swelled together in a crescendo inside of me. If I could only send out a text message or dial 911, maybe help would come.

I slipped the device out of my purse and almost dropped it when the reverend jerked me to one side so he could open the door wider. I tightened my hand around my phone and managed to keep it from falling. My pulse galloped along as I glanced down without moving my head. I pressed my thumb to the numbers 911. As I tried to hit the third number, McAllister released his grip on me and shoved me ahead of him through the open door. My thumb skittered to one side.

I looked down at my phone and made a hurried attempt to finish dialing. Before I could put the call through, however, a hand wrenched the device out of my grasp.

"I'll take that."

My eyes followed my phone and then flicked up to the speaker's face.

Cindy McAllister.

Her gray-blue eyes were cold and hard. She held my phone in one hand and a sharp, glinting blade in the other. I recognized it as the wickedly sharp letter opener from the reverend's desk. It had seemed like an innocent tool at the time, but now, with its point directed at my torso, it was a weapon.

A grin that I could only describe as maniacal curled Cindy's lips. She slid my phone into the pocket of her jeans. From the bulge in her other pocket, I gathered she had another phone on her as well.

A whimper caught my attention, and I jerked my head to the left. Susannah sat huddled on a chair, her wrists and ankles bound with rope, and a scarf tied around her face as a gag. Tears had smudged her mascara and left shiny tracks down her cheeks. Her wide, terrified eyes pleaded with me to help her.

"So you were in on this together," I said to the McAllisters, hoping to distract them until I came up with a way to get myself and Susannah out of our predicament. There was a slight shakiness to my voice but I was surprised it wasn't even less steady.

Cindy snorted, still pointing the letter opener at me. "Being in on it together would suggest that my husband had enough brains to be my equal partner."

"And I take it he doesn't?"

As I spoke, I took in the surroundings with my peripheral vision. The four of us stood in a long, narrow, windowless room that appeared to be a storage area for costumes and props. A lone bare bulb provided the only illumination, and a musty smell permeated the air.

"Of course he doesn't," Cindy replied.

"Now, Cindy, I'm not sure that's fair—" the reverend started.

"Oh, shut up, you fool!" Her nostrils flared and her grip tightened on the letter opener.

My eyes fixed on the point of the blade. It was about six inches away from me, and I didn't want it coming any closer.

It jerked in an unnerving fashion as Cindy continued to rant at her husband. "What have you ever done except jeopardize your position in the church?"

"Now hold on," McAllister cut in, but his wife wasn't interested in hearing him out.

"Shut up!"

Maybe he finally heard the note of crazy in her voice or saw it in her eyes, because he did as he was told.

Even though their short argument had provided me with a few more seconds to assess the situation, I still had no bright ideas. The door was the only escape route, but McAllister stood in front of it, blocking my way out of the room. Even if he hadn't been in the way, Cindy would probably jab me with the letter opener before I made it two steps, and I couldn't leave Susannah behind.

I eyed the bulge in Cindy's pocket where she had my phone. Considering that she was armed and had her husband to back her up, I didn't think it would turn out well if I tried to wrestle her to the ground.

No, I needed to keep them talking until I came up with a better solution.

"So you killed Jeremy?" I directed the question at Cindy.

"Of course I killed him," she snarled.

I decided to test out the rest of my theory. "Because he was blackmailing you? About your gambling addiction, or maybe the funds you stole from the church?"

Cindy's eyes narrowed. "I knew you'd been snooping. I saw you sneaking out of my office yesterday, you know. You weren't as stealthy as you thought."

So she was the one watching me from the window as I left.

I jumped back as she jabbed the point of the letter opener toward my stomach. My back hit the wall and

I plastered myself against it as Cindy advanced a step toward me, her weapon only an inch away from me now.

"You should have minded your own business. Now you have to pay for what you've done—snooping into my private life, encouraging that little brat . . ." She waved the letter opener in Susannah's direction before pointing it back at me. " . . . to rat on my good-for-nothing husband."

Susannah whimpered, but I didn't dare spare her more than a glance. I wanted to keep a close eye on the blade pointed at the spot just above my navel. I sucked in my stomach to put a little more room between myself and the weapon.

"If he's good for nothing," I said, "then why do you care about the truth coming out about what he said about the bishop and his congregation?"

"I am not good for nothing!" McAllister protested.

Cindy and I ignored him.

"Because if he goes down, I go down," Cindy replied, the ferocity in her voice making me wish I could melt through the wall behind me to get away from her. "If the bishop found out about the video, Peter would be finished. He'd be replaced."

"Ah." I thought I'd caught on. "And if that happened, his replacement—or somebody at least—would be bound to uncover the fact that you'd been helping yourself to church money."

Her nose twitched, and I knew I had it right.

"So Jeremy was or wasn't blackmailing you as well as your husband?" I wanted to know the answer as much as I wanted to buy myself some time. Even in my dire circumstances, I couldn't quell my curiosity.

"He wasn't. He only blackmailed Peter."

"But you still killed him to protect yourself."

"To protect us both," McAllister put in.

Cindy shot him a derisive look out of the corner of her eye. "Don't kid yourself. You could rot in hell for all I care. If it didn't mean I'd do so right along with you."

McAllister's mouth dropped open in shock, but I didn't give him a chance to say anything more to his wife.

"And you broke into Jeremy's suite?" I asked Cindy.

"I sent Peter to do that." She sneered at her husband. "He was supposed to retrieve the check he'd given Ralston, but he couldn't even do that right. Almost got caught by the police. What was he even thinking in the first place? Who gives a check to a blackmailer? Who?"

She jabbed the letter opener at me again as if to emphasize her disbelief at her husband's stupidity. I squeaked and sucked in my stomach even farther as the point of the blade met the fabric of my shirt. Another muffled sob escaped from Susannah, but I was in no position to comfort her. What comfort could I offer anyway? I still couldn't see a way out of our quandary.

"And what about the break-in at my apartment?" My voice sounded higher than usual, fear upping its pitch. "Did you send him to do that too?"

"So he could screw up again? Of course not. After the fire didn't do its job, I knew I had to be more direct."

So I was right. The murderer and arsonist were one and the same.

I gulped as her last words registered in my brain. "You went to my apartment to kill me?"

"You had to be silenced. You were interfering. When I discovered you weren't home, I decided to leave you a message in the meantime. Until I had a chance to try again."

I gulped again, not wanting to think about what would have happened if I hadn't gone to stay with JT.

"You overheard me talking to Susannah," I guessed. "Right before the fire."

"That's right. You think I don't know everything that goes on in his church? *Somebody* needs to be aware of things."

McAllister frowned. He must have been as aware as I was that the verbal jab was aimed at him.

I directed my next question at him. "Why did your sister tell me that Jeremy thought his fiancée was having an affair? She said that was what your supposed spiritual guidance conversation was about."

Mild surprise registered on the reverend's face. "She told you that?" He thought for a second. "I suppose she was trying to protect me. Perhaps she thought you'd let the matter drop if she gave you some sort of explanation for my, ah, association with Ralston."

"So she knew about the video?"

"Of course. I told her all about it. She's my closest ally, after all."

Cindy snorted and raised the letter opener. She pointed it at my throat, snapping my thoughts back to my present situation. My eyes remained glued to the blade, willing it not to come any closer.

The reverend's wife jerked her head to the right. "Go sit down."

I forced my eyes away from the weapon and looked in the direction she'd indicated. A second wooden chair sat empty next to Susannah. I didn't want to sit down, because I knew that an escape would only be more difficult if I let myself be tied up. At the same time, I still wasn't in any position to take on Cindy or her husband. The proximity of the letter opener's blade to my throat was far too precarious.

"Move it!"

The menace in her eyes would have been enough to make me obey even without the letter opener. I shuffled to the side to avoid the sharp blade and lowered myself into the chair. I reached a hand out to Susannah and gave her arm a squeeze. Fresh tears trickled out of her eyes. I tried to give her a reassuring smile but my mouth didn't cooperate.

"Make yourself useful for once," Cindy snapped at her husband. "Tie her up."

I sent a pleading look in McAllister's direction, hoping he wasn't as crazy or cruel as his wife. If I could get him to turn on Cindy, Susannah and I might have a chance of surviving this fiasco. Unfortunately, he avoided my gaze.

He grabbed a length of rope from a nearby shelf and brought it over to me. He cast a quick, sidelong glance at his wife, and I knew then that I couldn't count on him for any help. He was too scared of his wife to stand up to her. That was clear on his face.

While Cindy kept the point of her weapon trained at my throat, McAllister bound my hands behind the back of my chair. I tried to keep my wrists as far apart as possible without being obvious about it, but I didn't know how much good that would do me.

Susannah choked out another sob, and Cindy's eyes strayed in her direction, the point of the letter opener drifting to one side. I didn't know if I'd have another opportunity to make a move, so I kicked out at Cindy's knee. Her legs gave way and she stumbled, doubling over. The blade of the letter opener slipped across my upper left arm. I gasped but didn't hesitate. Throwing myself forward, chair and all, I drove my shoulder into her.

She screamed, the shrill sound filled with intense fury and a hint of lunacy. I fell to my knees and struggled beneath the chair that came down on top of me. I wiggled my arms and wrists toward the top of the chair's arrow back. I needed to free myself before Cindy recovered enough to retake control of the situation.

I almost had myself free, with only a few more inches to go, when strong hands grabbed my upper arms from behind and wrenched me to my feet. While maintaining a grip on one of my arms, McAllister righted my chair and shoved me back into it.

By then Cindy was back on her feet. She was breathing heavily, her normally neat and tidy hair wisping out in all directions. Her eyes were colder than ever, her mouth pinched with anger. She leaned in toward me and pressed the point of the letter opener to my neck as her husband held me down in the chair, one hand on each of my shoulders.

"That is the last time you will ever interfere with one of my plans."

The venom in her voice chilled my blood as it pounded through my body.

"Finish tying her up," she ordered McAllister.

He obeyed, using more rope to bind my torso to the back of my chair. Out of rope, he used scarves from a costume rack to tie my ankles to the chair legs.

"What are you planning to do?" I asked, doing my best to keep my voice from quaking with fear. "Even without my help, the police will eventually figure out that you killed Jeremy. And if anything happens to me and Susannah, they'll know you're responsible for that too."

"Gag her, will you?" Cindy said to her husband. "I'm sick of listening to her."

"The police know I'm here. They'll come looking for me."

McAllister stuffed a scarf in my mouth. I gagged and tried to spit it out, but he tied it firmly in a knot at the back of my head.

A cruel, satisfied smile spread across Cindy's face. "Much better."

I squirmed against my restraints, but that only made her smile more.

"Nobody will connect me to anything once you're out of the way," she said with unnerving confidence. "I'll simply tell everyone that you and the little brat were helping my husband search for some suitable props for the upcoming youth group play. Tragically, a fire started and you weren't able to escape." She smirked. "This old building is full of fire hazards, and the door to this little room has a rather unfortunate tendency to stick. I'll be upstairs in my office at the time, completely unaware of what's happening below me until I hear the sirens or smell the smoke. By then it will be too late for you and I'll be free to start a new life."

I shook my head. I wanted to tell her that she wouldn't get away with it. Not that she would listen to me. I didn't think she was giving the police and fire investigators enough credit. More likely than not, it wouldn't take them long to figure out that her story was fabricated, particularly if there was enough of Susannah and me remaining for them to figure out we'd been restrained.

Of course, the investigative skills of the police and fire departments weren't exactly of much help to Susannah and me right at that moment. They might help to get us ultimate justice, but they wouldn't save us from a fiery, unpleasant end.

I tipped my head back, looking up at McAllister, using my eyes to plead with him once again. This time he met my gaze, and I thought I detected a hint of uncertainty.

"Help us!" I tried to yell through my gag but all that came out was a desperate but indistinct noise.

Cindy understood me well enough. She laughed, reaching out and grabbing a frying pan off a shelf laden with props. "Don't bother looking to him for help," she said. "My darling husband is going to perish in the fire right along with you. That way I can pin the theft on him and be free of his idiocy."

My eyes widened. Maybe McAllister's did too, but I never found out. As I jerked my head back to look at him, Cindy swung the frying pan at his head.

I heard a sickening thud and McAllister crumpled to the ground behind me.

Susannah screamed against her gag. I craned my neck around to get a look at the reverend. He lay in a heap, unmoving.

Cindy dropped the frying pan on the floor. "And now it's time for me to exit stage left." She dug into the back pocket of her pants and withdrew a lighter. She smiled with a crazed glint in her eyes. "Goodbye."

She backed out of the door and slammed it shut. A moment later I caught my first whiff of smoke.

Chapter 25

THE PAIN IN my arm chose that inopportune time to vie for my attention. With my mouth gagged, I had to take deep breaths through my nose to help direct my thoughts away from the agony. A second, stronger waft of smoke did more than my steady breathing to sharpen my focus. Susannah must have smelled the smoke too. She squirmed in her chair, crying and trying to scream.

We had to get free.

I wiggled my wrists. The restraints weren't tight but they weren't loose enough for me to slip out of them. Not yet at least. Maybe I could work my way out of them in time, but time wasn't something I had.

I shifted my body weight from side to side, giving my chair an experimental rock. It felt rickety beneath me, and I hoped that would be the key to my freedom. I was only a couple feet from the nearest wall but I needed to get closer. By shuffling my feet and making bouncy, jerking motions with my body, I managed to inch my chair toward the wall.

When I thought I was close enough, I gripped one of the slats of the chair back with my bound hands and lifted the piece of furniture up off the ground as I tried to stand on my feet. It was awkward but the scarves restraining my ankles shifted up my legs enough that I was able to stand, bent over at the waist. I pivoted my body as hard as I could and slammed my chair against the wall. Wood cracked, but I remained strapped to the piece of furniture.

My arm protested with a fierce cut of pain, but I steadied myself and repeated the action, again and again. The third time was the charm. As I smashed the chair against the wall, it shattered, legs and slats breaking off the seat. The various pieces fell away from me, and I kicked and shimmied until the last bits clattered to the floor. The entire process had taken less than a minute, but I didn't have a single second to spare.

I dropped to my knees behind Susannah's chair, my back to her, holding my bound hands against hers. I couldn't speak to tell her what I wanted her to do, but I didn't need to. Her fingers fumbled against my wrists until they found the knot in the rope. We were lucky that Reverend McAllister wasn't great at tying knots. He must not have ever been a Boy Scout. Susannah had my wrists free in a matter of seconds, and I spun around to untie her.

As soon as she was free, I yanked the gag out of my mouth, and she did the same with hers. The smell of smoke had grown stronger as we worked, and the first wispy tendrils slithered through the crack beneath the door. Somewhere off in the distance a fire alarm rang a shrill, unceasing note. I hoped help would come, but at the same time I knew it would be too late.

I stumbled over pieces of broken chair to get to the door and placed my palm against it. It was warm.

"We can't go out that way."

"But it's the only exit!" Susannah sounded frantic.

I couldn't blame her.

I yanked two frilly gowns and a soldier's coat off a rack of costumes and shoved them at Susannah. "Try to block the cracks with these."

She did as she was told, stuffing the costumes into the cracks beneath and around the door. It helped to slow the influx of smoke, but I knew that time was slipping away from us, the seconds ticking in my head like a metronome turned up to full speed.

McAllister moaned on the floor, but his eyes only opened halfway. I ignored him. I had to if I didn't want us all to die from smoke inhalation in the next few minutes. I cast my eyes around the small room, searching for something strong and sturdy. I considered the frying pan at my feet for half a second but then pounced on an electric guitar. Its body was scratched and it had no strings, but I wasn't interested in making music.

I grabbed the instrument and hurried to the wall opposite from the door. I knocked against it with my fist, working my way from left to right and listening to the change in sounds. Satisfied that I'd located a spot between studs, I held the guitar by its neck with both hands.

"What are you doing?" Susannah asked.

I didn't bother to waste time answering. Instead, I swung the guitar as hard as I could. It broke a hole through the drywall.

Hope gave me greater strength, and I swung the instrument over and over again, smashing it against the wall, opening a wider hole with each impact.

Behind me Susannah coughed. "The smoke! Midori!"

"Help me." I dropped the guitar and ripped at the jagged drywall with my hands.

The sharp edges cut and scratched my skin, but I hardly noticed.

Susannah joined me, and we soon had a hole big enough to squeeze through.

And not a moment too soon.

The smoke had thickened, and flames crackled and popped on the other side of the door. Even across the room I could feel the heat. It pressed against my face, urging me to flee.

"Reverend!" I screamed at McAllister, my words ending with a coughing fit.

He moved one arm but did nothing else.

"Go!" I shouted to Susannah before turning back to McAllister.

I grabbed him under the arms, but knew right away that I wouldn't be able to move him on my own. He was too heavy. Somebody joined me in the murky dullness of the smoke-filled room and took some of McAllister's weight.

Susannah.

I wanted to scream at her again to leave, to save herself, but my coughs and protesting throat wouldn't let me. There wasn't time to argue with her anyway, and I needed her help to move the reverend.

Together we hauled him to his feet. He swayed and lurched but shuffled along, making our job easier. When we reached the wall, Susannah climbed through the hole first and half caught McAllister when I pushed him through. I climbed out after him and secured his arm around my shoulders.

I coughed and blinked as I took in our new location. We were in an unfamiliar hallway, but an exit sign glowed with a dull red light in the distance. With toxic smoke billowing out of the hole behind us, the three of us set off down the hall, Susannah and I supporting the reverend between us. We pushed through a heavy door and found ourselves in a shallow concrete stairwell, our heads just above ground level.

A symphony of light and sound greeted us. Rain pelted against the street and parked cars, a siren wailed in the distance, and a fire engine rumbled to a stop in front of the church. The lights on the emergency vehicle flashed brightly and voices called out over the jumble of other sounds.

Susannah and I only made it up one stair before McAllister's weight became too much for us. The three of us crumpled down into a heap, struggling to draw in cool fresh air between harsh coughs.

"Is there anyone else inside?"

I looked up at the firemen looming above us. "Not sure," I croaked.

A male voice shouted out orders and several firefighters raced past us. Another fixed an oxygen mask over McAllister's face as an ambulance turned onto the street, cutting its siren.

The next few minutes passed in a daze, but I was aware enough to notice that they felt like an eerie repeat of the scene that followed the previous fire. Someone helped me up the steps and away from the building. I sat down on the curb, leafy tree branches above me providing some shelter from the pouring rain. A female paramedic checked me over just as before, but this time tended to my arm rather than my hand.

"It's not bad enough to need stitches," the paramedic said as she cleaned the cut on my upper arm, "but I'll put a bandage on it for you."

I nodded, aware of her words and the pain in my arm but far more focused on what was happening around me. An ambulance pulled away from the crowd of emergency vehicles, carrying Reverend McAllister off to the hospital. At almost the same time, police officers arrived on the scene. A couple of them set to work herding the growing crowd of onlookers back from the church property and others conferred with firefighters.

A commotion at the front of the church drew my attention. A fireman held a hysterical Cindy McAllister by the arm. As he led her down the steps, past the hoses and away from the church, she screamed and clawed at his arm.

"My husband's still in there! You have to help him!"

I jumped up from my spot on the curb, startling

the paramedic as she finished bandaging my arm, and marched toward Cindy.

"Your husband's on the way to the hospital," I corrected her.

Her eyes widened at the sight of me. Fear flashed across her face but it was quickly replaced by fury. "You!"

She spat the word out, and I was glad I was far enough away to avoid her spittle. The distance between us was good for another reason. Her face contorted with rage, Cindy lunged at me. I leapt backward, out of her reach. She lurched toward me again, her fingernails ready to rake down my face.

Cindy's fireman escort grabbed her from behind. "Ma'am, I need you to calm down."

She struggled against his strong grip, her screams wild and high-pitched.

Three police officers ran over to help the fireman. Even when surrounded, Cindy continued to flail and fight, her angry eyes locked on me.

My heart jumped around in my throat as the police officers pushed the reverend's wife to the ground and cuffed her hands behind her back. Finally, the fight seemed to go out of her and she sagged into the wet grass, her body shaking with sobs.

Two of the police officers pulled her to her feet and the third stepped in my direction.

"Are you all right?" he asked me.

I nodded, unable to take my eyes off the sorry, sopping wet figure that was Cindy McAllister. "She started the fire." My voice was rough and I paused to ward off a bout of coughing. "She tied up Susannah and me and knocked out her husband."

The policeman looked at me with an odd expression. "And why would she do that?"

I hugged myself, only then realizing that I was soaking wet and chilled to the bone. "She's a murderer." My words came out heavy with exhaustion. "I think I need to speak to Detective Bachman or Detective Salnikova. They'll want to know about this right away."

I reached for my purse, only to discover that I didn't have it. "My purse is inside still. And Cindy McAllister took my phone." I didn't mean to sound as upset as I did, but the events of the past hour had caught up with me. "All my identification . . . And how will I call the detectives? Can I get my phone back?" I swiveled around to watch the other two police officers escort Cindy toward one of the parked cruisers.

"Hold on a moment," the officer at my side said in a calming voice. "If she's got your phone, we'll make sure it gets back to you. As for your other belongings, we'll have to wait and see if they've survived the fire."

I closed my eyes in disappointment. I knew he was right, but I didn't like the thought of having to replace my credit cards and identification. At least I hadn't had a whole lot of cash in my wallet.

I opened my eyes and tried to focus on what was most important. "And the detectives?" I gestured in Cindy's direction as an officer guided her into the backseat of the cruiser. "She's done far more than cause a ruckus on the church lawn, you know."

"I'll get in touch with the detectives for you."

I hugged myself again. Rain still pelted down from the sky, soaking my clothes and plastering my hair against my head. My arm felt as though it had a knife—or a letter opener—stuck into it, and my recently healed throat was scratchy and sore.

All I wanted to do was go home, or at least to JT's house. With Cindy safely in custody I could go back to my apartment, but I wasn't sure I wanted to be without company right away. It was a moot point anyway. I needed to speak to the detectives before I could go anywhere.

Another thought struck me.

"My students." I put a hand to my head and groaned. "I really need my phone," I said to the police officer. "My violin students will start showing up at my studio. I need to cancel their lessons, and all my students' contact information is in my phone."

The officer nodded with understanding, and I noted that he had kind brown eyes. He probably wasn't much older than I was. "Why don't you go take shelter under a tree," he suggested. "I'll see what I can do about your phone."

"Thank you."

As the officer walked off toward the cruiser where Cindy was sequestered, I wandered back toward my spot at the curb. Susannah wasn't far off. She stood huddled under one of the many large trees lining the street. She was crying, and a female police officer had her arm around her. I considered going over to help comfort her until a familiar voice called my name.

"Dori!"

Relief whooshed over me, and I rushed over to JT and hugged him. He returned the hug and a sharp pain shot through my injured arm. I yelped and jumped back.

"You're hurt? What happened? Not another fire?"

The worry in his eyes was touching.

"I've got a cut on my arm. Nothing serious. And yes, there was another fire. Deliberately set."

"Dori, this is like some weird déjà vu experience. What the hell is going on?"

Déjà vu was right. But this was an experience I definitely could have done without repeating. "When I came looking for Susannah, the McAllisters snatched me. I think Cindy must have used Susannah's phone to lure me here, or forced her to text me, because they already had her tied up. After the reverend tied me up too, Cindy whacked him on the head with a frying pan and set the fire. She meant for us all to burn to death."

JT ran a hand through his damp hair. "Are you saying she's the murderer?"

"That's exactly what I'm saying. And an arsonist twice over. She's also the one who trashed my apartment."

"And she even wanted to kill her husband?" JT sounded incredulous.

I couldn't blame him. It was a lot to take in. "Yes. She doesn't seem too fond of him, and I think he figured out that she was the one who stole the money from the church."

"So the whole gambling thing was relevant after all?"

"More than relevant. It's what set her off down the

slippery slope to her crazy crime spree." I leaned against him, careful to spare my injured arm. "I'm glad you're here, JT."

He put an arm around my shoulder, and I closed my eyes, listening to the comforting beat of his heart. When I reopened them, I spotted the brown-eyed police officer heading in our direction with what looked like my phone in his hand.

"I have a feeling this is going to be a long, long day," I said to JT, still leaning against him.

He gave my shoulder a squeeze. "No matter how long it is, I'm right here with you."

I tilted my head back so he could see my grateful smile.

Even though I'd been the target of attempted murder more than once over the past week, I considered myself lucky. Lucky to be alive, and lucky to have a friend like JT.

Chapter 26

TWO DAYS LATER my life had regained some normalcy. I was back to teaching my students, and the following week the orchestra would return to our usual rehearsal space at the Abrams Center. I no longer had any reason to return to the church, and I planned to stay well away from it. Even if the McAllisters were no longer there, I didn't need to stir up any unpleasant memories. If I ever had the urge to attend a church service, I'd do so elsewhere.

I'd heard through Detective Salnikova that the reverend had suffered a minor concussion as a result of getting hit with the frying pan, but he was otherwise fine. Physically, at any rate. He was still in a whole lot of trouble, even though Susannah's video had only been shared with the police. The fact that he'd be going to jail for his involvement in his wife's crimes was enough to lose him his position with the church.

With Cindy McAllister locked away awaiting trial, I

had moved back to my apartment. The burn on my hand had healed enough that it no longer bothered me, and I could play my violin without pain. The cut on my arm had mended, and the smoke-induced scratchiness in my throat had all but disappeared.

Even though I was no longer camped out at JT's house, I stuck around after my last student of the day left the studio. It was Friday evening, and JT and I had plans.

After a delivery boy brought pizza to the front door, JT and I got comfortable on his couch with drinks and food. Finnegan settled on the floor between us, his brown eyes keeping a sharp lookout for any bits of food that might drop to his level.

"How was your day?" JT asked as he passed me a can of root beer.

I popped the top. "Blissfully without incident."

"You mean you managed to stay out of trouble?"

I elbowed him in the ribs and nearly spilled my root beer. I took a long sip and swallowed the delicious, fizzy liquid. "I'll have you know that I was instrumental in solving several crimes. If not for me, the police would still be looking for the killer."

"True. But you scared me half to death, you know that? I got worried when you didn't answer my texts or phone calls, and when I got to the church and saw all the commotion . . ."

"I know. The whole thing scared me too. But it's over now."

"And Susannah?"

I selected a piece of pepperoni pizza and took an experimental bite. It was hot. "I talked to her last night. She's upset, of course. Did you know that Cindy lured her to the church with a text from my phone?"

"How did she manage that?"

"She must have used my phone when I left it in her office while I talked to her sister-in-law. Sneaky woman. I had no clue. She also sent Susannah a threatening e-mail." I paused to blow on my pizza. "I think Susannah's a strong kid though, despite her tendency to cry a lot."

"What about Ray? He didn't have anything to do with the murder in the end?"

"Nope. But he did break into Jeremy's basement suite. Apparently he was hoping to recover some marijuana he'd sold to Jeremy the day before his death. So he could resell it to someone else, I guess."

JT picked up a piece of pizza. "And you're doing all right now?" His eyes watched me carefully.

"I did have a nightmare last night," I admitted. "But I'll be okay. I'm looking forward to getting back into my regular routine. Teaching, rehearsals, hanging out. No fires, no crazy murderers." I tested my pizza again. It was cool enough to eat, so I took a bite.

"Speaking of rehearsals," JT said, "how are things between you and Clausen?"

I chewed and swallowed. "I think it'll be okay. Maybe a little awkward at times, but okay."

"You're not going to turn him in for lying about his previous job?"

I shook my head. I'd thought about that over the last couple of days. I didn't want to cause a kerfuffle in the orchestra, and even if I no longer held Hans in the highest esteem personally, he was a good conductor. And I wasn't vindictive. If someone found out down the line, maybe he'd be in trouble, but I didn't want to be the one to stir things up.

In fact, there was only one thing I wanted to do right at the moment.

"Let's get this marathon started."

JT popped open his can of root beer. "Where do you want to start tonight?"

"Right at the beginning."

He picked up the remote and cued *The X-Files* pilot.

I settled deeper into the couch cushions and smiled with contentment.

Life was good.

Acknowledgments

Thank you to Nicole Bates, Sarah Blair, and Sarah Henning for being such amazing critique partners and such great friends. Sincere thanks also to my agent, Jessica Faust, for believing in *Dead Ringer* and for finding it a home, and to my editor at HarperCollins, Rebecca Lucash, for her enthusiasm and guidance.

About the Author

SARAH FOX was born and raised in Vancouver, British Columbia, where she developed a love for mysteries at a young age. When not writing novels or working as a legal writer, she is often reading her way through a stack of books or spending time outdoors with her English Springer Spaniel.

www.facebook.com/authorsarahfox
www.witnessimpulse.com

Discover great authors, exclusive offers, and more at hc.com.

CPSIA information can be obtained
at www.ICGtesting.com
Printed in the USA
JSHW030722090623
42967JS00008B/178

9 780062 413031